DEATH AND DECEPTION

A VICTORIAN BOOK CLUB MYSTERY

CALLIE HUTTON

This book is a work of fiction. Names, characters, places, and incidents are the product of the author's imagination or are used fictitiously. Any resemblance to actual events, locales, or persons, living or dead, is coincidental.

All rights reserved, including the right to reproduce, distribute, or transmit in any form or by any means. For information regarding subsidiary rights, please contact the Author.

Author's website: http://calliehutton.com/

Cover design by Anna Greene

Manufactured in the United States of America

First Edition December 2022

ABOUT THE BOOK

After almost a year of marriage, Lord William Wethington and Lady Amy Wethington have put aside their sleuthing skills to prepare for their first child. 'Twould be an easy thing except to their dismay, dead bodies are once again popping up.

A corpse discovered floating in the Roman Baths was startling enough, but the unfortunate victim turns out to be Amy's and her sister-in-law Eloise's midwife, Mrs. Jane Fleming.

"Do not get involved," Lord William warns.

"We are ordering you not to entangle yourself," incompetent Bath Police Detectives Carson and Marsh state.

Lady Amy reluctantly agrees and takes up a questionable hobby that William swears will eventually poison him.

Then another body shows up.

Now, really, what's a bored mystery writer to do?

* * *

Receive a free book and stay up to date with new releases and sales!
http://calliehutton.com/newsletter/

AUTHOR'S NOTE

For those readers who are familiar with my Merry Misfits of Bath series, you might recognize Dr. Rayne Stevens and Lord Sterling from The Doctor and the Libertine.

1

June 1892
Bath, England

Lord William Wethington cringed as his wife of one year, Lady Amy Wethington, glared across the bedchamber at him, her hands on her hips. "You promised I would be able to continue writing once we married. If I remember correctly—and I do—it was the one condition I insisted upon when I accepted you."

They were preparing to retire for the night, and his wife looked tired. He'd already consulted with her midwife, Mrs. Jane Fleming, who had agreed that Amy should rest more. "Yes, I did, my dear, but you are six months into your confinement, and you must cut down on your work. I feel it is taxing you. I heard you crying last night as you pounded away on that infernal noisy typing machine."

She raised her chin. "I was not crying; I was merely feeling the pain of my main character. It is what a good author does. And furthermore, that wonderful machine cuts down the amount of time it takes to finish a book."

William sighed, knowing this was not going to be an easy conversation. "If I remember correctly—and I do—" He grinned as he used her very same words, then continued, "Your publisher didn't even give you a deadline for this book since you are in a delicate way."

Amy narrowed her eyes. "I knew I should not have told you that bit of information. However, that matters not. I have my own standards, and it has always been my intention to finish this book before the baby arrives."

"I do not agree, wife." He walked toward her and placed his hands on her shoulders. "The last thing you need is to push yourself and put more of a strain on your body." He kissed her forehead. "I do worry about you, you know."

She huffed and turned to climb into bed. The fact that she didn't continue the discussion told him much. His spitfire wife would not have given up so easily. Could it be he'd won the argument?

Almost as if she'd read his mind, she said, "And do not congratulate yourself on having succeeded. I am merely too tired to argue." She shifted onto her side and watched him enter the bed.

After climbing in behind her, he said, "Aha! You see, love, that is my point." He leaned over and kissed her cheek. "Good night."

What he really wanted to do was retire to his country home until after the baby was born. He could easily run his estates from there, and the move would get his wife out of the foul city. Fresh air, paths to walk, and good food were the best things for pregnant women. Not stress, city air, and manuscript deadlines.

In fact, he mused, a permanent move would be for the best, but Amy's family were all in Bath now that her brother and father had moved their businesses from London. There was also her Aunt Margaret who practically raised her that Amy would most likely be loath to leave.

He was sure he'd also have to fight an additional battle with her brother Michael, whose wife was Amy's best friend and also enceinte. Then there were their book club friends, church family, and of course, her publisher.

Maybe if he prevailed upon Lady Margaret to step in and attempt to convince Amy to work less, it might go better.

William rolled onto his back and glanced over at Amy who was already asleep. Mrs. Fleming had assured him that his wife was in the best of health and even though at seven and twenty years was not as young as other first-time mothers, she saw no reason why things should not go well.

He'd thought about approaching her publisher to request he encourage her once again to cease trying to finish the book, but if she ever found out, he would need to move to the other side of the earth. That was, if his bruised body could make the journey.

With all of that ruminating in his mind, he finally fell asleep.

* * *

THE NEXT MORNING, he joined Amy at the breakfast table. She appeared a tad lethargic and kept yawning.

"Why did you leave the bed if you are still tired?" he asked as he placed the napkin on his lap. With a nod to the footman in attendance who poured his coffee, he studied his wife's features. Yes. She was definitely peaked.

She rested her chin on her upraised hand. "Husband, you may officially congratulate yourself."

He raised his eyebrows, hoping, but not expecting her to bow to his wishes about writing. "Why is that?"

Amy studied her plate and sighed. "Not only am I especially

tired at the end of each day, but my gestating muse has apparently flown out the window. For the first time in my writing career, I cannot think of plot points, twists, and red herrings."

"Since I assume you are not referring to food items, it appears you will set your work aside for now."

She waved her finger at him. "Yes. For now. I fully intend to continue my current novel once the baby is born and things have settled down. Hopefully, I will then regain my normal frame of mind." She picked up her fork again. "One hopes, anyway."

"I have a great deal of faith in you."

"The problem is, I know without my writing, I will remain restless. I do need something to fill my time."

"Needlepoint?"

She pulled a face. "No. That is not one of my skills."

"Gardening?"

She shook her head. "I tried to grow some pretty flowers in the area where the gardener keeps such a lovely spot." She shrugged. "They died, and he suggested I take up needlepoint."

He didn't mention knitting since she'd tried that once before and the resulting 'item' was eventually trashed. He still had no idea what it was she'd been knitting but was grateful she hadn't presented it to him as a gift, expecting him to know what the devil it was.

"Painting?"

"That would require an investment in brushes, canvases, and paint."

William smiled at her attempt to economize. "We can certainly afford it."

"I will keep it in mind, but I don't feel a strong pull toward the idea. Aunt Margaret has always been the artist in the family. Just another attribute of hers I did not inherit."

Once he finished his breakfast of sausages, eggs and the scrumptious scones Cook produced a few times a week, he wiped his mouth and stood. "I am off, my dear. I've meetings with some of the other members of Parliament to discuss a new bill we wish to present at the next session."

Amy tilted her head to receive his kiss on her cheek.

William walked to the doorway, stopped, and turned. "I suggest you take a nap today."

Amy waved him off, placing her other hand over her mouth to stifle a yawn.

* * *

"I HONESTLY DO NOT UNDERSTAND why I keep Mrs. Fleming on as my midwife. She is rude, condescending, and unlikeable." Lady Eloise Davenport, Amy's sister-in-law and best friend, reached for another pastry. "She even told me I needed to cut down on my eating because I was growing too large."

Amy smiled and kept her opinion to herself, lest she hurt Eloise's feelings. She was a good month behind Amy in her pregnancy, but she had gained about a half stone more.

They were spending their afternoon visiting, something they did each day. Luckily for Amy, when Eloise and Michael eloped last year, Michael had already moved his business to Bath, so it made sense to rent a townhouse for them to live in, near enough to Amy and William that they were able to maintain their close relationship. Michael had claimed to have no desire to retire to his country estate.

But what Eloise said about their mutual midwife was certainly true. Amy didn't find her very likeable herself. "I agree," she said. "But I'm afraid I am stuck with her, though. William did quite a bit of research when we learned I was increasing. Mrs. Fleming, as she's told us many times before, has been trained and certified as many practicing midwives have not. He said he wanted the best for me."

"How sweet," Eloise said, munching on the apple tart. "Michael hasn't said that, but I know he feels that way."

"True," Amy nodded, sipping her tea. "He's been my brother for twenty-seven years, and I can tell you he is not one to put his feelings into words."

"Yes, I know," Eloise added, "but he does have his ways to show me." She grinned and a slight blush appeared on her face. Since they were discussing her brother, Amy did not want to continue the conversation along *that* line.

"Lady Wethington, Mrs. Fleming has called." Filbert, the butler who manned the front door, entered the drawing room.

Amy turned toward the door. "I wasn't aware I am due for a visit," she said to Eloise. She looked back at the butler. "Nevertheless, please show Mrs. Fleming in."

The two women looked up expectantly when Mrs. Fleming entered the room. "Good afternoon, Mrs. Fleming, to what do we owe this visit?"

The midwife raised her sharp chin, as if Amy was challenging her. She really was not a pleasant person. "I know it is a bit early, but I have taken on two new mothers and according to my list, this was the best time for me to see you." Mrs. Fleming regarded Eloise. "Since you are here, Lady Davenport, I can take a quick assessment of you as well, since you are next on my list."

Amy glanced at Filbert who lingered at the door. "Please have Cook send in hot tea."

Mrs. Fleming waved her hand. "No need, Lady Wethington. I will do my examination and be on my way." She eyed their teacups and pastry plates. "I am much too busy to spend my precious time socializing."

Amy drew in a breath at her comment as the midwife began with a series of questions about Amy's health and general welfare. "Any depressive or negative thoughts?"

Besides you?

"No. You might be interested to know that I put my recent book aside until after the baby is born. Lord Wethington thought the stress and strain were not good for me or the baby."

"A very wise man, my lady. Because you tend to write dark matters, it is the general opinion among those of us who are *properly trained and certified* that a mother's negative thoughts can affect the child."

Amy and Eloise shared an amused glance. Mrs. Fleming was always very proud of the fact that she was one of only a few *properly trained and certified* midwives in Bath.

Once she ascertained that Amy was fit, she turned her attention toward Eloise. "I see you are still eating too much." She pointed to a piece of the apple tart Eloise popped into her mouth.

Jumping to her friend's defense, Amy said, "I am somewhat knowledgeable about pregnancy, Mrs. Fleming, having done quite a bit of reading on the matter. The current thoughts are an expecting mother should eat and drink whatever appeals, and as much as she likes."

Mrs. Fleming's face turned bright red, then she adopted a patronizing demeanor. "Lady Wethington, I bow to your superiority in matters of murder, based on your dubious hobby of writing such things, but I assure you, I am thoroughly educated and well-informed on the subject of pregnancy and childbirth. It is *our* thought that too much eating makes for a heavy baby, and therefore a more difficult birth." She began her assessment of Eloise.

Well, then.

The woman managed to insult both her clients in less than ten minutes. Rather than argue the point with the woman, once she was through, Amy merely stood and smoothed out her skirts, a signal that the midwife's examination of the women was finished. "I will show you to the door."

Mrs. Fleming hurriedly gathered her things, and chin thrust forward, marched behind Amy to the entrance. Amy turned to her and offered what she hoped looked more like a smile than the scowl she was afraid was all she could manage. Not waiting for Filbert, Amy opened the door. "Have a good day, Mrs. Fleming."

Mrs. Fleming nodded and marched through the door which Amy closed with a bit more enthusiasm than necessary.

"Well, I never," Amy said as she joined Eloise in the drawing room. "That woman might be *properly trained and certified,* but she certainly does not comport herself as caring and kind."

As if to dispute the midwife's advice, Amy sat across from Eloise, reached for another tart from the tray, and took a large bite. "Take that, Mrs. Fleming."

They both laughed as the crumbs fell from Amy's mouth in a most unflattering and unladylike display.

2

*A*my took William's arm as they left their carriage and proceeded to Atkinson & Tucker Booksellers where they met every Thursday to discuss books. William had fond memories of the store and book club since he'd met Amy there. His mother met her husband, Mr. Edward Colbert, there as well when the then widow decided to make her home with William a couple of years before.

It had been difficult at first accepting that a man was romantically interested in his mother. His mother! But once he saw how happy they were together, he pushed his awkwardness aside and wished them well.

Because it had taken three attempts before Amy could find matching shoes, they had arrived after most of the other members. His stepfather, Mr. Colbert—he could never think of him by any other title since he'd known him as such since he first joined the book club years before—was already at the front of the room, shuffling through papers. He'd acted as moderator for the group for as long as William had been a member.

As usual, William's mother was seated in the front row. Mr.

Colbert always wanted her up front so he could gaze at her throughout the meeting. William shook his head. He had to remind himself more than once that his mother was happy, and that was all that mattered.

The Misses Penelope and Gertrude O'Neill, sisters who dressed alike as if they were twins but didn't resemble each other at all, waved at them and moved in their direction. They were sweet older women they also knew from church, and William was still amazed that they had joined a mystery book club.

William helped Amy to a seat just as Mr. Colbert called the meeting to order. As was normal procedure, Eloise raced into the room just as Mr. Colbert began to speak. She hurried over to where William and Amy sat. She was out of breath and gave them both a big smile.

William leaned over and spoke softly. "I've told you before we would be more than happy to pick you up on the way to the bookstore each week."

"I know. And I really did intend to send along a note asking you to do that, but Michael was in the middle of a story about his growing strained relationship with his father, and not having the heart to cut him short, I didn't have time to wait for my carriage to be brought around."

William looked aghast. "Does he know you left without the carriage? Whatever is wrong with you, Eloise?"

Eloise blushed. "I waved down a hackney." She held her finger to her lips and nodded to Mr. Colbert.

"I have an interesting proposal for all of you tonight." Mr. Colbert studied the group in front of him.

William looked around at the familiar faces: Lord Temple and his daughter, Abigail, Mr. Davidson and his special friend, Mr. Rawlings, Mrs. Morton, Lady Forester, and of course the O'Neill sisters.

Mr. Colbert continued. "We have always, as you know, read

and discussed mystery books." He looked at Amy. "And having my own daughter-in-law, better known in the publishing world as E. D. Burton, a well-known and respected mystery author, it has been wonderful to read some of her work as well."

Slight applause followed, along with Amy's blush.

Mr. Colbert cleared his throat. "I'd like to suggest we change things a bit. My lovely wife has suggested that we read some of Miss Austen's works."

A groan came from Mr. Davidson's direction, which was no surprise because he was a tad difficult to deal with. Both William and Amy had suffered run-ins with the man.

"I think trying something new is wonderful," Lady Forester said.

Of course, all the women in the room nodded yes. Davidson didn't say anything further, but slumped in his chair, his arms crossed. Whenever Mr. Rawlings was with him, his behavior improved. Almost as if he needed a nanny to keep him polite. Had Mr. Rawlings been missing, William was certain an argument would have ensued.

"May I make a suggestion?" Eloise asked.

Mr. Colbert nodded. "Yes, of course, Lady Davenport."

"I think we should read Miss Austen's book, *Pride and Prejudice*. I always liked the alliterative title. Just like *Sense and Sensibility*."

Mr. Davidson waved his hand in the air. "Surely, my lady, you don't purchase your books by the cover? That seems foolish to me."

Eloise drew in a breath and straightened her spine. "I never mentioned the cover, Mr. Davidson. Mayhap you should pay better attention."

Giggles erupted from a few of the women, but Mr. Colbert looked like a teacher who had just realized he'd lost control of the classroom.

After a sharp jab to his side by his loving wife, William said, "I happen to agree that perhaps it is time to try something new."

Mr. Colbert looked relieved. "Thank you, my lord." He picked up his papers and said, "I had a few suggestions, but since Lady Davenport has made a couple of her own, why don't we have a vote. Those who prefer *Pride and Prejudice*, raise your hand."

He counted and wrote on his notes. "Those who would like to read and discuss *Sense and Sensibility*?"

William looked around. It appeared there were more votes for *Pride and Prejudice*.

"*Pride and Prejudice* it is, then." Mr. Colbert winked at his wife in the front row. William guessed that was the book she had suggested to Colbert.

They spent some time finishing up the discussion of their last book and then Mr. Colbert called an end to the meeting.

William helped Amy up from the chair, then turned to assist Eloise. Before they were able to take one step, his mother hurried over to them. "Oh, my dear, aren't you looking lovely," she said to Amy. She turned briefly to Eloise. "And you too, dear."

His mother placed her hands on Amy's shoulders and stared into her eyes. "Are you taking proper care of yourself?" She looked at William. "Is she taking proper care of herself?"

Before he could answer she said, "She looks a bit tired. Perhaps these evening meetings aren't good for her."

She glanced at William again. "Do you think these evening meetings are good for her?"

"Mother, Amy is standing right here. She can certainly speak for herself."

Mr. Colbert walked up to them and slapped William on the back. "Are you taking good care of our Amy?"

Eloise waved her hand. "I'm here, too."

Mother looked back at her. "You look wonderful, Lady Davenport." She glanced at her tummy and said, "You might want to watch the desserts, though."

* * *

Amy spent three days trying to find something to keep her brain occupied. The gardener had already chased her off, reminding her of the flower debacle. She attempted to mend a pair of William's socks but managed to sew the top to the bottom of one of them. She doubted he would miss them once she tossed them into the rubbish.

She took out the yarn and needles from her attempt to knit something a couple of years before. A nice, pretty blanket for the baby, she thought. She spent an entire morning shopping on Milsom Street for the perfect soft, lovely yarn.

Pleased with her purchase, she hurried home and began her project. After several attempts, ripping out the stitches numerous times and cursing her inability to do simple things, she put it aside. Currently, it gathered dust alongside William's sock.

Why was she not capable in things all women could do? Aunt Margaret, of course, could knit, sew, sketch, paint, play the pianoforte, and probably fix a hole in the roof. Why hadn't any of her capabilities passed down to her?

She'd had all the proper lessons growing up. She could speak a passable French, name all the Kings and Queens, could add, subtract, multiply, and divide numbers, and knew the proper bow to the Queen. Of course, lacking an invitation to join Her Majesty for tea, practicing that talent would not help to pass the time until the baby arrived.

Her fingers itched to work on her typing machine. But aside from promising William she would put it aside for now, she really felt lost when she thought about her current story.

She drew in a deep breath when she had the frightening idea that perhaps motherhood had taken away all her writing ability!

Could that happen? She must ask Mrs. Fleming the next time she saw her. Of course, she would probably laugh at her and pat her on the head like some pet dog.

Speaking of dogs, her dear Persephone had been peculiar since she'd given birth to puppies a couple of years before. She must still be mad about them giving them all away. She sighed and pondered her life.

"Dearest, are you sitting here all by yourself wallowing in self-pity?" Aunt Margaret's familiar and comforting voice filled her sitting room where she'd been wallowing in self-pity.

"Aunt Margaret!" She jumped up—well, lumbered up actually—and hugged her aunt. "It is so good to see you. Can you stay for tea?"

Her aunt slipped off her gloves and gracefully sat on the settee across from Amy. "Of course. I didn't make the trip to see my dear niece without expecting tea."

Amy rang for tea and settled back down again, her heart lighter with Aunt Margaret just being in the room. The woman had practically raised her and was all things Amy was not. But she loved her and always felt better when she was around.

"I understand you are not writing."

"Yes. I promised William I would stop for a while—he thinks it's too taxing for me."

When Aunt Margaret waved her hand in dismissal, Amy added, "But, in all fairness, I seem to have lost my muse anyway. I was reduced to tears the other night because I couldn't keep my train of thought." She chewed her lower lip. "Do you believe that can happen? I mean, can motherhood affect your brain?"

Aunt Margaret smoothed out her skirt. "My dear, motherhood will indeed affect your brain. I don't know about writing, but I am familiar with too many women whose brains seemed to turn to mush once the urchins were born." She shook her head. "I will never understand what is so delightful about a burping, wailing, nasty-nappy creature." She shivered.

She leaned over and patted Amy on the knee. "However, I have no doubt that you will regain all your writing talent once the baby arrives." She looked at her with horror. "You are going to have a nurse and a nanny, are you not?"

Amy shrugged. "A nurse for sure, especially in the beginning, but I'm not certain about a nanny. I mean, suppose she isn't careful enough or harms the baby?"

Aunt Margaret stared at her with wide eyes. "Please do not tell me the mushy brain has already started."

Just then the footman entered, pushing in a tea cart. Amy was more than pleased to have Aunt Margaret take over the pouring and fixing of the tea. As in all things, she was very graceful in her task.

Where Amy was short and carried almost a stone more than she should even before she was pregnant, Aunt Margaret was willowy, lissome, and efficient.

Amy took a sip of tea and reached for a biscuit. "How is Papa? I haven't seen him in a while."

Aunt Margaret placed her teacup in the saucer in front of her. She and Amy's father, Aunt Margaret's brother, Franklin, Marquess of Winchester, had an ongoing battle about his frustration with his sister's refusal to allow him to run her life.

"Fighting with your brother again."

Amy rolled her eyes. "Is he still annoyed with Michael for marrying Eloise? Gracious that was ages ago."

"No. I think he's gotten over it since she is about to produce one of his grandchildren." She patted Amy's hand. "With both of you expecting babies in the near future, one would think he had better things to think about than how Michael is running his part of their businesses."

They both looked up as William entered the sitting room.

"What are you doing home so early? I assumed your meetings would take all day."

He sat alongside her, and she realized he was looking strange.

"What is it?"

William took her hand. "I'm afraid I have bad news."

Amy placed the biscuit in her hand back on the small plate, her mouth immediately drying up. "I don't like bad news."

He brushed a few crumbs off her skirt. "I'm afraid no one does, love, but I wanted to be the one to tell you before you heard it elsewhere."

"What is it, William?" Aunt Margaret asked, her growing concern visible on her face.

He wrapped his hand around Amy's and looked between the two women. "Mrs. Fleming is dead."

"Who is Mrs. Fleming?" her aunt asked.

Still in shock, Amy just continued to stare at William. He turned toward Aunt Margaret. "She is—rather was—Amy's and Eloise's midwife."

"She told us she just took on two new mothers," Amy said, still trying to grasp what he'd just told her. "Was she in an accident of some sort?"

William patted her hand. "Not exactly. She was found floating in the Roman Baths this morning when the employees opened the building. I'm afraid they believe she was murdered."

3

"Murdered?" Amy was having a hard time catching her breath. "I must admit I wasn't too fond of the woman, but I can't imagine one of her clients disliked her that much."

Persephone picked that moment to wander into the sitting room and jump onto William's lap. He and the dog did not have a warm relationship and Amy was convinced her pet was jealous of William and purposely worked quite hard to make his life miserable.

William rolled his eyes. "Persephone, down."

The dog continued to sit there and stare at him. William shook his head and turned his attention back to Amy. "I'm afraid there is no more information than that at the moment."

"Where did you hear this?" Her brain had finally resurrected itself. They'd been through this before—unfortunately—and she was beginning to feel as though they would be plagued with suspicious deaths for the rest of their lives. She shivered at the thought.

"At my club. I stopped there for luncheon and met one of our members, Mr. Scott. It turned out he employs a maid who was friendly with the worker at the Roman Baths who found the body, a Mrs. Garfield."

"Dearest, you are not a healthy person to be around," Aunt Margaret said as she picked up her teacup.

Amy sighed. "I know."

William cleared his throat and squeezed her hand. "I want to make it perfectly clear that you will not involve yourself in this matter."

"I see no reason why I should. The other matters we dealt with involved us, but aside from being my midwife, I have no connection to Mrs. Fleming."

William released a breath. "Splendid," he said as he stood, dumping Persephone from his lap. "Now, I must leave you lovely ladies. I am late for an appointment." He leaned over and kissed Amy on the head and left the room.

Aunt Margaret shook her head. "What was Mrs. Fleming like? You mentioned you were not too fond of her."

Amy shifted in her seat, annoyed that pregnancy was uncomfortable. "She is—was—one of a few midwives who were properly trained and certified. Currently, there is a push to have all midwives do so. William selected her after we interviewed several midwives. Eloise employed her as well."

"Why did you dislike her?"

Just then Eloise entered the sitting room as usual, never waiting to be announced. "Did you hear about Mrs. Fleming?" She was out of breath, most likely having eschewed a carriage and hurried over despite Michael's request she use a carriage if she was travelling more than a short way. Eloise, of course, never bowed to his requests unless it was something with which she agreed.

"Sit down and catch your breath, Eloise. It is not good for the baby for you to be rushing about," Aunt Margaret said.

Eloise sat and fanned herself with her hand. "I know, but I was so anxious after Michael told me the news I couldn't sit still and wait for the carriage to be brought around." She reached for an elderberry tart.

"How did you feel about Mrs. Fleming?" Aunt Margaret asked. "Amy was about to tell me her thoughts right before you entered."

Eloise swallowed and wiped her mouth with a napkin. "I didn't care for her. She was efficient, I must say, but her manner was anything but warm."

Aunt Margaret turned to Amy. "And you felt the same way?"

"Yes. She was downright rude on some occasions."

Eloise jumped in. "She was always telling me not to eat so much," she huffed. "I am eating for two people," she said as she reached for a chocolate biscuit. She touched the teapot on the table and said, "Amy, can you send for more tea? This is cold. And perhaps some small sandwiches. It's been a while since luncheon."

Amy and Aunt Margaret shared an amused glance.

Her aunt stood and shook out her skirts. "I will ask Cook to send it up. I would love to stay and hear more about this poor dead woman, but I have an appointment with my modiste." She waved at Amy as she began to stand. "Stay there, I can certainly see my way out. And I know where the kitchen is."

"Will you be at the Assembly this Saturday?" Amy asked.

Aunt Margaret smiled. "Yes. I will, in fact."

"Then we will see you there," Amy added.

With another kiss on Amy's head, Aunt Margaret gracefully exited the room, leaving behind her soft scent of lavender and vanilla. Both Amy and Eloise watched her graceful exit.

With everyone kissing her on the head, she was beginning to feel like a child.

Eloise sighed and swallowed. "I wish I had the grace and charm of your aunt. She is always so well put together and never looks lost or confused."

"That is because she never is lost or confused. What I don't understand is how I am blood related to her and she practically raised me, and yet I have none of her good traits."

"Maybe your baby will take after Aunt Margaret."

Amy raised her brows. "I do not wish to have a graceful son."

"That is true. I was thinking more of a daughter."

Amy shrugged as she took a bite of a cookie and pondered the unfairness of life and the mystery of inherited traits. Or lack thereof.

* * *

WILLIAM STOOD and shook Mr. Wilson's hand. He and his man of business had just completed their weekly meeting. Since Wilson's office was currently under repair, they met at The Bath & County Club where William had been a member since he'd returned from university years before.

Once Wilson left, William planned to enjoy a small drink before he returned home. He called for a brandy and had taken one sip when his brother-in-law, Michael, the Earl of Davenport, plopped into the chair across from him.

Once he was settled with his own drink, he swirled the liquid around in the glass and studied William.

"What is it, Davenport? You look as though you are anxious to say something but thinking about how to begin."

He took a sip. "I guess you've heard about our wives' midwife found floating in the Roman Baths this morning?"

"Yes. I heard about it here, in fact."

"Did you tell my sister? I imagine she will be anxious to take on an investigation again."

"No." William shook his head. "Not at all. I've already told her she is not to involve herself in another murder."

Davenport smiled. "And she agreed?"

"She doesn't need to agree. I am her husband. When I tell her to do something or not to do something, she must obey."

They garnered quite a bit of attention as Davenport roared with laughter. William shifted in his seat in agitation. "What is so funny?"

"You," Davenport said. "I seem to remember that your wife is my sister, Lady Amy Wethington? Is that correct?"

"If you have something to say, man, just say it."

"I believe you are fooling yourself if you think she will ignore this. The woman was her midwife."

"And your wife's midwife as well, I might add."

Michael frowned. "Yes. But Eloise is not the type to involve herself in something like this."

William took a sip. "Our wives are thick as thieves. We shall see."

His brother-in-law leaned forward and dangled his drink between his knees. "I'm having trouble with my father."

"Indeed?"

"Yes."

Michael swirled the liquid in his glass and studied it. "As you know, my father and I have been in business together for years. Right after I returned from university, we became partners. Aside from that little dust-up between us last year, everything has gone well."

He swallowed and signaled for more brandy. "He was against the move to Bath, and it had taken me a couple of years to get him to do it. I was proven right because we are doing better than we have in years."

"What is the problem, then?"

Davenport sat back and rested his foot on his knee. "I want to continue moving forward. I have plans for another business that my research indicates would be quite successful, but we must move now."

"Ah. And Franklin is against it?"

"Yes. Emphatically. He wants to continue to cling to the old way of things. Another matter I want to do is invest in railroads, and he says they won't last." Michael shook his head and stood. "Do you see how beneficial it could be?"

"Yes. I have a bit of money in railroad stock myself. My man of business and solicitor have both investigated and they assure me after all these years, railroads are here to stay and getting into the manufacturing side of it is a good thing."

"It's good to have you on my side." With those words, he downed the rest of his drink, gave him a slight salute, and left the club.

William didn't think he was on his brother-in-law's 'side'. He just agreed that railroads were a good place to put one's money. He was ready to leave the club himself when Amy's father, Franklin, Lord Winchester, entered and made a beeline for him. William stood and held out his hand. "Good evening, my lord."

"Good evening, Wethington. Do you mind if I join you?"

"Not at all." William looked around and waved for a footman to bring brandy. He hadn't planned on having another one. If this continued, he'd be too soused to make it to his carriage.

After the preliminaries of asking after his daughter's health, Franklin took a sip of his brandy and shook his head. "It is a sad day when one has trouble with his son." He pointed his finger at William. "Remember that. One day—maybe soon—you will have a son." He shook his head. "They reach an age where they think they know more than you."

William groaned inwardly. He knew where this was going and really didn't want to be in the middle of it. He nodded at his father-in-law.

"I've always been conservative in my business decisions." He pointed a finger at William. "And I'm successful. I have more money than I need, and my children and sister are content." He gave William a look that had him hurriedly saying, "Of course, Amy is not merely content, but quite happy, and it appears Michael is as well, although Margaret could use a slight shove into marriage."

He stared into space for a moment, then said, "My son. He wants to take on some of these newer things that I say hold off on, railroads in particular. Let's see what happens with it."

William shifted in his seat. Good grief, the Bath station had been built fifty-two years prior. "I have some railroad stock myself, Franklin, and I'm looking into the manufacturing end of it now."

The man waved at him. "I still don't trust them. The next thing you know, some fool will come up with a horseless carriage, and my son will want to throw money at that." He finished his drink and placed the glass on the table in front of them. Shaking his head, he stood and nodded at William. "It was nice talking to you. I'm pleased to have you on my side in this."

I'm pleased to have you on my side in this?

He watched Franklin leave the club with his familiar determined gait. Well, that was certainly surreal. He'd offered no opinions that Franklin or Michael would have considered on their side. The only thing he'd said was that he, too, had railroad investments.

It was time to leave. See what his wife was up to.

He entered the house and handed his coat and hat off to Filbert at the door. "Where is Lady Wethington?"

"I believe she is in the kitchen, my lord."

That was a surprise. He never knew Amy to show interest in the kitchen. When she and her aunt lived in the Winchester townhouse, they both avoided anything to do with meal preparation.

He stepped into the room and came to an abrupt halt. Flour

was everywhere. Broken eggshells littered the work counter and what looked like milk puddled on the floor.

Cook was sitting at the back of the kitchen in a daze, fanning herself. Amy turned to him, also covered in flour. "Oh, you're home. Wonderful. I have decided to take up baking to keep me busy until the baby arrives."

Amy picked up something that William would be hard pressed to identify. It was white, flat, and soggy. She beamed at him. "Look what I made today!"

She looked so very proud of herself he had to swallow the laugh that was trying very hard to emerge. "Very nice." Should he ask what it was? That would most likely hurt her feelings. He looked frantically at Cook who just shook her head and shrugged. No help there.

Trying to guess what the lump of whatever it was, he asked, "Will we eat it for dinner, or save it for later?"

Amy frowned. "Dinner, of course. For dessert."

Ah. It must be a confection of sorts. Before he had the chance to comment on her effort, Filbert entered the kitchen. "My lord, there are two men here to speak with you and my lady." He handed a card to him.

William glanced at it and pinched the bridge of his nose. He looked over at Amy. "Our friends, Detectives Marsh and Carson."

Amy groaned and collapsed into the chair behind her.

4

Detectives Marsh and Carson had plagued William and Amy for years. As far as they were concerned, the detectives were sloppy and incompetent. Since William and Amy had been unfortunate enough to be involved in murders before, they had clashed with the detectives many times.

Amy placed her cake on the table and walked to the kitchen mirror. She was a mess. She turned to William. "I cannot meet them looking like this. They will have to return or wait while I bathe and change my clothes."

"I will speak with them and see if I can answer any questions they have. If not, I will suggest to them that they return at a designated time."

"Thank you," Amy said.

William was gone and back within minutes. "They are determined to wait until you feel presentable."

"Very well, but I will not rush my bath to suit them." She used the back stairs from the kitchen to the bedchamber floor, grumbling to herself. After grabbing the items she needed for her bath, she made her way down the hallway to the bathing room.

Even though she had planned on taking as much time as she needed, the anxiety to get the interview with the detectives over with spurred her to finish in record time.

With no time to dry her hair, she braided it and wrapped it around her head. She struggled into her front fastening corset and dress. Doing things for herself was getting harder with the extra bulk. She might have to do as William suggested and hire a lady's maid. She and Aunt Margaret had shared the services of Sophie when she lived at the Winchester townhouse, but the maid remained with Aunt Margaret when Amy married and moved, so she had learned how to live without one.

Because she couldn't find matching shoes, she chose to wear her house slippers since her dress was long enough to cover her feet. Yes, it was time to hire a lady's maid.

The two detectives and William all stood as she entered the drawing room. Amy greeted the men and took a seat next to William. "Is there a particular reason you're visiting us tonight, detectives? Because it is growing close to our dinner time."

Detective Edwin Marsh was tall, lanky, with what Amy always thought of as sad eyes. His partner, Detective Ralph Carson, was the opposite of Marsh with his shorter, more rotund visage. Most of the times they'd been visited and questioned by the detectives, it was Marsh who did the notetaking while Detective Carson fired questions at them. As Marsh pulled out the small notepad he always carried with him, it appeared nothing had changed.

"Lady Wethington, I understand Mrs. Jane Fleming was your midwife." Detective Carson began his inquisition. She'd learned from past meetings with him that it was best to answer as briefly as possible.

"Yes."

Carson continued to stare at her. She stared back.

"Do you know of any reason why someone would want her dead?"

"No."

Marsh was scribbling away frantically. She wondered what he was writing since she hadn't said anything worthwhile.

Detective Carson continued. "I understand your brother's wife, Lady Eloise Davenport, was also one of Mrs. Fleming's clients."

"Yes."

"I understand you are with child."

The temptation was to point out to the not-too-brilliant man that Mrs. Fleming would not have been her midwife if she wasn't pregnant, but her promise to keep her answers simple prevailed.

"Yes."

William cleared his throat. "Frankly, Detective, I do not see the reason for these questions. It is obvious to anyone looking at my wife that she is carrying a child. Also, it is clear that my wife would have no need for a midwife if she wasn't in this condition." He stood, glaring at the men. "If there is nothing more worthwhile that you wish to ask her, you must excuse us since, as Lady Wethington pointed out, it is close to our dinner time."

Surprisingly, both men lumbered to their feet, and Marsh closed his notepad and slipped it into his pocket. Detective Carson pointed his finger at Amy. "We have been through this before with the two of you. We. Do. Not. Want you interfering with our investigation."

"We have no intention of doing so. Lady Wethington is busy with planning for the baby, and I want nothing less than getting involved with the Bath Police. Again." William moved toward the door, and the detectives followed. He waved them from the door to the entrance hall where Filbert awaited them. "Good evening, detectives."

William placed his hand at Amy's lower back, and they moved into the dining room.

"I think they only came here to look us both in the face and warn us off," Amy said as she took her seat. She sniffed as she shook out her napkin and placed it on her lap. "There was absolutely nothing in their questioning that made rushing my bath necessary."

* * *

THURSDAY MORNING. It was the day of Mrs. Fleming's funeral. Despite William's protests, Amy was attending the event. Eloise was going also, with Michael grousing as much as William. Despite their complaints, neither man offered to go with them, so Eloise and Amy entered the Wethington carriage and set off for St. Michael's.

The mystery writer in Amy had her eyeing various people in the church, looking for guilt. It was well known that the murderer often showed up at the funeral. Of course, Detective Marsh and Detective Carson were standing at the back of the church watching all the attendees.

Eloise leaned over and whispered, "He looks guilty." She gestured with her head to a man in the front pew who was bent over and looked bereaved. "He's pretending," Eloise added.

Although she promised William—and herself—that she would not become involved with the midwife's death, she took a close look at the man Eloise indicated. Did he look guilty? It was hard to tell with his back to them. He was hunched over as if in grief, but he might have a back condition. Then she took a deep breath and cleared her mind. She would not fall into this again. She had a baby on the way.

She moved her thoughts in another direction. With the promising results of the baking she'd been doing, she might even open a bakery one day. In between her writing, of course. And taking care of her baby. With the nurse. If the woman was good enough, that is.

As with most funerals, it was boring. Not that a funeral should be entertaining but sitting on a hard bench was not something her growing body enjoyed.

Occasionally, she snuck a look behind her at the two detectives. Marsh was, of course, scribbling in his notepad.

The eulogy was short, given by the pastor. No one else spoke. They all sat for about thirty minutes while one somber, gloomy composition after another was played by the church organist.

Finally, the service ended, and they all made their way outside. The man who Eloise thought looked guilty announced to the crowd that there would be a luncheon in the Fellowship Hall following the burial of Mrs. Fleming in the church graveyard.

"I could tolerate a bite to eat," Eloise said.

Amy would have preferred to go home and start the new recipe she'd found in an old book in William's library, but she would not abandon her friend. "Then we shall go to the graveyard first and then Fellowship Hall."

The man who'd made the announcement stood by the gravesite, his head down, his hands clasped in front of him. The pastor spoke briefly—perhaps he was hungry, too—and within minutes it seemed, they were all headed for the luncheon.

Amy and Eloise filled their plates and took a seat near the back of the room. "Good afternoon, Lady Wethington."

Amy looked up and groaned to see Detectives Carson and Marsh standing in front of them, holding filled plates. "Do you mind if we join you?"

Yes. I mind if you join us, but my aunt raised me better than to tell you no.

"Not at all, detectives. Please join us." She waved at the empty chairs across from her and Eloise.

Once they took their seats, she looked at Eloise and said,

"May I make known to you Detective Marsh and Detective Carson." She turned to the men. "This is Lady Eloise Davenport."

Both men nodded. They remained silent as they all ate, but Amy was quite suspicious. Not that they had attended the funeral since that was a common practice, but that they stayed for the luncheon and sat with them. She knew something was coming that she wasn't going to like but she refused to let it interfere with her food.

"I am going back to get another one of those small berry pies," Eloise said as she wiped her mouth with a napkin and placed it alongside her empty plate. "They are very good. Would you like another one?"

"No. Thank you. I believe I've had enough."

Eloise stood and headed to the table where all the food had been placed. She returned with two pieces.

"You will be pleased to know that we have solved the problem of Mrs. Fleming's death." Detective Marsh smirked. It was almost the first time she saw the man's face since he always had his head down, writing in his notepad.

Amy had no idea murder was merely a problem, but since dealing with these two men on other cases, nothing really surprised her where they were concerned. "Indeed?"

Eloise stopped eating to study the two men.

"Yes. We have ascertained the Roman Baths employee, Mrs. Garfield, who found the body is the murderer."

They found the murderer already? Mrs. Fleming was barely in her grave, and these two incompetent men were satisfied that they had found the killer?

"And since you are willing to tell me this, I assume you won't mind if I ask why you believe Mrs. Garfield killed Mrs. Fleming?"

"It is very simple."

Of course, everything with you two is simple. Starting with your brains.

"Mrs. Garfield and Mrs. Fleming were long-time enemies, you might say. No one is too sure how it all started, but since Mrs. Garfield works there, and the body was found there, it all fits."

Amy didn't think anything these detectives came up with was worth pursuing, but she couldn't help herself. It was almost like when she was a child, and she had a loose tooth she constantly jiggled all the time. "They have been nemeses for a long time? Then why did Mrs. Garfield suddenly kill Mrs. Fleming?"

Carson shrugged. "Mrs. Garfield won't say, keeps saying she's innocent. But all murderers say that."

"How did Mrs. Fleming end up floating in the Roman Baths?"

"We presume the victim went to the Roman Baths to continue an argument, and in anger, Mrs. Garfield pushed her into the bath and held her under until she drowned."

Amy was speechless. That explanation was so weak that she had to struggle to keep from laughing. "And you, of course, have a witness to this? I mean the Baths are full of visitors all the hours they are open."

"Ah, but there are times when the Baths are not open."

She shook her head in confusion but decided to just move on. "I assume you have arrested Mrs. Garfield?"

"Yes."

"May I ask why you are here then if the case is solved?"

"Normal procedure."

She really didn't want to hear what they said about that, anyway. She looked over at Eloise who had finished off the two pieces of pie. "Are you ready to leave?"

Eloise studied the dessert table once more but said, "Yes. I'm ready."

Detectives Carson and Marsh stood as Amy and Eloise climbed to their feet. "Another reason we are here, Lady Wethington," Detective Marsh said, "is to warn you to forget all about this murder since the case is solved. I do not want to hear about you roaming around Bath asking questions."

Amy smiled and nodded, took Eloise's arm, and they left. Once outside, she pulled Eloise close to her and said, "We have a case to solve."

5

"No, we do not have a case to solve," Eloise said. "Michael already warned me that you would do this, and he forbade me to get involved."

"Is that so? Well, William told me the same thing, and while I agreed with him at the time, it has now come to my attention that in addition to the poor woman wrongly accused of Mrs. Fleming's death, there is a murderer out there who will not pay for his crime."

"Why are you so sure the detectives are wrong?"

Amy blew out a breath and began to count on her fingers. "They were wrong in St. Vincent's murder, wrong in Mr. Harding's murder, and the same in my cousin Alice's death. I have no reason to believe they are correct in this one either. And it was way too fast and easy. Their favorite way to solve things."

"That is true."

Amy looked around as they strolled back to her carriage, along with numerous other guests from the luncheon. "I don't know why I'm surprised, but it seems strange to me that there are so many mourners at Mrs. Fleming's funeral."

Eloise shrugged. "She was a midwife. Perhaps a lot of her

former patients are here." She took the footman's hand as he helped her into the carriage. Once they were both settled, she said, "If you are insistent on getting involved in this, how do you plan to go about it? I wasn't a part of the other deaths, so I'm not sure how one starts such a thing."

Amy tapped her lips as the carriage started up. "First, I would need to learn about her life. Who were her friends, who were her clients. Was she married? I assume since she was 'Mrs. Fleming' that she was either married or a widow."

"And there was that man who seemed to be directing the funeral."

Amy smiled. "You mean the one who you said looked guilty?"

Eloise nodded. "If I were getting involved in this, that is the man I would look at first. With the way he seemed to take over, I think he might be her husband. Or brother."

"But you are not getting involved?"

"No."

Amy let her thoughts wander as the carriage made its way to Eloise's townhouse. She was more interested in the contention between Mrs. Fleming and Mrs. Garfield. Although she dismissed out of hand the theory the detectives had, it would be interesting to know what this lengthy dissension was all about.

"Will you and William be at the Assembly this Saturday?" Eloise asked as the carriage came to a halt. "Michael promised to take me since we haven't been there in a few weeks."

"Yes. We will probably go. I don't know how much longer I will be able to appear in public without embarrassing myself."

"Yes," Eloise said as the footman opened the door. "We might as well have a bit of social life before it all stops." She leaned over and kissed Amy on the cheek. "I will see you Saturday, then."

As the footman started to close the door, Amy said, "Please have the driver go to the Roman Baths instead of my home."

He nodded, closed the door, and shouted the information to the driver.

Once they arrived, Amy climbed from the carriage and walked around the area where the Baths were, along with the beautiful and majestic Abbey. She'd always been fascinated with the history of the Roman Baths and enjoyed visiting it on occasion.

The Baths dated back to Roman times. The area had originally begun as a temple, and then in the early decades of Roman British rule, the town of Aquae Sulis grew around it. The Baths were restored several times over the years and eventually became the town of Bath and drew visitors from all over Britain, but primarily London. The baths were rumored to restore one's health, and people lined up daily to drink some of the liquid from the Mendip Hills, which was the source of water for the Baths.

She strolled the area around the water, stood in line for her drink, and spoke to a few of the employees who were not busy. Everyone she spoke with was adamant that Mrs. Garfield did not murder Mrs. Fleming, and the police were all idiots.

She agreed.

It was a nice visit but turned up nothing in the way of information she could use. She learned that Mrs. Garfield was a lovely woman, admired by her coworkers, who had been employed at the Baths for years, was the granddaughter of an Anglican bishop, had one son who moved to America, and she had, indeed, crossed swords with Mrs. Fleming. However, the employees she spoke with had nothing good to say about Mrs. Fleming.

She agreed with that, also.

Gathering as much information as she could, she returned to her carriage and directed her driver Randolph to bring her home. She had to make notes and see what she could do to correct the misinformed detectives.

* * *

WILLIAM NODDED at the man at the door of the Assembly who took his hat and Amy's cape. They made their way into the large room with the lovely blue walls and numerous chandeliers. The orchestra members were tuning their instruments but had not yet started to play.

"Oh, there is Aunt Margaret," Amy said.

They headed in the woman's direction. As always, Lady Margaret looked graceful and stunning. Her slender body showed off the rose-colored gown with black lace on the bodice and cuffs. William grinned, willing to bet any amount that she had on matching shoes, too. Something his wife had a hard time accomplishing.

Lady Margaret was busy speaking with a man William did not know.

"Aunt Margaret," Amy said as they approached the couple. "How nice to see you here."

Lady Margaret turned and smiled at her niece. "And you as well, Amy." The women hugged, and then Lady Margaret took the arm of the gentleman with her. "May I make known to you Jonathan, Marquess of Exeter." She turned to the gentleman. "Jonathan, this is my niece and her husband, Lord and Lady Wethington."

They all did the usual nodding and curtseying. William and Exeter shook hands. "Exeter? I know the name, of course, but I don't believe we've ever met," William said.

"No. I am sure of it. You are most likely thinking of the former Exeter. I have only recently come into the title. The prior Exeter was my uncle, a recluse for years. He passed several weeks ago. I haven't had a chance to make myself known to Parliament yet, either, which is a grave oversight on my part." He offered a warm smile.

William was certain Amy would love to draw more information from her aunt about the marquess. Lady Margaret had always seemed to have a male admirer about but remained steadfastly single.

"We're here." Eloise hurried up to them, Michael right behind her, joining their small circle.

After introductions were made, the musicians began a waltz, for which William was most grateful because he didn't want Amy doing any of the strenuous dances. He didn't dare mention it was because of her added bulk because he was sure she would take that as an insult.

The three couples proceeded to the floor. It was about thirty seconds into the dance when Amy said, "I wonder how long Aunt Margaret has known Exeter."

"I'm quite sure, my dear, that you will soon find out. I've never known you to pass up an opportunity to uncover information."

"Yes. That is true. That is also why I am such a successful mystery author." He had to admit she looked quite adorable when she displayed that smug grin.

"If he's recently come into his title, I wonder how Aunt Margaret met him." She paused. "I wonder where he was before now." She twisted in his arms to look at the couple as they waltzed by. "He is quite handsome, don't you think?"

William raised his brows. "I don't generally look at men and gauge their handsomeness, my dear." He bent in closer. "Neither should you, wife."

He could sense the frustration in Amy as she continued to study them. He bent close to her ear. "Sweetheart, just enjoy the dance for now, and you can inundate your aunt with questions this week. I am sure you are already planning a visit."

"Oh, yes."

When the music came to an end, they wandered toward the refreshment tables. Bowls of lemonade were displayed along with plates of cakes, biscuits, and tarts.

Michael and Eloise had already arrived at the table and the woman's plate was piled with sweets. Michael bent close to her ear and said something that she apparently didn't like. She shook her head, whispered something back, and he smiled and patted her shoulder.

William touched Amy on her elbow. "Do you want some refreshments?"

"I would like a lemonade."

"Sister, have you thought about another midwife? I was just speaking with Eloise about it. I'm sure you are both sad at the passing of Mrs. Fleming, but you need to think about someone to take her place," Michael said as William and Amy joined them at the small table against the wall where other attendees had gathered.

Eloise turned to Amy. "We do have to think about that."

"I shall ask at Bath United Hospital once again," William said. "It was where we obtained Mrs. Fleming's recommendation. We certainly want someone who is trained and certified as Mrs. Fleming was."

"And she let us know that on a regular basis," Eloise said as she wiped her mouth with a napkin.

After about another hour and one more waltz, William looked at his wife and frowned. "You look a bit peaked, dear. Would you like to return home?"

She shrugged. "Since Aunt Margaret and Lord Exeter have already left without me getting any more information, I don't see a reason to remain. I'm too cumbersome to do much dancing"—she cast him a dare-to-agree glare—"so I concur it's time to leave."

Just as they were retrieving their belongings, a woman

hurried up to them. "Lady Wethington," she said once she arrived, out of breath.

"Yes," Amy answered, a slight smile on her face.

"I understand you and your sister-in-law are looking for a new midwife since poor Mrs. Fleming's passing."

"Yes. That is true. Do you recommend someone?"

"Indeed I do. I am Mrs. Oldbridge, and my sister, Mrs. Phillipa Penrose, is a midwife. She can take on new mothers."

William cleared his throat. "If you don't mind, Mrs. Oldbridge, can you send around a note with the information?" He reached into his jacket pocket and pulled out his card. "Here is our information. I wish to get my wife home now, as she is feeling weary."

"Oh, of course." She smiled and took the card. "Phillipa will be so happy to gain new clients." She looked around and lowered her voice. "It was because of Mrs. Fleming that she's had a hard time finding new mothers. And her with no husband and a little girl to care for." She shook her head. "Not to speak ill of the dead, but she was a mean one, Mrs. Fleming."

Amy took William's arm, and they made their way to the carriage. "That was an interesting comment," Amy said.

"Do not dwell on it, my dear."

6

*A*my looked with satisfaction at the treat she had baked. Cook had tried to help her, but she was determined to do it all herself since she had Cook's recipe for Petit Fours right in front of her, so she'd shooed her off and took over the kitchen.

She pulled out her timepiece and groaned. Eloise and Mrs. Penrose, the midwife who was recommended to them, were both set to arrive in about fifteen minutes. She hurried up the back stairs to the bathing room and gave herself a quick wash, returned to her room to change her dress and fix her hair.

As she reached the bottom of the staircase, Filbert said, "My lady, Lady Davenport and Mrs. Penrose have arrived. You will find them in the drawing room. Shall I send for tea?"

"Yes, that would be nice. Ask Cook not to send in the Petit Fours I just made because I want to save them to surprise his lordship at dinner tonight."

She swore Filbert hid a smile, but she dismissed it and joined the ladies in the drawing room.

Mrs. Penrose stood when Amy entered the room. She

appeared younger than Mrs. Fleming, which made her wonder if William would object to employing her.

"Good afternoon, Mrs. Penrose I presume?"

The woman gave her a slight dip and smiled. "Yes, and you are Lady Wethington?"

"That is correct." Amy waved at her. "Please, take a seat. I have ordered tea so perhaps we can get to know each other while we wait for it."

Amy greeted Eloise and took the chair next to her. Mrs. Penrose shifted in her seat, her back stiffened. "First of all, I would like to warn you that Mrs. Fleming did her worst to try to keep me from getting new clients. I say this because you might have already heard some of her lies or will in the future."

Well, then.

That was certainly a different approach to introducing oneself and one's services to a new client.

"I'm afraid I have heard nothing about you until your sister approached me at the Assembly last Saturday."

"You will," she said.

Feeling a bit rattled at this introduction, Amy turned to Eloise who looked as befuddled as she felt.

Eloise cleared her throat to garner Mrs. Penrose's attention. "Mrs. Penrose. Can you tell us a little bit about your midwifery? How long have you been seeing mothers?"

"At least ten years. Right after my daughter, Beatrice, was born. I had helped another midwife up until my little girl was born. Once I recovered enough, I began to take on my own clients."

"Are you certified?" Amy asked.

She did not imagine the snap of anger in Mrs. Penrose's eyes at her question.

"I have years of experience, my lady. I have followed all the new ideas about cleanliness and washing one's hands. My mothers love me, and I would be happy to procure several references for you."

Just then Filbert returned to the drawing room pushing a tea cart. He moved it across the room to where the ladies sat and left it next to Amy. "Is there anything else, my lady?"

Amy viewed the cart. "No. That is fine."

She took her time pouring everyone's tea and passing around the plate of sandwiches and biscuits. She was pleased to see that Cook did not include her Petit Fours. She wanted to surprise William with them.

"Tell us about your daughter, Mrs. Penrose," Amy said as she blew on her cup of tea.

The woman patted the corners of her eyes. "My little Beatrice is the most wonderful child in the world. However, she is not a well girl." She took a moment to compose herself while Eloise refilled her plate.

Taking a deep breath, Mrs. Penrose continued. "Beatrice was only three years when she developed tuberculosis. That was bad enough, and while I prayed so hard that the disease wouldn't take her, it left her with weak lungs and a weak heart."

"Oh, I am so sorry," Amy said.

"Our doctor has tried various treatments on her, but so far nothing has helped. However, every time he tries a new medicine or procedure, it costs money. As a widow, I don't always have the funds he needs."

She wiped her eyes again. "That is why it has been so disturbing that Mrs. Fleming has spread lies about me and my clients." She shook her head and took a sip of tea.

"Why would she do that? Do you know?" Eloise asked.

Mrs. Penrose's eyes flashed. "She is—rather was—an evil person. She knew my daughter needed treatment for her troubles, but it didn't stop her from taking away clients that I had already secured."

Amy studied her for a moment. "May I ask what lies she spread about you?"

"Yes, indeed, because if you start to ask about me, you will hear some of them." She wiped her upper lip. "She has told people that more of my new mothers die than hers do."

That was certainly a skin crawling comment since all about-to-be-mothers fear the childbirth process and like to think all will turn out well, even though they know the risk of death of the mother or baby is possible.

"I don't mean to be insulting, but is that true?"

Mrs. Penrose straightened in her seat. "All midwives lose a mother or two, my lady. But my losses are no more than normal."

She declined to ask her what 'normal' was. "That was not very kind of her to do that." She really didn't know what else to say. No expectant mother wanted to dwell on the possible death of her or her baby.

"Just so," Mrs. Penrose said and took another sip of tea.

Amy peered over at Eloise who looked a tad uncomfortable. "I will be happy to speak with some of your clients. My husband, of course, will be involved in the decision, as will my brother, Lady Davenport's husband."

"I would like that, my lady. I have many happy clients." She fumbled in her reticule and withdrew a piece of paper. "Here is a list. I composed it this morning, hoping you would ask for it. I added their directions so you can send around a note if you wish to or visit them in person."

Amy reached for the paper and gave it a quick perusal.

They finished their tea with mundane chatting, since Amy didn't want to hear any more about mothers lost in childbirth.

Eventually when the conversation waned, Amy stood and Mrs. Penrose jumped up.

"Lady Davenport and I will speak with these people and get back to you."

The woman looked relieved and gave a slight dip. "Thank you so much, my ladies. I look forward to hearing from you."

Filbert appeared, obviously close enough to the room to hear the conversation. "My butler will see you out," Amy said.

She thanked them again and left with a smile on her face.

Amy collapsed into her seat and looked over at Eloise. "It appears Mrs. Fleming had a number of enemies."

"Based on the number of mourners at her funeral, she also had a lot of friends," Eloise said.

"Or enemies who wanted to make sure she was truly dead and buried."

A FEW HOURS LATER, she and William sat in the drawing room enjoying a before dinner drink. "I have no intention of employing a midwife who I haven't met." William took a final sip of his drink. "And frankly, I'm a little concerned that she mentioned her differences with Mrs. Fleming. Speaking ill of another colleague doesn't seem to be the professional way to attract new clients."

Amy placed her empty sherry glass on the table in front of her. "According to Mrs. Penrose, it was Mrs. Fleming speaking poorly of *her* skills and treatment of *her* patients that caused a rift between them and also initiated her losing clients."

He glanced at his empty glass, shrugged, and placed it on the table in front of him. "Nevertheless, I intend to visit with Bath United Hospital in the morning to see who they have to recommend."

"And I shall go with you."

William opened his mouth to speak just as Filbert entered the room. "My lord, my lady, dinner is ready."

"Thank you." William turned to Amy and took her arm. As they strolled down the corridor to the dining room, she said, "I am anxious for you to eat the lovely Petit Fours I made for you today."

William smiled and squeezed her hand, looking a bit fearful.

* * *

IN THE YEAR EIGHTEEN TWENTY-SIX, the City Infirmary and Dispensary joined with the Casualty Hospital to form Bath United Hospital. Located in the Weston suburb of Bath, it served Bath and surrounding areas. The combined institution opened in a building designed by John Pinch the Elder on Beau Street.

When William had visited before, he'd been very impressed with the doctor he spoke with. Hopefully, he would be able to see the same man. He patted his pocket where he had the paper from his last visit, then pulled it out and studied it as he walked through the lobby, Amy alongside him.

"Do you know some women are going to hospital to give birth? It's becoming the fashionable thing to do," she said.

"What do you think? Would you prefer to do that?"

Amy smiled and shook her head. "I believe your mother would be brokenhearted if she was unable to attend me. She did deliver two children. Perhaps we should have brought her with us."

"No need, dear." Egad, the last thing he wanted to discuss with his mother present was childbirth. When the time came, he had planned to be at his club, drink in hand, awaiting the news, surrounded by friends. Until his mother informed him he would be at home, with no drink, and maybe a friend or two. Or Mr. Colbert. He knew she was right but based on what he'd heard from men who had gone through it, it seemed damned uncomfortable to listen to something he preferred not to hear.

They stepped up to the young man seated at the desk. "We

are Lord and Lady Wethington. We wish to speak with Dr. Dudley. Is he available?"

"Do you have an appointment?" the man asked.

"No. But I did send around a note the other day that I would be stopping by today. If he is unavailable, I can ask my questions of another doctor. It's just that I spoke with Dr. Dudley before."

The young man stood. "You may take a seat over there. I will see if the doctor is available."

They were only settled for a short time when the young man returned. "You are fortunate. Dr. Dudley is here and available. Please follow me."

He took them through a maze of corridors before they came to an area that was apparently newly built. The smell of medicine and sickness was less prevalent in this section.

A tall, slender man, Dr. Dudley wore spectacles that he kept pushing up his nose. He was about forty or so years and had a very soothing and caring look about him. But his eyes were as sharp as a swordman's blade. He stood as they walked into his office. "Lord Wethington. A pleasure to see you again."

"Thank you, doctor. May I introduce you to my wife, Lady Wethington."

The doctor dipped his head. "A pleasure to meet you, my lady." He waved at the two chairs in front of his desk. "Please, have a seat."

Once they were settled, the doctor said, "How may I be of assistance to you?"

William leaned forward. "As you know, I was here a few months ago seeking a recommendation for a midwife. You suggested Mrs. Fleming, who we were quite satisfied with. However, I'm sure you have heard she passed away, and now we need another recommendation."

The doctor put his palms together and tapped his lips with

his index fingers. "Yes. I did hear about her unfortunate end." He shook his head. "I wonder if they caught the villain yet."

"I don't know," William said smoothly before his wife could jump in. He just wanted a recommendation, not to delve into the poor woman's murder.

"If I may, Doctor?" Amy said. She fumbled in her reticule and pulled out a paper. "I have received one recommendation, and I would like your opinion. A Mrs. Penrose."

"Is that Mrs. Phillipa Penrose?"

"Yes."

He leaned back and placed his elbows on the arm rests. "I hear she is a fine midwife. Her clients seem happy with her. She is not certified, though, if that is an issue with you—"

"It is," William said.

"I know she has a sick daughter that she is supporting by herself." He started to speak and then stopped.

"What is it, Dr. Dudley?" Amy asked.

"This has absolutely nothing to do with her skills as a midwife, but it would be remiss if I didn't mention that she arrived in Bath a few years ago under a cloud."

"What was that?" William asked.

He still seemed reluctant to speak but continued. "She had been detained—but then released by the police—on a charge of murder."

"Murder!" they both said.

"Yes. Her elderly father. It happened in Bristol from what I understand."

William sucked in a breath. "How did her father die?"

"Drowned. In his bath."

7

"Drowned?" Eloise said as she stared at Amy.

"Yes. Dr. Dudley felt the need to tell us even though she was never convicted."

Eloise grabbed Amy's arm. "Don't you find it peculiar that Mrs. Penrose had a strong dislike for Mrs. Fleming and then Mrs. Fleming drowns, and Mrs. Penrose had been under suspicion for drowning her father?"

"Indeed."

"I don't know about you, but I wouldn't feel comfortable having Mrs. Penrose as my midwife," Eloise said.

Amy nodded. "William has already crossed her off the list. But this is interesting. Dr. Dudley referred us to a Dr. Stevens." She paused. "A woman!"

"A woman doctor? How very odd. What did William say about that?"

"He was as taken aback as was I, but he wrote her information down and said we were to visit with her."

It was a lovely early summer day, and they were enjoying an afternoon repast at a small outdoor teahouse located on the pavilion between the Abbey and the Roman Baths.

"Since we are the ones who will need the services of the doctor, I think the two of us should go see her first." Eloise took the last biscuit on the tray in front of them.

"That is an excellent idea! I would love to meet a woman doctor and ask her things I probably wouldn't ask with our husbands present."

Eloise began to gather up her things. "We shall go now."

"What? I don't have her information."

"No matter. If William wrote it down, it must be somewhere in the library at your house."

Catching her enthusiasm, Amy lumbered up. "Yes. You are correct. William placed the paper on his desk when we got home from our visit with Dr. Dudley."

Once the carriage was on its way to Wethington House, Amy said, "I find myself drawn into Mrs. Fleming's murder more each day. Although they have arrested that woman, we seem to run into people who had a dislike for her."

"Don't let William know."

She sniffed. "I feel no need to tell him everything I do."

Eloise shook her head. "I've never seen William mad at you. In fact, I get the feeling that your antics amuse him most times, but if you do become involved and he finds out, I think you may see a different side of Lord Wethington."

"Oh, don't be silly," Amy said. "He would never harm me."

"Of course not. But you might find yourself locked in your bedchamber until your confinement ends."

"I won't do anything dangerous. I will merely ask a few questions about Mrs. Penrose." Amy shifted in her seat, trying to get comfortable. "For instance, since she has applied to be retained by William and me to deliver our baby, it would be perfectly normal to inquire. In fact, I shall look at the list she gave us of references and speak with one or two of those women. I will send around a note and ask if I might stop by. I don't see anything dangerous or harmful in that."

"I hope William agrees with you."

When they arrived at Wethington House, Amy asked her footman who arrived to help her out of the carriage to retrieve the list from William's desk. Ordinarily, she wouldn't make that request, but she found all this scurrying about with her extra weight was quite fatiguing.

With the paper clutched in Amy's hand, they made their way to the direction Dr. Dudley had provided, the light traffic making for a brief trip. Eloise looked out the window as the carriage slowed down. "It appears we have arrived."

They climbed the few steps and knocked on the simple wooden, albeit expensive, door that held a plaque in gold lettering. *Clinic of Dr. Rayne Stevens*. A very tall man answered, a friendly smile on his face. "How may we help you, ladies?"

Amy smiled back. "I am Lady Wethington, and this is my friend and sister-in-law, Lady Davenport. If Dr. Stevens has a few minutes, we would like to speak with her. I know we should have sent word ahead of time, but we were out and about anyway, and thought to stop by."

He glanced down at their swollen bellies and smiled again. "Of course, my ladies. Please follow me to the waiting room, and I will advise Dr. Stevens of your arrival."

"Thank you." They followed the man down a corridor. The smell of medicine and something stronger filled the air. Soft mumbling came from behind a closed door.

"Here we are, my ladies." The man waved them into a room.

The room was much more pleasant than she'd expected for a medical facility. Soft rose and green colors dominated the space, with a lovely carpet, several comfortable chairs, and floor-to-ceiling windows that let in plenty of light.

They were barely settled when a man arrived and offered a slight bow. "Lady Wethington. How very nice to see you again, although the last time we met you were Lady Amy Lovell."

Amy's brows rose. "Lord Sterling?"

She remembered him from the time Papa had insisted she must have a Season in London and find a husband. Not fitting in well with the Upper Ten Thousand, especially the young ladies born and bred for their 'Seasons', it was a disaster. After fumbling her way through two years of the various events, always saying the wrong thing, missing dance steps, and spilling drinks on her gowns, she convinced her papa to allow her to return to Bath.

With a great deal of reluctance on his part and relief on hers, he permitted her escape.

"I saw you several years ago when you were very much a part of the London *ton*. What brings you here?" she asked.

Lord Sterling had always been pleasant to her, although if memory served, he was more than pleasant to all women. She'd heard he had some sort of a tragedy in his family, which drove him into a few years of dissipation, but because the only information she had about anyone from London was from Michael, her knowledge of *ton* goings-on was scarce.

It appeared whatever caused him to dip into rakishness was well behind him.

"Excuse me, my lord, allow me to introduce you to Lady Eloise Davenport. She is married to my brother, Michael."

Lord Sterling nodded in Eloise's direction. "A pleasure, my lady." He looked back at Amy, placing his hands on his hips, and leaned back on his heels, a grin on his handsome face. "I am married to Dr. Stevens."

Amy's jaw dropped, and she continued to stare at him.

"I take care of her books," he continued, despite her stunned expression. "The woman would never get paid if I didn't step in. I'm usually here once or twice a week in the afternoons."

His lordship burst out laughing. "I see you are surprised."

"I don't mean to offend, my lord, but surprised hardly covers it."

Just then a lovely woman wearing a long white apron over a

dark blue wool dress entered the room. She was quite pretty, with her hair pinned into a sensible topknot, the wisps of which were falling around her face. "Are you charming my patients again, my dear?"

Lord Sterling smiled widely and wrapped his arm around the woman's waist, which told Amy she must be Dr. Stevens. "Of course. It is part of the service we provide." He leaned over and kissed her cheek.

Dr. Stevens laughed and pushed him away. "Off with you. I hear ledgers calling your name." She looked at the two women. "I assume you are Lady Wethington and Lady Davenport?"

"Yes." Amy felt her face flush with the interaction between Lord Sterling and the doctor. It was obvious they had a very happy marriage, something not always seen in the *ton*.

The doctor smiled at Amy and Eloise as she took a seat across from them. "I have asked John, the man who guards our door, to send for tea since this is a perfect time for me to take my afternoon break. If I don't, Sterling becomes grumpy." She patted her slightly swollen belly. "He wants to make sure his son is well fed, and his mother is off her feet for a little while."

"How do you know what the baby is?" Eloise asked.

Dr. Stevens offered a very warm smile. "I don't. I'm a doctor, not a fortune teller. But this is our second child, the first being our beautiful daughter, Lady Madeline. Sterling insists this one is a boy."

She looked up. "Oh, here is the tea." The man who greeted them at the door pushed in a cart with the usual tea refreshments. Dr. Stevens fixed tea and passed around the plate of small sandwiches.

Still full after their trip to the tea shop, Amy passed on the food. Eloise put a few tidbits on her plate.

They kept the conversation light as they shared their tea. Once they wiped their mouths and sat back, Dr. Stevens said, "How can I assist you ladies today?"

Amy sat forward. "As you can see, we are in a family way. We are both due in a few months."

Dr. Stevens changed from light and carefree to serious as she adopted her doctor persona. "Yes, I see that."

"We both had Mrs. Fleming as our midwife. Are you familiar with her?"

The doctor hesitated for a moment, then said, "Yes. I am. Her work is exceptional."

Eloise joined in. "Are you aware that she has passed away?"

"Sadly, yes. Although the unfortunate woman made enemies easily, I can't imagine her making anyone so angry that they would kill her." She shook her head.

They took a moment of silence, then Amy said, "Lady Davenport and I need a new midwife. My husband, Lord Wethington, secured your name from Dr. Dudley who was most impressed with you."

Dr. Stevens dipped her head. "Dr. Dudley is a very nice man, and a wonderful doctor. One of the few who accepted me when I took over my father's practice. I am honored that he mentioned my name."

"Are you in a position, Dr. Stevens, to accept two new mothers?" Amy held her breath. Everything they'd seen and heard so far made Dr. Stevens an excellent choice to replace Mrs. Fleming.

"Yes, indeed, my lady." She checked the timepiece pinned to her apron. "If you both have the time now, I would like to do an examination and gather some medical information. Can you do that? It will take no more than thirty or forty minutes."

Amy and Eloise looked at each other and nodded. "Yes, doctor, we will be more than happy to do that," Amy said.

* * *

WILLIAM BOUNDED up the steps to his front door, quite happy with his day's work. He'd met with his solicitor to set up a trust fund for the new baby. He also made certain all his affairs were in order now that he and Amy were to become parents. Amy, herself, had a considerable sum set aside by her brother, Michael, who had handled all the royalties from her books over the years. When they married, William saw no reason to change that.

He smiled at the idea of having a child of his own. He'd have to speak with Amy soon about decorating the nursery. Hopefully, that would keep her from sticking her nose into the investigation of Mrs. Fleming's death.

Or continuing her baking efforts. Dear God, he didn't know if he would survive this new adventure of hers. He had found it necessary to seek a stomach tisane from Cook just about every night. But he would never hurt her feelings about her efforts.

"Where is her ladyship?" he asked as he handed his hat and gloves to Filbert.

"Lady Wethington is in her sitting room, my lord. She returned from an outing about thirty minutes ago."

Amy was lying on the settee in front of the window in her sitting room. Her eyes were closed, and from her steady breathing it appeared she was asleep. Rather than disturb her, he took the soft comfortable blanket at the bottom of their bed and covered her. He then left and proceeded to the library where he poured himself a small brandy.

He walked to the window and stared out at the light rain that had just started. After a few minutes, he wandered to his desk and picked up a folded newspaper. In the center of the page of legal notices was an item that had been circled with a dark pencil.

He walked back to the window and held the paper up to read it. It was a copy of the *Bristol Mercury*, which they received by the post twice a week. The circled item said:

Banns announcements:
Mr. Ronald Fleming and Mrs. Catherine Seiber announce their intention to marry on 21 July 1892. If an individual has reason to believe this marriage is not lawful, please contact Church of the Holy Trinity with St. Edmund, Bristol.

"I SEE YOU FOUND THE NOTICE," Amy said as she walked into the room, looking as though she just woke up from her nap.

"Yes. However, who are these people and why are you interested in their marriage?"

"I have reason to believe Mrs. Fleming's husband was named Ronald. It appears quite helpful that his wife died so he could marry someone else less than a month after her funeral."

William drew himself up and glared at her. "*Amy.* I see no reason why that should concern you. If for some reason that is correct, you can turn the information over to our detective friends and forget about it."

"*William.*" She pointed to the paper he held. "Do you *honestly* believe they will admit that once again they were wrong and will pursue this?"

"My *honesty* is not in question here, wife. With a child on the way, you have much to take care of. Just because we were involved in previous police matters in the past does not mean you should do so again." He tapped the paper with his finger. "I do not—I repeat *do not*—want you putting yourself in danger."

With those words, he tore the newspaper in quarters and tossed it into the cold fireplace. He tugged on his jacket cuffs. "Would you care for a sherry before dinner, my love?"

She glared at him while Persephone barked and growled in

his direction. She wished she had spent the time teaching her beloved dog to bite on command.

8

William had just left to take a tour of a business Lord Melville had recommended for investment purposes. Amy sat in her sitting room, going through Cook's recipes for something sweet to make for the evening's dessert. It took her a while to find the old book of recipes because Cook had put it somewhere she'd never done before and then forgotten where. Luckily, Amy had found it for her.

She awaited Eloise's arrival. She'd convinced herself that she was not putting herself in danger if she and Eloise merely stopped by Mrs. Mallory's home, one of the women on Mrs. Penrose's list, to discuss the midwife. Afterward, they would take a stroll in Victoria Park and chat with some of the people they met along the way. It was a lovely day, sunny with a mild breeze. Just the thing for two expectant ladies to take advantage of since Dr. Stevens had pointed out to them that mild exercise was good for their condition.

She'd found it quite suspicious that the banns for Mr. Fleming's upcoming marriage were announced in a Bristol newspaper instead of the *Bath Chronicle*. She had no idea where the Mrs. Catherine Seiber resided, but Mr. Fleming was certainly a

Bath resident, and any banns should have been posted locally. That was the point of advertising them.

Mr. Fleming and Mrs. Penrose were the only two people on her list of suspects. Not that she was keeping an actual list of suspects. After all, both the detectives and William had told her not to get involved in the murder.

She sniffed. She wasn't involved; she merely wanted to chat with a reference given to her and then take a walk on a lovely summer day.

Her attention was taken with Filbert as he appeared at the doorway. "Lady Davenport has arrived."

"Thank you. Has my carriage been brought around?"

"Yes, it awaits you out front."

Amy placed the book of recipes on the top of her desk and walked the short distance to their bedchamber and gathered her gloves, hat, and cape. Although Eloise would have arrived in her own carriage, Amy felt the Wethington carriage was more comfortable so they would switch to hers for their trek.

She took one last look in the mirror and glanced down at her feet. She was quite pleased to have found the other half of her favorite pair of walking boots. Well, actually she hadn't found them. Persephone must have grown tired of her constant complaining about missing shoes and rummaged through her closet until she found the boot, dragged it to her, and dropped it at her feet.

After greetings and hugs, bonnets tied, and gloves pulled on, Amy and Eloise climbed into the carriage and settled in.

"I think we should stop somewhere for tea after our visit with Mrs. Mallory before we take our stroll. It's been a while since luncheon," Eloise said.

Amy held in her grin; the woman was a walking eating machine. "I could use a cup of tea, actually." She tapped on the ceiling of the carriage to signal they were ready to leave. She had already given the direction to Randolph.

Amy leaned forward. "I must tell you about a very interesting thing that has happened."

Eloise shifted forward. "What? You certainly have my attention."

Amy lowered her voice as if their conversation could be heard outside the window of the carriage. "Mrs. Fleming's husband is getting married. Er, remarried."

Eloise blew out a breath and leaned back. "That doesn't look good."

"Absolutely not."

"How do you know this?"

"There was an announcement in the Bristol newspaper, announcing banns for a Mr. Ronald Fleming and a Mrs. Catherine Seiber."

Just then the carriage came to a rolling stop, and Randolph jumped down. He opened the door and said, "We have arrived at the direction, my lady."

"Thank you."

The two women made their way up the steps to a nice townhouse. While not in the fashionable part of Bath, it was still a very decent neighborhood. When they knocked, the door was opened by a young maid in a typical uniform with a mobcap on her head. She dipped. "Good afternoon, ladies. Mrs. Mallory awaits you in the drawing room."

She did not offer to take their capes and bonnets, so it appeared Mrs. Mallory was not expecting them to stay long.

Mrs. Mallory was a young woman, not even Amy's age. She held an infant in her arms who was sleeping. She offered a warm smile. "I hope you don't mind. I'll need to make this a quick interview since my older son is about to awaken from his nap."

"This won't take long," Amy said. "I am Lady Wethington, and this is my friend and sister-in-law, Lady Davenport."

She acknowledged them with a slight nod. "How can I help you?"

"Mrs. Penrose has given us your name as a reference for her services. Lady Davenport and I find ourselves in need of a new midwife."

"Oh, dear," she said. "Was Mrs. Fleming your midwife?"

Amy nodded. "Yes."

"I wish I could say I was sorry to hear of her death, but she was a very bitter woman." She shook her head. "I have no idea why, but she tried her best to ruin Mrs. Penrose's reputation."

"How did you find Mrs. Penrose to be in her handling of you?"

Mrs. Mallory stopped for a minute. "She was very skilled in her work. I felt most comfortable with her services."

Eloise leaned forward. "Did you find her to be easy to deal with?"

The young mother laughed. "If you are trying to ask if she was kinder than Mrs. Fleming, the answer is yes. She did have a quick temper, I might add, but otherwise I had no issues with her."

It appeared they weren't going to get any more information, so Amy stood, Eloise following her lead. "I thank you very much, Mrs. Mallory, and I wish you well with your new baby and older son."

"Thank you. I would walk you out, but I prefer not to disturb the little one." She nodded at the infant in her arms.

"That is fine. We can see ourselves out." Amy led the way out of the room and to the front door. The same young maid greeted them and let them out. They descended the steps and entered the carriage.

"That visit didn't tell us much," Eloise said.

"True. But I was interested in her comment about Mrs. Penrose's temper. That seemed to be an odd thing for a patient to say."

It was a short ride from the Mallory residence to the area surrounding the Baths and the Abbey. After the short stroll from the mews, they arrived at the outdoor tea shop they favored.

The beautiful weather made sitting outside the best possible choice. Only a few tables were occupied, and Amy and Eloise took the one in the corner with a perfect view of the Roman Baths and the Abbey.

"I had wanted to bring you the newspaper announcement of Mr. Fleming's upcoming nuptials, but William tore that section and tossed it into the fireplace. I tried to piece it together, but it ripped right where the wording was."

Eloise smirked. "I told you William would not be happy if you got involved in this."

Amy shrugged.

They chatted about other things until the waiter delivered their order. Once he was gone and they fixed their tea, Eloise said, "These sandwiches look wonderful! Oh, look, Amy, watercress and cream cheese. And smoked salmon!"

"Oh, ladies!" A woman's voice interrupted Amy as she began to speak. She looked over her shoulder at Mrs. Penrose waving at them and making her way to their table.

Amy groaned. Eloise took a bite of a sandwich.

Mrs. Penrose made herself comfortable—uninvited—at their table. "How fortuitous. You are just the women I wanted to see. I am so pleased."

"Yes, fortuitous," Amy mumbled. "Would you care for tea?"

* * *

William settled comfortably in his favorite chair at the club and took a sip of the brandy he'd been looking forward to all day. Feeling quite content, he picked up the newspaper on the table in front of him and shook it loose.

It had been a profitable and enlightening day. The meetings with his man of business, Mr. Frank Wilson, and then his solicitor, Mr. Alfred Lawrence, had resulted in the finalization of the new venture which would increase his financial stability and secure the future for his family. It was quite a good feeling to be a family man. At one time, he eschewed the idea of marriage since there were other male relatives able to step up to his title if he suffered an early death.

Then he met Lady Amy at the Mystery Book Club, admired her for some time, and after arriving at her house one evening to loan her a book, he stumbled across a distraught Lady Amy and a dead body in her library. The rest was history.

"Wethington!" Amy's brother, Michael, strolled up and settled into the chair across from him.

William lowered the newspaper. "Good afternoon, Davenport. You seem quite cheerful."

Michael waved at the footman to bring him a brandy. He turned to William and rubbed his hands together. "Yes. I am feeling quite enthusiastic for my businesses right now."

William studied his brother-in-law. He did look quite excited. "What news do you have?"

"My father and I have gone our separate ways." He saluted William with his glass and took a sip of brandy.

"Indeed! That is certainly a surprise. I didn't realize your differences were that severe. I believe you have been partners for years."

In his enthusiasm, Davenport had finished his brandy and signaled for another. He glanced at William's glass. "Are you ready for a refill?"

William placed his hand over the top. "No. I think I will hold onto this one for a while." Davenport was certainly thrilled by his news. He could hardly sit still.

"As you are aware, we have been partners in business since I left university. But lately, we seem to have two different directions for our businesses as I told you once before. I'm looking toward the future, and he is still in doing everything the same way." He shook his head. "It was time."

The next thirty or so minutes were spent with Michael congratulating himself on his move and laying out all the plans he had for his businesses. By now, William had consumed two brandies and was anxious to get home and relax. Forget business, even though he'd had a rewarding day.

He placed his glass on the table in front of him and stood. "I wish you the very best, Davenport. I'm happy for you since you believe this is the right thing." He straightened his jacket. "Now I must be on my way."

Michael snapped his fingers. "Wait a moment, and I will walk out with you." He downed the rest of his drink and they walked to the door.

It looked as though their sunny day had disappeared. Ominous looking clouds were gathering. Since William had ridden his horse, he was anxious to leave.

They walked to their horses which the doorman brought from the mews behind the club. He swung his leg over his horse, Major, and headed home. The rain started before he reached his townhouse, but fortunately it remained only a light drizzle.

He shook off his wet jacket and handed it to Filbert. "Where is her ladyship?"

"I believe Lady Wethington is in the library, my lord. Shall I send in your valet with a dry jacket?"

"Yes. Please do."

Amy sat on the settee in front of the window, apparently watching the raindrops slide down the glass. She had a book on her lap. She turned as he entered and gave him a warm smile, which was the one thing he needed to shake off the chill from the rain. "Good afternoon, husband." She looked him up and down. "I see the rain caught you a bit."

He walked to her and sat alongside her. She slid over to make room. "Luckily, I avoided most of it. How was your day?"

"Productive."

William leaned back and rested his booted foot on his knee.

Amy shifted in her chair to face him. "Eloise and I visited with one of Mrs. Penrose's references today."

William frowned. "Why did you do that? I thought we decided on Dr. Stevens." He immediately wished the words back again, not wanting to know precisely what his wife was up to. He had a strong suspicion that her visit to this woman was not just to determine the other midwife's capabilities, but since he preferred not to stroll down that lane, he said, "Where the devil is my dry jacket?"

"Yes, we did decide on Dr. Stevens. But it didn't hurt to see what Mrs. Penrose's references had to say. I'm still not convinced the detectives have the right person under arrest. As good citizens, we should be willing to step up and see that justice is served."

"Here we are, my lord." Stevenson, his newest valet since his previous one took a pension, entered the room, holding out a dry jacket.

"Thank you," he mumbled, allowing the man to help him into it.

Just then a very small, furry creature toddled into the library. William pointed at the thing. "What in heaven's name is that?"

"Do not change the subject, William."

"I am not changing the subject; I am merely trying to identify a creature in my house. I know it is not Persephone since this one is darker and smaller."

Amy walked over and picked the thing up. "This is a kitten."

He shook his head, already reaching for his handkerchief. "I cannot have a kitten in the house. I am allergic to them." He sneezed.

Twice. And pointed to the door. "Out."

Amy drew herself up. "Me or the kitten?"

He couldn't suggest they both leave the room since she was still fixated on the murder, and he wanted to straighten her out about further investigation. The tears following would not be worth it. "Amy, love. I cannot have a kitten in the house."

"Then you are in luck, my lord, because this is Eloise's kitten. Michael is against pets of any sort, and she wants me to keep this one—very briefly—until she can change Michael's mind."

A headache was in his future, he could feel it coming on. "I think I will go for a walk in the garden."

Amy glanced at the window. "It's raining."

He stopped and pinched the bridge of his nose.

Amy walked over to him and patted him on the arm. "I shall put the kitten in the kitchen."

Sneeze.

She walked away and then turned back. "I have another wonderful surprise for your dessert tonight my lord. Three-layer apple upside down cake."

9

*L*ively conversation and spirited music greeted Amy and William as they entered the Assembly the following Saturday evening. To keep peace in her marriage, Amy said no more about Mrs. Fleming, hoping William would believe she had lost interest in the matter, but the occasional way he studied her said no.

She thought back to the meeting with Mrs. Penrose the other day when she'd approached her and Eloise at the tea shop. Neither one of them had wanted to tell the midwife that they had already secured the services of Dr. Stevens, so they gently avoided giving her a definite answer. Even if they had not arranged for the doctor to attend them, they would have been especially reluctant after hearing that her father had drowned in his bathtub and one of her references mentioned her bad temper.

Focusing on the evening ahead, Amy decided to try her best to speak to as many people as possible to gather information on Mrs. Penrose, Mr. Fleming, and his betrothed, Mrs. Seiber. As a good mystery writer, she should also add Mrs. Garfield who sat in gaol for the murder to her list. To be honest with herself, the only reason she had not added her was because the inept detectives thought she was the guilty one, which almost definitely made it not her.

As they made their way across the floor, William leaned in close to her. "Do not be offended my dear, but you look a tad peaked. If you decide at any time to return home, just let me know."

Despite wanting to snap at him for treating her as though she were old and withered, he, unfortunately, was correct. Evening entertainments no longer held her interest. All she wanted after dinner was to slip into something soft and comfortable and read a good book, with a nice cup of tea, William sipping on his brandy as he read his book alongside her. Carrying a child was quite fatiguing.

"Aunt Margaret, I had hoped you would stop by for a visit this week," Amy said as they approached the small group of friends and hugged the woman. She still wanted to get information on Lord Exeter, who was again accompanying her aunt to the Assembly. He stood with his arm around her waist which told her a lot without Aunt Margaret having to say a word. A very pleased looking Aunt Margaret, she noted.

"I had planned to, but the week just flew by." She looked at Exeter and grinned.

Well, then.

"How is your baking project going?" Aunt Margaret asked.

She could have sworn she heard a choking sound come from William, but when she looked at him, he appeared normal.

"Excellent. I made Petit Fours this week. They were wonderful, weren't they, dear?" She looked at William who nodded.

"Indeed."

"I must stop by for tea this week and sample some of these wonderful baked goodies you are making," Aunt Margaret said.

"You know I always love to have you join me for tea, Aunt."

Amy looked around the room, her eyes quickly returning to Mrs. Penrose who had just entered the room in the company of three other women. It would be an uncomfortable conversation with her since she was expecting an answer about using her services, but she needed to speak with her to gather any information that might place the midwife higher up on her list of suspects.

She and Eloise were able to put her off once, but Amy was certain she would not be put off forever. She seemed to be a forceful sort.

"Did you see who just entered the room?" Eloise's voice in her ear had her turning toward her sister-in-law.

"When did you get here?"

"Just now. We were right behind Mrs. Penrose and her friends. What shall we do if she tries to corner us here?"

"This is becoming ridiculous, you know. We cannot avoid the woman for the rest of our pregnancy." Amy glanced over Eloise's shoulder. "Oh, no. Here she comes."

Amy grabbed William's sleeve. He leaned down, concern in his eyes. "Is something the matter, sweetheart?"

"No. I mean, yes." She took a deep breath and pressed on. "Remember Dr. Stevens, the one Dr. Dudley recommended to us as a substitute for Mrs. Fleming?"

"Yes, I know, dear. I intended to see Dr. Stevens myself this week."

"Well, no reason to. Eloise and I visited with her this week and agreed to have her act as our midwife."

William's lips tightened. "You are my wife. I will make the final decision on who will attend you."

Annoyed at his high-handedness, she decided to put off her retort to that when she darted a glance at Mrs. Penrose, who was making her way across the floor. "Oh, do not concern yourself, husband, she is wonderful. I will tell you all about her as soon as we arrive home." She lowered her voice and sped up, tripping over her words as Mrs. Penrose bore down on them. "Mrs. Penrose, who wanted to be our midwife is about to step up to us. Eloise and I have put her off once, but she is quite adamant that she needs an answer. I haven't yet told her about Dr. Stevens, so you must tell her that *you* arranged for Dr. Stevens without me knowing it."

She took in a deep breath and gave the woman a huge smile as William shook his head, as if to clear his brain. "Good evening, Mrs. Penrose." She turned to William who was still looking a bit befuddled. "May I introduce Mrs. Penrose to you, husband? Mrs. Penrose, this is my husband, Lord William Wethington." She thought perhaps adding his title might intimidate the woman a tad so breaking the news to her would go smoother.

Or not.

"It is a pleasure to meet you, Mrs. Penrose." He appeared to be repeating her hurried words over in his mind.

"I am so glad to meet you, my lord. I had hoped Lady Wethington has spoken to you about my services."

"Er, no. I mean, yes." He looked at Amy. "Isn't that so, dear?"

"Yes."

They both turned their attention to Mrs. Penrose who looked very confused. She cleared her throat. "Well, have you made a decision?"

"No." Amy said.

"Yes." William uttered at the same time. He looked over at her, threw up his hands and walked away.

Honestly, the man could not seem to get anything straight. She looked back at Mrs. Penrose. If she told the midwife she was not going to be needed, that would prevent her having a reason to speak with her, enough to ascertain whether she should remain on the suspect list. Since she'd said 'no' before William said 'yes', one would think he would follow suit.

"I'm afraid my husband and I are still mulling it over." She took Mrs. Penrose by the arm and walked her away from the group. "You've given us some recommendations to contact, and unfortunately I haven't had the time to do that."

There was no reason to tell her that although Mrs. Mallory had been happy with her services, she mentioned a bad temper. "Perhaps you can give me some information about yourself, which will help in making our decision."

When the woman looked confused—goodness, what was it with people tonight—she said, "I believe you mentioned you had a daughter? No husband?"

"That would be correct. I am certain I told you at our interview that I am a widow. My husband died a few years ago."

"Oh, I'm so sorry. Was he ill?"

"No. An accident."

Bells went off in her head. She didn't want to appear morbid, but for purposes of her investigation, she had to know about poor Mr. Penrose. "What sort of accident?"

Mrs. Penrose frowned. "It was a strange thing. Mr. Penrose had too much to drink one night—that was his way, you see— and slipped off the icy bridge crossing over the river near where we lived close to Stroud."

"Oh. Then what?"

"Knocked himself out and then drowned."

* * *

"It seems much too coincidental that Mrs. Penrose's husband and father both drowned," Amy mused.

The Monday afternoon following the Assembly, Eloise reached for a small egg salad sandwich on the tea tray Amy's butler had just placed in front of them. "As did Mrs. Fleming."

"Yes. But the question remains, how do we prove that she is the culprit?"

Eloise frowned. "Then you've given up on the others on your suspect list?"

Amy shook her head. "Not at all. Don't forget Mr. Fleming is ready to marry another woman with his wife barely in her grave. It would be very foolish to eliminate him."

"Ah, it appears despite your husband's request to avoid getting involved in the Fleming murder, you have decided to eschew his wishes," Aunt Margaret said as she sailed through the doorway of Amy's drawing room, looking as graceful and elegant as always.

"Aunt Margaret!" Amy attempted to hop up, but instead just shifted to the edge of the couch as her aunt held up her hand to stop her. She leaned over and kissed her on the cheek. "No need to get up, dearest, it would be far too embarrassing to watch you try to do that."

Amy huffed. "Now I'm not quite sure I am happy to see you."

Aunt Margaret patted her cheek. "You are always happy to see me, my dear." She looked over at Eloise. "Good afternoon, Eloise."

Since her mouth was full, Eloise merely nodded.

Once she was settled and had poured her own tea, she turned to Amy. "Are any of these delightful tidbits from your baking efforts?"

"No. I save those for dinner so William can enjoy them."

Aunt Margaret stirred her tea. "Then you must have me for dinner one evening."

"Of course, I would love that." Amy cleared her throat. "And it would be quite lovely if you brought Lord Exeter with you as well. If you give me a date that works for you, I shall be happy to send him an invitation."

Expecting her aunt to dismiss her suggestion since she had never gone as far as allowing her family to meet any of her beaus, Amy was quite taken aback when Aunt Margaret said, "I know it's short notice, but Friday would be nice. His lordship plans a trip to London next week." She glanced at Amy. "Close your mouth, dear. It is quite unladylike." She smiled and took a sip of tea.

"You didn't answer my question when I arrived, but I assume you are pursuing the drowning of your midwife even though I am certain William has ordered you not to do so?"

Amy nodded. "I am completely unable to believe that the two inept detectives have found the right person so quickly." She shifted on the settee. "Do you know Mr. Fleming—the drowned woman's husband—has already announced banns of matrimony?"

Aunt Margaret's brows rose. "Indeed?"

Eloise swallowed. "Yes, he plans a wedding in only a few weeks."

"That's somewhat scandalous," Aunt Margaret said. She placed her cup in the saucer in front of her and turned her attention to Amy. "You can imagine what a surprise it was to me when Lord Exeter mentioned he knows Mr. Fleming. It seems they were schoolmates at university and even engaged in a small business together several years ago."

Amy and Eloise looked at each other and grinned.

***

"My dear, even though you have it all settled with Dr. Stevens, I would like to meet the woman myself," William said as he took a piece of fish from the tray the footman held at dinner that evening.

"Yes, I would like that," Amy said. "I think you will be quite impressed with her." She waved her fork around. "We were stunned to learn she is married to Lord Sterling."

William's eyes grew wide. "Indeed? That is quite interesting. I wonder how the man feels about his wife not only working, but as a doctor. It is not considered proper work for a lady. Or for any woman, that is."

"Actually, he seemed quite happy. Proud, almost. He has taken on the job of balancing her books. He claimed if he didn't do it, his wife would never be paid."

Amy took a sip of her wine. "If I remember correctly, he suffered some sort of family issue a few years ago and soon developed a reputation as quite the libertine. The fact that *she* married *him* surprises me more."

"I will send around a note to the doctor asking for a day and time we can both meet with her," William said.

"That reminds me. I've invited Aunt Margaret and Lord Exeter for dinner Friday. She stopped in today to visit and mentioned that Exeter knows Mr. Fleming."

"Amy..."

"What?" She tried to look innocent but wasn't sure she was managing it.

"Why the fact that Aunt Margaret's friend knows the man whose wife was recently murdered gives me second thoughts to this dinner invitation you've extended?"

Amy shrugged. "I know not of what you speak. Aunt Margaret mentioned she was looking forward to sampling one of my baking efforts and I suggested she come for dinner. Then when I mentioned she might want to extend the invitation to Lord Exeter and she agreed, I was quite surprised. And pleased."

"And how did Mr. Fleming's name come into the conversation?"

She huffed. "I had nothing to do with it. She merely mentioned there was a connection between the two men. *After* I extended the invitation. I shall also include Eloise and Michael and your parents if you're concerned that I will be badgering the man with questions all evening."

William wiped his mouth and placed his napkin alongside

his plate. "How convenient that your aunt's beau knows Mr. Fleming."

A footman cleared their places as Amy ruminated on the dinner with Lord Exeter and how she could question him without actually questioning him.

"My lady, Cook would like to know if you are ready for dessert?"

Amy clapped her hands. "Oh, yes. Indeed." She looked at William. "You will never guess what wonderful dessert I made today."

He gulped. "No, my dear. I cannot imagine what you've done this time."

She studied him for a minute, his words going through her mind, not quite sure what he meant by that. Just as she was about to ask him, the footman returned with her cake and a tea set. "Here we are, my lady."

She beamed at William as the cake was set in front of them. "Doesn't it look wonderful?"

"Ah. Yes. It truly does. Now what type of cake is this?"

"Three-layer chocolate cake."

William examined it. "Indeed? One would think having three layers there would be a bit more to it. In other words, maybe a little higher?"

Amy studied her masterpiece. "No. That's the way it turned out. There is a possibility I could have put more baking powder into it, but I'm sure I followed the directions explicitly."

"Well, then. Let's give it a go," William said as a piece of the thing was placed in front of him. He took one bite and his eyes watered. "Um, lovely, my dear. I do wish I hadn't eaten so much of the fish, though. I am truly quite full."

Amy took a bite. "I might have used a tad more salt than necessary, but otherwise it is quite good." She smiled at him.

William nodded and slowly edged the plate away from him.

He patted his stomach. "Yes, quite good, indeed." He took a deep breath and immediately sneezed.

Again.

And again.

And again.

He looked around as a small ball of fur wandered under the table and wound itself around his ankle. He backed his chair up so quickly, he almost hit the footman standing against the wall behind him. "What is this?" he shouted.

Amy leaned down to take the small kitten into her arms.

"Take that out of the room," William said just before he sneezed again. "Why is it in my house again?"

"I'm sorry. I had her hidden in a box at the back of the kitchen."

Sneeze.

She grimaced. "Eloise is still hiding it from Michael."

William stood, his handkerchief at his nose. "I'm sorry, but no. It cannot stay here." He left the dining room, the sound of his sneezes echoing throughout the house.

Amy sighed and rubbed the little kitten's stomach. "I'm afraid Eloise is going to have to deal with this problem herself."

10

"Lord Exeter, it is so nice of you to join us." Amy greeted her aunt's gentleman friend as he and Aunt Margaret entered the drawing room where Amy and William were enjoying a drink before dinner.

"Thank you for having me, Lady Wethington." Exeter walked over to where William stood and extended his arm. "Good evening to you, Wethington."

"And to you as well. What would you like to drink?" William asked.

As Aunt Margaret and Exeter told William their preferences, Eloise and Michael entered the room. "Ho, I see we are just in time for libations," Michael said, rubbing his hands.

They were followed on their heels by William's mother and stepfather, Mr. Colbert, and Lady Lily Colbert, who made a beeline to Amy to inspect her middle. Satisfied at how she looked, she patted her on the cheek and turned to William and offered her cheek for a kiss.

"What would you like to drink, Mother, Mr. Colbert?"

"Now, William, I think it's time you called me Edward, instead of this Mr. Colbert stuff."

William nodded and cleared his throat. "What would you like, Edward?"

Mr. Colbert asked for a brandy, and William's mother requested a sherry, which the other women were drinking.

Once everyone was settled with their preferred drinks, William said, "Exeter, how do you find dealing with your new title?" He turned to Michael and said, "Exeter only inherited the title from an elderly uncle several months ago."

Michael nodded and Exeter continued, "My uncle's affairs were, unfortunately, in terrible shape. His—mine now—country estate was in shambles. The tenants remaining there are on the verge of starvation." He shook his head and took a sip of his drink. "I have done some emergency repairs and provided necessary resources for them to allow some planting just to keep them on the property so I can rebuild what was once a profitable estate." He turned to Aunt Margaret and patted her hand. "Lady Margaret has been most helpful in her suggestions."

Edward leaned forward. "Do you find, as other estate holders have, that with so many moving to the city to obtain factory jobs it is hard to keep the younger men on the farms?"

"Yes. Indeed. To keep the estate, I've come up with a few ideas to improve what we have." He swirled his drink around. "As you say, it will never be as productive and profitable as in years past. But that is the way of things, and we must move with the times. Fortunately, I did not need to depend on my uncle's estate to keep myself solvent."

Anxious to move the conversation closer to what she wanted to know, Amy said, "I understand you are friends with Mr. Fleming?"

Silence enough to fill a cavern ensued as seven pairs of eyes looked in her direction.

William cleared his throat and threw a warning glance at Amy. Eloise covered her mouth, attempting to hide her giggle.

Exeter nodded. "Yes, indeed. It was a shame about his wife. I went to university with Fleming. We engaged in a small, somewhat unprofitable business venture when we left university, which eventually failed. I only see the man occasionally now."

"I understand—" Amy began when William cut in. "So, tell me, Exeter, do you plan to venture into Parliament sometime soon? I remember you mentioned you hadn't been able to do that yet."

Amy glared at him but took a sip of her drink. Wisely, she had the foresight to arrange the seating at the dining table so that Exeter was to her right where she sat at the head of the table.

Exeter nodded. "As you say. I have yet to wet my toes, so to speak, but I plan—"

"Dinner is served, my lord, my lady." Filbert stood in the doorway to the drawing room his usual steady self, the perfection of manservant.

Shuffling ensued as they put their drinks down, ladies smoothed out their skirts, and the group made a short procession to the dining room. William leaned down toward Amy. "Do not begin a conversation about Mr. Fleming."

She merely smiled up at him and nodded. "Yes, dear."

He frowned.

Amy settled at one end of the table, and William at the other. She had Exeter on her right and Lady Lily on her left. Thankfully, Michael seemed to have engaged her mother-in-law in a conversation.

"Your aunt tells me you are a renowned mystery author," Exeter said as he scooped his spoon into the lovely clear broth with pieces of chicken in it.

"Yes. I have written several books."

"You must tell me the names so I can read them. I am quite fond of mystery books." He swallowed a spoonful of soup. "I assume you do not write under your own name?"

Amy shook her head. "No. When I received my very first contract, my father was most insistent that no one learn my identity. So, I use the *nom de plume* E. D. Burton."

He reeled back. "Indeed? I have read a couple of your books. Very good, I might add."

Amy felt the familiar pleasure when someone recognized her work. "Thank you very much, my lord. It pleases me to know you enjoyed them."

"But now I assume it is known that you are the famous author?"

She felt her cheeks redden. "I don't really believe I am famous, my lord, but yes, I have been revealed as the author, even though I continue to write under my pseudonym."

"How did that revelation come about?"

She grinned, remembering William's proposal. "Well, when Lord Wethington proposed to me, I told him I would accept on one condition."

Exeter threw his head back and laughed. "Don't continue. I can guess. You would accept his hand in marriage if he allowed you to disclose yourself?"

Amy nodded. "Quite true."

He wiped his mouth and placed his spoon alongside his empty bowl. "Would you have accepted him if he refused to allow that?"

She smiled. "What do you think?"

He studied her for a moment, then glanced down the table at William who was in a deep conversation with Aunt Margaret. "I think yes. You two seem very well suited."

"I was quite certain he would agree. Maybe that is why I made it a condition, because I was sure of his answer." She thought for a moment. "It never occurred to me that he would say no."

"Do you ever get involved in real mysteries?"

Amy almost swallowed her tongue. Was it truly possible

that Lord Exeter made the opening statement that would allow her to question him? She could tell William later, in all honesty, that she did *not* begin a conversation with his lordship about the murder.

Deciding to start off easy, so as not to frighten the man, she said, "Once in a while." She noted that William was still engaged in conversation. "In fact, I am quite interested in the untimely death of Mrs. Fleming."

"Yes. Very sad. And to think the detectives found the culprit so quickly."

"Hmm. That does seem a bit odd to me, truth be told."

"As a mystery writer, my lady, what are your thoughts on it?"

Her insides were jumping with glee. She still had to take it slow with the man, though, since she didn't want to appear morbid or overly interested in the death of his friend's wife.

"I must admit that I do not necessarily believe the detectives have come up with the right suspect."

"Indeed? And why is that?"

She thought for a minute on how to express her opinion without disparaging the detectives too harshly. "I think they named their suspect much too quickly." She turned in her seat, so she faced him. "The morning after Mrs. Fleming's body was found they already had Mrs. Garfield under arrest. Whatever happened to doing a complete investigation?"

"Something you would do if you were writing the story?"

"Of course." She leaned to the side as the footman placed platters of lamb, potatoes, curried lobster with rice, roast capon, with platters of boiled vegetables in the center of the table.

Once they were out of the way, she said, "First of all, you must realize as an author, there have to be several of what we call red herrings to distract the reader. Therefore, an author would never name the murderer at the very beginning."

Exeter smiled at her. "Ah, but we are talking real life here, not fiction."

Amy cleared her throat. "Also, I have watched the two detectives who are on this case in other matters, and I must say my faith in their ability to find the right suspect is quite challenged."

Exeter laughed again. "In other words, you don't think they are competent."

She shook her head. "No. Not at all." She waited for a minute then said, "Have you kept in touch with Mr. Fleming these past years?"

He shook his head. "Not really. I mean, we meet on occasion at some social event. He's also a member of my club. Like me, he prefers Bath life to London."

Taking only a moment to think it over, she said, "Are you aware that Mr. Fleming has announced his intention to remarry in a few weeks?"

Her dinner partner frowned. "No. I did not know that, but then again, as I said, we really haven't spent much time in each other's company the last few years." He thought for a moment. "I wish I could say I am surprised, but I really am not."

Her heart sped up. She leaned in closer. "Ah, why do you say that?"

She might have looked a tad too interested because he said, "I really do not wish to gossip."

Botheration. Here she was sure she would find out something that would help advance Mr. Fleming to the top of the suspect list, but suddenly Exeter became close-mouthed.

"I certainly understand that. Gossip is so messy." She shook her head and ate a few bites. When it seemed Exeter wasn't going to say anything else, she opened her mouth to speak when William addressed him. "Exeter, I am taking a trip to London next week. I wonder if you would be interested in joining me. I can introduce you to people at my club who you will be dealing with once you are involved in Parliament."

"That sounds like a wonderful idea, Wethington. I had planned a trip myself so this would be quite helpful. I look forward to it."

Then to her dismay, Eloise, sitting on Exeter's other side asked him a question.

* * *

UNBEKNOWNST TO AMY, William had been watching her conversation with Exeter all through dinner. Of course, being too far from them and having to converse with Lady Margaret on one side and his stepfather on the other, who was quite talkative, had kept William from hearing anything from the other end of the table.

His wife didn't seem to understand that in her condition, she was much more vulnerable. Not that he ever really approved of her getting involved in murder investigations, but he wished she would focus more on the upcoming birth of their child.

Other women knitted blankets and garments for a new baby. She should be spending her time interviewing nurses for the baby and decorating the nursery. While he knew she was just as excited as he was about becoming a parent, the normal 'women' type activities just didn't seem to hold her interest enough to keep her from getting herself into trouble.

"My lady, did you want dessert served in here, or shall we bring it with the tea cart into the drawing room?" Although Filbert addressed Amy, his words stopped the conversations.

Amy looked down the table at all their guests. "I have been baking some lovely confections." She looked at William. "Haven't I, dear?"

"Yes." He held in his groan, not wanting his guests to insult his wife, but it would be almost impossible for any of her *confections* to be edible.

"I think tea and dessert in the drawing room would be best, Filbert. Thank you. And don't forget the two pies I made this afternoon."

"Oh, my lady. I am so very sorry. Cook told me there was an unfortunate accident with the pies."

Amy looked stricken. "Oh, dear. What happened?"

Filbert cleared his throat, and it was apparent to William by the butler's demeanor that he was about to tell a Banbury tale. "Cook said she placed the pies on the counter to cool and unfortunately, one of the kitchen helpers slipped and knocked them both to the ground."

William's heart broke at the look on his wife's face, but he was able to take a deep breath after Filbert's announcement. "It is all right, my dear. There will be other dinners where you can provide a dessert," he said.

Amy nodded. "Yes, I believe that is so."

She looked back at the butler. "Do we have anything for dessert, then?"

Filbert smiled. "As a matter of fact, yes. Cook made some lovely puddings this afternoon, so we can serve them."

"How very convenient."

Before anything else could be said about pies, puddings, or desserts in general, William stood. "I believe the gentlemen will take their after-dinner port in the drawing room with the ladies."

The group stood and wandered from the room. Amy walked up to William. "Do you find anything wrong with my baked goods?"

William ran his finger along the inside of his cravat. "No, of course not, my love. It's too bad about the pies."

She nodded. "Yes. Too bad."

They had barely settled into their seats when Filbert once again arrived at the door to the drawing room. "My lord, there is a caller here to see you."

William left the room and headed to the entrance hall. "Who is it?"

"It is me, Wethington. I need to speak to you about this matter between my son and me." Amy's father, Lord Winchester followed on Filbert's heels.

"Michael is here right now, Winchester. Would you care to join us in the drawing room for a bit, then we can speak later?"

Winchester lowered his voice. "I prefer to speak with you in private. My son and I have some differences, and I do not wish to alert him to our conversation. I wouldn't disturb you, but this is a matter that must be handled tomorrow."

Damnation. Just what he needed now. If he absconded from the group he would have to explain to Winchester's daughter, son, daughter-in-law, and sister that the man had arrived—unexpectedly—and now wanted some private time with him. It was especially awkward because he hadn't realized it until now that everyone in Winchester's family was here except him. That was indeed a misstep.

"What is it?" Amy walked up to them. "Papa! What brings you here?"

"I need a few minutes with your husband." He waved his hand in his usual dismissive way. "You may go back to your guests, and he will join you shortly."

Footsteps sounded. "Father. What are you doing here?" Michael joined the growing group huddling in the entrance way, Eloise right behind him.

"None of your business, son. I need to speak with Wethington." His abrupt tone had Michael frowning.

"Franklin!" Amy's Aunt Margaret added to the body count. "Why are you here? Is something the matter?"

William was at the point where he would have preferred to be eating Amy's pies at the table and pretending to enjoy it. He looked up as the Colberts and Lord Exeter joined the group.

"Anything wrong, Wethington?" Mr. Colbert—Edward—asked.

William dropped his head into his hands and groaned.

11

After a few minor delays, William and Lord Exeter set off for London on a cloudy Tuesday morning. By Thursday afternoon, Amy had to admit that she was left a bit lost with him gone, which amazed her. Even though William was usually in and out all day, tending to whatever it was he tended to, the house still seemed too quiet and empty.

She baked a few more batches of biscuits, but with William not there to appreciate her efforts, it had lost its appeal. She'd even been so listless that she bought another needlepoint which took up barely an hour before she tossed it aside and then foolishly picked up the knitting she'd started. No surprise, that hadn't held her interest either.

Eloise had been feeling a tad under the weather so Amy hadn't even had her best friend to distract her. Aunt Margaret had been busy—with what she hadn't disclosed when Amy had sent her a note. Then she chastised herself. Honestly, the man had only been gone for three days. She'd spent most of her adult life by herself. Well, while maybe not alone, certainly without William.

That evening was the book club meeting, and she was

already finished with her copy of *Sense and Sensibility* that the group had chosen to read after *Pride and Prejudice*. Mr. Davidson and Mr. Rawlings had skipped the last two meetings, which was unusual. Most likely they were just not that enthused about reading Miss Austen's work.

Happy to finally have something to do outside the house, she asked for a tray to be sent to her bedchamber since she didn't want to spend another meal in the dining room staring at the walls. Eloise had sent around a note that she felt better and would be joining Amy for the trip to the bookstore for the meeting.

Amy studied herself in her mirror as she took one last look at her attire. Everything seemed in place, and she even had matching shoes on. She picked up her copy of *Sense and Sensibility* and headed downstairs.

"Off to your meeting, my lady?" Filbert asked.

"Yes. I am looking forward to it. It is quiet here since his lordship left."

"Indeed." He smiled as he opened the door and bent to her ear. "You might want to adjust your hat, my lady."

She took a quick look in the mirror, shifted the hat, and smiled.

The butler grinned back, then assumed his usual formal demeanor. "The carriage is ready for you. Have a good evening."

Amy had barely settled into her seat when the carriage drew up in front of Eloise's house. Michael walked his wife down the steps to the carriage and helped her in. "You are growing quite large, wife," he said.

Eloise huffed and said, "I suggest the next time we add to our family, husband, that you carry the baby."

With a chortle, Michael closed the carriage door and tapped on the side, signaling Randolph to move forward.

Eloise shifted around until she was comfortable. "I am

growing quite weary of everyone telling me how large I am." Her eyes narrowed as she studied Amy. "Why am I bigger than you, and you are due almost a month before me?"

For the sake of friendship, Amy declined to mention the enormous amounts of food Eloise consumed. "Perhaps you are carrying a boy, and me a girl. Surely a boy baby would be larger than a girl?"

"Perhaps."

They remained silent with their own thoughts as the carriage made its way through Bath to Atkinson & Tucker bookstore. The sight of the store always raised her spirits. She really should have made a trip here after William left to select a few books to read. That would certainly have given her something to pass the time.

Just the smell brought happiness to her as they entered the store and browsed for a few minutes. After choosing two books that looked interesting, they joined the rest of the group in the meeting room at the back of the store.

"Oh, Amy, dear, I'm so glad you made it tonight. I was afraid with William gone you would not come." Her mother-in-law, Lady Lily, gave her a hug and then placed her hands on her shoulders and studied her. "Are you eating enough?"

"Yes. My appetite is wonderful," Amy said.

She cupped her cheeks with her hands. "Be sure to take good care of yourself. That is my grandchild you are carrying."

"I know." Amy hoped the remark didn't come out as terse as she thought. If it had, her mother-in-law chose to ignore it.

She turned to Eloise. "You are looking well, my dear. I see you are certainly getting enough to eat."

Eloise attempted a smile, but Amy saw it more as a grimace. Poor Eloise. Everyone was always commenting on her size and appetite.

The Misses O'Neill joined them, marveling once again on

DEATH AND DECEPTION

their swollen tummies, and luckily—or wisely—made no comment to Eloise about her size.

It appeared Mr. Rawlings and Mr. Davidson had decided to return to the fold. They stood with Lord Temple and Mr. Colbert, apparently in a lively discussion with Mr. Davidson's arms swinging around as he made his point.

Lady Forester and Lady Abigail joined their group, also commenting on how well they looked. Amy really wished they would get off this subject, afraid someone would eventually comment on Eloise.

Mr. Colbert's voice broke into their conversation. "If you will all take a seat, I think we can begin the meeting shortly. We're waiting for just a couple more members."

"Come, dear, you must get off your feet," Lady Forester said as she took Amy's elbow and moved her in the direction of the comfortable chairs scattered around the room. "Where is his lordship? I never see you without him by your side."

They settled next to each other on one of the settees. "He is on a short business trip to London. He left Tuesday morning. I expect him home by the end of the weekend."

Lady Forester patted her hand. "And how are you doing with the unfortunate death of your midwife?"

It didn't seem like the appropriate place to discuss murder—but then again it was a murder mystery book club. "It was quite a shock. Of course, when anyone dies unexpectedly like that, it tends to unnerve one."

The group continued to settle in, while Mr. Colbert conversed with his wife who, of course, sat right in front, so he could gaze upon her while he conducted the meeting.

"Yes. It was sad," Lady Forester continued. "From what I understand, though—as much as I hate to gossip—she was not very well liked."

Amy perked up. "Did you know her?"

Lady Forester shifted closer. "Yes. She was a member of my

church—St. Michael's—although she hadn't attended very much recently." She thought for a minute. "I guess poor Mrs. Devon is, if not happy, at least relieved now that her court case can be dismissed."

Surprise shot through Amy. She sat forward. "Who is Mrs. Devon?"

Lady Forester leaned in close and looked around to make sure they were not being overheard. No one was paying them any mind. "My dear, didn't you hear about the battle being fought between poor Mrs. Fleming and Mrs. Devon?"

She shook her head, her heart giving an extra thump at possibly receiving some very helpful information.

"The two women were cousins and at one time very close. However, the way the story goes, Mrs. Devon's mother, Mrs. Mary Stoker, promised a very expensive piece of jewelry—a diamond necklace, I believe that was given to her by her grandmother—to her daughter, but before the woman could claim it, Mrs. Fleming acquired it from a very befuddled Mrs. Stoker who thought she was giving it to Mrs. Devon." She patted Amy's arm. "She had grown grew quite confused in her last months."

"Oh, how awful."

"Indeed." Lady Forester nodded. "When Mrs. Devon learned of her cousin's perfidy, she attempted to retrieve it from her, but Mrs. Fleming refused to give it up, saying Mrs. Stoker had changed her mind and wanted her to have it."

"I am not one to wish anyone ill, mind you, but it seems to me that Mrs. Fleming made enough enemies in her life that I am not completely surprised that she ended up…you know," Amy said.

She sat back in her chair, taking all the information in. Not knowing Mrs. Devon, there was no way she could assess if she were the type to actually murder someone. That was a big step to take. "Does Mrs. Devon also attend your church?"

"Yes, she does. I usually see her every Sunday." Lady Forester patted Amy's hand. "I'm sorry, dear, but we got sidetracked. I was curious about the loss of your midwife. Have you found another one?"

Wishing to continue the conversation about Mrs. Devon instead, but not wanting to be rude, she said, "As a matter of fact, we did. Lady Davenport and I visited with Dr. Stevens here in Bath." She grinned. "Dr. Stevens is a woman."

Lady Forester's brows rose, and she clutched the pearls at her throat. "Surely, you would never secure the services of a female doctor?"

Hmm. That was a surprise. One would think a woman would be thrilled to learn of a female who made it through medical training and had her own practice. "As a matter of fact, both Lady Davenport and I have asked Dr. Stevens to attend us."

Lady Forester leaned close. "I don't think Lord Wethington will be happy about that."

"Oh, but he is. He is very happy."

She shook her head and tsked. "Young people. I don't understand. Some things are proper, and others are not."

Before Amy could ask any more questions about Mrs. Devon, Mr. Colbert called the meeting to order and began by asking the usual questions about everyone's thoughts on the book. Since Amy had read the book several times, she was able to answer questions without giving it all her attention.

Mrs. Devon would obviously make it to the list of suspects. If she was having no results with her lawsuit, she might very well have taken upon herself to retrieve it. But why drown her at the Roman Baths?

The group decided on one of Amy's books as their next selection which made Amy very happy despite Davidson scowling in her direction. For goodness's sake, the man was so grumpy all the time. It amazed her that he had a friendship with Mr. Rawlings who was so pleasant and cheerful.

Eloise kept shifting around in her chair, it being apparent she was uncomfortable. As much as Amy wanted to speak further with Lady Forester, she felt sorry for her sister-in-law. Once the meeting closed, Eloise cast her a pleading glance.

As they rose to go, Amy placed her hand on Lady Forester's forearm. "I like to try different churches on occasion. I think I would enjoy attending service at your church on Sunday. I was there briefly at Mrs. Fleming's funeral and found St. Michael's Church quite lovely." She sent up a prayer that God would forgive that little lie but then again, a house of worship was still a house of worship.

Lady Forester's face lit up with pleasure. "Oh, my dear, we would simply love to have you. Our pastor is a lovely young man who gives the most inspirational sermons." As they began to walk toward the door, she said, "I would prefer to send my carriage for you, so you don't need to worry about getting there or looking for me. Service is at eleven o'clock, so will half past ten be acceptable to you?"

"Yes, that would be fine."

"We generally have what we call a 'potluck' luncheon after the service in our Fellowship Hall. Everyone brings a small contribution."

"Oh, I would love to bring some of my biscuits or tarts." She smiled, then looked over at Eloise who sounded like she was choking.

Lady Forester held the door open as Amy and Eloise passed through, "No need, my dear. Guests are not required to contribute."

"That is very nice," Eloise said. By this time, she was practically dragging herself to the carriage door Randolph held open. "I am so uncomfortable. I must take this corset off."

They all offered hugs to each other, and Amy and Eloise

climbed into Amy's carriage, and they set off. "Maybe I should bring some baked goods to the church potluck anyway," Amy said as the driver moved the carriage into the traffic.

"No, I don't think so." Eloise jumped in. "You might offend Lady Forester since you are her guest."

"Yes. That is true."

* * *

THE FOLLOWING SUNDAY MORNING, Amy prepared for church, spending the time assuring herself she was merely meeting Lady Forester and anyone else at her church to expand her circle of friends. If this Mrs. Devon made an appearance, then that would be fine.

The fact that William was still in London and would not know of her foray from their usual church was a plus. Not that she would keep it a secret from him, of course. That was not an obedient wife's way. Of course, if he asked her where she went to church while he was gone, she would have to tell. Nil chances of that, however.

At precisely half past ten, Lady Forester's footman arrived at her door. She checked herself in the mirror, checked her hat, checked her matching shoes, and felt confident all was well.

"My lady, you might want to rearrange the buttons on your pelisse."

Botheration, Filbert had caught her again. She sighed, righted herself, and descended the steps to the waiting carriage.

After greeting Lady Forester, Amy settled into the seat of the very comfortable carriage. Her hostess gave her some history of the church as they made their way through the light Sunday morning traffic.

St. Michael's church was situated on Walcot Street, fronting

Northgate Street. The looming south tower of the church was a prominent fixture on Bath's skyline. It was a lovely old church.

Congregants streamed into the building as she and her hostess climbed out of the carriage with the footman's assistance. Amy shook out her skirts and rearranged herself.

"Oh, goodness, there is Mrs. Devon now," Lady Forester said as she took Amy's arm. "I see her frequently at church, but it is noteworthy that she is only a few steps from us."

A large woman in a very large lavender hat faced away from them, amid a conversation with two other women. Amy assumed one of them was Mrs. Devon since Lady Forester steered her in the group's direction. As they approached the group the woman turned to face Amy and Lady Forester.

"Matilda, how very nice to see you." She air kissed Lady Forester's cheek.

"Mrs. Petrina Devon, I would like you to meet a friend of mine, Lady Amy Wethington, who is visiting with us today."

She looked over at Amy whose eyes grew wide. Before she could think of how rude it sounded, Amy blurted out. "*You* are Mrs. Devon?"

12

*A*my could not believe she was staring into the face of her nemesis from when she had attended Lady Finch's School for Young Ladies of Quality years before. Then she had been Miss Petrina Spencer, the bane of her existence.

"Oh my goodness, Lady Amy. I haven't seen you in years, my dear." The woman had the nerve to air kiss her cheeks. She glanced down at Amy's middle and wagging her finger, said, "I see you have been busy."

Still unable to comprehend that she was looking directly at Petrina Spencer—who was now Mrs. Devon—she found it difficult to access her voice.

Petrina, however, had no problem rattling on. "The last I heard when I spoke with some of our schoolmates a few years ago, you were still unmarried. It looks like you managed to bring someone up to scratch after all." The woman's giggle was supposed to make Amy feel like she wasn't being insulted, but of course she was.

"Yes. It took all my effort and feminine wiles to drag Lord Wethington to the altar."

Mrs. Devon laughed as if that was the funniest thing she

had heard in years. Lady Forester gave Amy a strange look, and she decided if she was going to get any information from Mrs. Devon, she would need to put aside any animosity toward her.

"Lady Wethington is my guest this morning." Lady Forester turned to Amy. "Is it not strange that you know each other?"

Finally able to take a deep breath, Amy said, "Yes. It is quite strange. But then Bath is a small city, and there weren't too many young ladies' schools."

"Is that where you know each other then?"

Mrs. Devon waved her hand in the air. "Oh yes, we were quite good friends during our school years."

Amy's eyes grew wide. She held many unpleasant memories of this woman, but the one that had been first in her mind was the short story contest the school held each year.

Just beginning to feel as though she might have some talent as a writer, Amy had spent hours writing a lovely story about a young girl and a puppy she found and had to convince her parents to allow her to keep. Pleased with her work, she left it lying on the desk in the room she shared with another young lady, Miss Serena Jackson.

Two days later when it came time to turn the story in, she could not find it. She and Miss Jackson searched the room high and low, but it didn't show up. Upset at having lost it, her disappointment turned to outrage and anger when Miss Petrina Spencer received first prize in the contest. With Amy's story!

The witch had stolen it and recopied it into her own handwriting and turned it in. Amy attempted to convince Lady Finch that it was her story, but Miss Spencer had cried when accused and since her father was a generous donor to the school, it was no surprise when Lady Finch agreed with Miss Spencer.

Since that event was the last of a string of difficulties she'd had with the girl, Amy was able to convince Papa and Lady

Margaret to remove her from the school. To this day, she'd never seen the woman again.

After introducing the other ladies who had been conversing with Mrs. Devon, Lady Forester said, "I think we should proceed into church."

It was a lovely old building, and Amy tried her best to concentrate on the sermon the pastor gave. But her mind was on Mrs. Devon and how she was going to be able to get some information from her without wanting to dump a cup of hot tea over her head.

"Is everything okay, Lady Amy? You seem distracted." Lady Forester took her arm as they left the church.

"I'm sorry if I appear that way. I always enjoy the Sunday services, and I'm afraid I found myself comparing your pastor to mine." She leaned in, hoping she didn't sound like a fool. "I know I should not have been doing that."

Lady Forester patted her hand. "I am sure you're missing Lord William, too."

"Yes." Although true, it was as good an excuse as any. "He should return this evening."

The congregants moved to the church Fellowship Hall where Amy had attended the meal after Mrs. Fleming's funeral. Lady Forester had sent her potluck offering over to the hall with her footman before they had entered the church.

Now she had to figure out a way to maneuver them so that they sat with Mrs. Devon, as much as Amy did not want to even speak with her. But that was the reason for the switch in churches, so she might as well seize the opportunity that would most likely never happen again.

"Oh, there's Mrs. Devon." Amy turned to Lady Forester. "I would very much like to sit with her if we may. It would be nice to catch up with a former classmate." The last words were so difficult to say, Amy almost gagged on them.

"Very well. I think that's a splendid idea." Her hostess

headed them toward Mrs. Devon and the other women she had been speaking with earlier.

"Woo hoo, Mrs. Devon." Lady Forester hurried them along. "Lady Amy would love to catch up with you. May we join you at your table?"

"Of course."

Amy had to admit the Demon Devon looked a tad curious since she was obviously aware that Amy knew she'd stolen her story, but to benefit her investigation, she would swallow her pride and smile.

A very difficult effort indeed.

As was generally the method used for this sort of gathering, each table was requested to take their plates to the long line of offerings. Amy picked a few items that looked delightful since it had been a few hours since breakfast. She really should have brought some biscuits or perhaps a pie as a contribution, but it was too late to concern herself with it now.

Once they were all settled and the pastor blessed the food, chatter began as the congregants shared a meal. Amy's issue was how to bring up the death of Mrs. Devon's cousin without sounding like some sort of ghoul?

After considering it for a bit while she ate, she realized she had the perfect reason to do so and at the same time flaunt her success. Of course, it would be better if she could get Lady Forester to mention her books.

Almost as if she'd read her mind, Lady Forester wiped her mouth with her napkin and addressed Mrs. Devon. "Did you know your former schoolmate is a well-known mystery author?"

Amy would never forget for the rest of her life the surprise on Mrs. Devon's face and the triumph she felt at seeing it.

"Indeed?" She barely got the word out as Amy smiled sweetly at her.

"Yes. She has even won awards for her work," Lady Forester continued.

Mrs. Devon looked as though she had swallowed a slice of lemon. Since it was expected of her, she really had no choice but to comment. "That is quite strange. I visit the bookstore on a regular basis, and don't remember seeing your name among the selections."

Amy waved her arm. "Oh, I don't write under my own name." She didn't continue, wanting her foe to ask.

Mrs. Devon cleared her throat and stepped right into it. "And what name is that, Lady Amy?"

"E. D. Burton." She smiled and took a sip of tea.

The woman gasped. "You are the mystery author, E. D. Burton?" She looked over at Lady Forester, seeming to want her to deny it.

"Yes, indeed, Mrs. Devon. Our Lady Amy is E. D. Burton."

Amy could not help herself. "I have been writing since, oh, I would say my childhood years."

Now that the subject had been brought up, she needed to take advantage of it while Mrs. Devon was still ruminating on what she'd just heard. Amy took a small bite of a wonderful lemon tart. She really must try making this herself. "I find myself very interested in all manner of mysteries."

Mrs. Devon shuddered. "I, on the other hand, find such things quite unpleasant." She leaned in and whispered. "My cousin was recently involved in a most nasty form of demise."

Amy found it quite hard to keep from laughing at the way the woman referred to murder. But then again, if it was a relative of hers, perhaps she would find it hard to speak of, too. Except the purpose of this trip to Lady Forester's church was to see if Mrs. Devon was the type who could murder her cousin.

Based on her experience with the woman, she could see her doing all sorts of nasty deeds, but murder was a rather serious step to take. "I am sorry to hear that, but the unfortunate event had come to my attention since she was my midwife."

Mrs. Devon drew back and placed her hand at her throat. "Is that so? My goodness, the world is a very small place." She shook her head. "I'm just glad they found the culprit so quickly and have her under arrest."

In for a penny, in for a pound. "And you agree with whom they have charged?"

She shrugged. "Why wouldn't I? The police know what they are doing."

Amy could tell Mrs. Devon stories about their less than spectacular Bath police detectives that would curl her very straight hair, but that was not the direction in which she wanted the conversation to go. "Do you not think it was rather fast?"

Mrs. Devon's eyes narrowed. "Do I understand that you do not agree?"

Was that a bit of guilt? Annoyance? Fear?

"Not necessarily. I guess I'm just thinking that when I write my books I don't have the true culprit identified immediately." She smiled. "That would make for a very boring book, don't you agree?"

Mrs. Devon nodded. "I've read a few of your books." She looked like she was chewing something nasty.

Amy relished the moment "Is that so? I hope you enjoyed them."

"I did." She placed her napkin alongside her plate and rested her hands in her lap. "My cousin and I didn't get along, you know."

Hmm. Confession time? Since there was no reason for her to know that she played ignorant. "No. I was not aware."

Mrs. Devon studied her for a moment. "How did you find her to work with when she was your midwife?"

Uh, oh. This was getting into sticky territory here. She

didn't want to offer her opinion on the woman, she wanted Mrs. Devon's opinion.

"She was extremely competent. She was a duly trained and certified midwife."

Mrs. Devon shrugged. "I know. She was always touting her credentials." She leaned in and lowered her voice. "We were not close."

Since she'd already admitted they didn't get along, it was no surprise that they weren't close. However, Amy tsked. "It is sad when family members do not get along well."

She huffed. "She stole my mother's heirloom necklace."

Well, this was certainly easier than she thought it would be. But then again, would she admit as much if she was the person who killed Mrs. Fleming for the jewelry? While her pregnancy befuddled brain tried to sort that out, she said, "That wasn't very nice of her. Did you get your piece back now that she is gone?"

Mrs. Devon gave her a terse nod. "I certainly did. I went right to the court and told them now that she was dead, I wanted my mother's jewelry returned. Since no one else had laid claim to it, they agreed."

Apparently, the woman did not realize she was incriminating herself, but Amy was not about to enlighten her. Not wanting to make her feel as though she was under interrogation, she switched the subject to other matters, but her former schoolmate had certainly given her something to think about.

She was definitely being added to the suspect list.

* * *

ELOISE BURST into her sitting room later that afternoon, carrying that dreadful kitten. "Eloise, I've told you that William is very allergic to that cat. I can't keep her here."

She dumped the small ball of fur onto Amy's lap. "Just one

more time. I promise. I almost have Michael convinced that we should have a pet."

"Ah, another gathering of the mothers-to-be." Aunt Margaret glided into the sitting room and sat across from Eloise and Amy. "I ordered tea."

"Thank you. I was about to ask Amy to do that," Eloise said as she took the kitten from Amy and placed it in her lap.

Lady Margaret's eyes grew wide as she studied the kitten. "What is that bedraggled thing, Eloise, dear?"

"A kitten. I found it not long ago, but Michael is not convinced he wants a pet in the house."

"I have a pet in the house," Aunt Margaret said, referring to her thirty-year-old cockatoo, Othello, who quoted Shakespeare. "However, I do not cuddle him in my lap."

"And I have Persephone," Amy added.

The short discussion on animals and pets apparently over, Amy shifted in her aunt's direction. "Not that I'm unhappy to see you, aunt, but what brings you here this afternoon?"

"Exeter and William are returning on the three o'clock train from London this afternoon," she said as she crossed her legs in a most graceful manner.

"Why do you know that, and I don't?" Amy had to admit she was a bit miffed. After all, William was her *husband*.

"Do not fret, niece. Exeter told me before they left that he had to be back in Bath no later than five o'clock today. As the only train left that would have them back in time for five o'clock is the three o'clock train, it makes sense." She nodded to the footman who brought in the tea cart. Aunt Margaret poured the tea and fixed it as everyone liked it.

Eloise reached for a small sandwich of watercress. "Lady Margaret, you are so smart."

"And graceful, and kind, and generous, and talented…" Amy mumbled.

"My goodness, are we grumpy today, Amy?" Aunt Margaret asked.

"Perhaps a bit. I should have taken my nap earlier this afternoon, but I kept waiting for William to return home. Of course, had I known there was a specific time they needed to be back, I might have done so."

Aunt Margaret smiled and sipped her tea.

After only a few minutes of visiting, the front door opened, and male voices drifted up from the entrance hall. "It sounds as though the men are home," Eloise said as she reached for a biscuit.

Amy noticed a distinct look of pleasure on Aunt Margaret's face. She really needed to delve into the relationship between her and Lord Exeter.

The men entered the room; William immediately looked her over and smiled. What, did the man expect that she would have given birth while he was gone? Goodness, she was indeed grumpy.

He immediately sneezed.

Eloise jumped up. "Oh, dear. I think it best to find another place to store my little kitten."

He sneezed again.

Exeter walked over to Aunt Margaret and extended his hand. She took it and stood, shaking out her skirts. "We will be on our way."

Hmm. That was interesting. She'd never seen her aunt in the company of a man more than once.

In the meantime, Eloise scooted to the door and left with the kitten in her arms.

William sneezed again. He glared at Amy and then took the seat next to her as the guests left. He removed his handkerchief from his pocket and wiped his nose. "I don't wish my return to start off unpleasant, but please do not allow that animal in the house, my dear. I've asked you that before."

"I know. I don't ask her to bring it over, she just shows up with it."

"The next time she does—" His words were interrupted by Filbert who stood at the sitting room doorway.

"My lord, my lady, you have visitors."

They looked at each other with raised brows. She wasn't expecting anyone else.

"Tell whoever it is we are unavailable." William turned to speak with her when Filbert placed a card into William's hand.

He looked down and groaned.

Detective Ralph Carson, Bath City Police

13

"Detectives, I see no reason why you should be bothering my wife and me. You were the ones who told us to stay out of your investigation, and yet here you are again." William began his speech as he walked through the door of the drawing room, Amy right behind him.

"You are correct, my lord. We did tell you—and your wife," he looked directly at Amy, "to stay out of our investigation."

"Then why the devil are you here?" William asked.

"Can we please sit?" Detective Carson asked.

Once they were all settled, and Detective Marsh had his ever-present notebook out, Carson leaned back on the settee and looked directly at Amy.

"Where did you attend church this morning, Lady Wethington?"

William hopped up. "This is outrageous. There can be no reason why which church we attend is any of the police's business. If you must know, we attend St. Swithin's, which we've done for years. Now I must ask you to leave before I need to have my butler throw you out."

Carson continued to stare at Amy. "My lady?"

William looked down at his wife who was shifting in the chair, her face flushed. She cleared her throat and mumbled, "St. Michael's."

Marsh scribbled in his notepad.

William sat back down and took Amy's hand. "What is this about Amy?"

Looking decidedly uncomfortable, she shrugged, but it was obvious from her face—which she was never able to keep from showing her feelings—that whatever was going on, she knew about it.

"And why did you attend a different church, Lady Wethington?" Carson continued.

She stiffened her back and raised her chin. "I was invited by a friend from my book club to join her for service and a potluck luncheon afterward."

"Uh, huh." Carson continued to stare at her.

"I have no idea why I must explain myself to you, detective, but my husband has been in London for the past several days and since he would not be with me to attend church, I decided to accept my friend's offer." She leaned forward; whatever it had been that was making her uneasy had now turned to anger. "I didn't realize it was a citizen's duty to report to the police on which church one attends on a given Sunday."

Ignoring her outburst, Carson continued. "Did you meet a Mrs. Devon at the service and meal following?"

Amy sniffed. "I did."

"Why?"

Still confused on whatever it was that was going on, William had a sinking feeling that Amy had not obeyed his request to stay out of the police's investigation.

"She was a friend from my school days."

Yes. A lie. He could read it on her face.

Carson continued to study her, making William very nervous as well as Amy it appeared, since she continued to fidget in her chair. "Had you planned on meeting her?"

"No. I didn't even know she attended church there."

Lie number two.

Amy's fingers twisted in her lap, and he was growing more concerned by the minute. Whatever had his wife gotten into now? "Detective, instead of asking all these questions, which it appears to me you already know the answers, I must insist you leave unless you plan to charge my wife with attending the wrong church on a Sunday. And provide me with the law that states that. I will see that we give a donation in your name to both churches." He stood, hoping the detectives would follow.

They didn't.

He sat back down.

Amy took his hand. Ice cold.

That did not look good.

At that point, Detective Carson chose to stand, his hands behind his back. "Once again I must warn you to stay out of our investigation—"

William hopped back up again. He was beginning to feel like a jack-in-the-box. "Wait just a minute. You already have a woman charged with the crime and sitting in gaol the last I heard. What investigation are you speaking of? Has there been another murder?"

"No. The same one," Marsh mumbled and continued to write.

William frowned. "I'm confused."

Carson cleared his throat and attempted to increase his height by stretching his neck. It didn't work. "Mrs. Garfield is no longer under suspicion."

After a few seconds for William to assimilate that information, he said, "Is my wife a suspect?"

"No."

"Am I a suspect?"

"No."

"Anyone in my household? Servants, staff members?"

"No."

"Then I am done with this interview." He walked to the door and summoned Filbert. "Show the men out, please."

He reached for Amy's hand—which was even colder—and the two of them left the room, climbed the stairs, and entered their bedchamber. Once the door was closed, William leaned against it and crossed his arms over his chest.

"I would like to know exactly what that visit from the detectives was all about."

* * *

SHE COULDN'T HELP but surmise that perhaps Mrs. Devon was the one now under suspicion. Mayhap the woman had bragged to the wrong person about how she got her jewelry back after Mrs. Fleming was murdered.

She sat on the bed and arranged her skirts, attempting to look innocent. "I don't know why you think I have any reason to explain their visit."

He sat alongside her. "Why did you go to St. Michael's church today?"

Hopping up and placing her hands on her hips would have given her an upper hand in the conversation, but her swollen body would not permit hopping up and she wasn't sure where her hips were even located anymore. Instead, she leaned back, placing her hands behind her and crossed her fingers.

"As I explained to the detective—which I find quite ridiculous—Lady Forester and I had a conversation at the book club meeting, and she asked me to attend her service since you were out of town, and they were having a potluck luncheon."

"Who is Mrs. Devon?"

Amy shrugged, making sure her fingers remained crossed. "Someone I met at the church service. However, as I told the detective, it turned out she had been a former schoolmate of mine years ago."

William stood and ran his fingers through his hair. "It makes me very nervous when you get involved in these things. Just because you write mysteries doesn't grant you the ability to solve real-life murders."

Amy's jaw dropped. "I believe pregnancy has affected my hearing, my lord. Did you just say I don't have the ability to solve murders? Do you even remember the past few years when the incompetent detectives who just visited us were going in the wrong direction and we—you and I—together—solved the murders?"

"We were lucky."

If only she had something heavy to hurl at his head. However, before William attempted to extract another promise from her, she decided changing the subject would be helpful. "I am quite tired, husband. If we are through with this discussion, I would like to take a short nap before dinner."

He immediately looked shamefaced. "I'm sorry, my love. I didn't mean to badger you, but I want a promise from you that—"

Amy stretched and yawned, quite loudly and said, "I think my brain would be working much better if I had some sleep." Without waiting for him to continue, she toed off her shoes, crawled across the bed, pulled the cozy blanket folded at the bottom of the bed, and covered her entire body.

Including her head.

She held her breath until she heard the door close, then moved the blanket down and rolled onto her back, staring at the canopy. Mrs. Garfield is out of gaol and Mrs. Devon was in the detectives' sights. How very interesting.

She would need to give this some thought. However, in between yawns she allowed that, as she was lying in bed anyway, she might as well take a nap.

* * *

WILLIAM WANDERED to the library and poured himself a glass of brandy. He checked his timepiece. A quarter to six. Dinner wouldn't be for another hour or so. He had hoped to spend the time with Amy, catching up on what she'd been doing while he was gone.

Apparently, what she'd been doing was sticking her nose into police business again. It was notable, however, that the police released the woman Amy had said from the start had been arrested too quickly. Now they seemed to be focused on this Mrs. Devon.

He would love to know what Amy discovered when she met with Lady Forester and Mrs. Devon at St. Michael's church. Not that he wanted to get involved in another murder, of course, but since he and Amy had worked before in finding true culprits, he found his interest in the matter piqued.

He took another sip of brandy and considered what he did know about the matter. Giving it more thought, he wondered about Mr. Fleming. He certainly didn't take much time in finding another woman to marry. It was disgraceful, and he couldn't help but wonder why the husband wasn't on the detectives' list. But then, he might very well be.

He firmly pushed away the thought that teased his mind. If he got involved, he could keep Amy out of trouble. He sighed, swirling the liquid in his glass. Why wasn't she like other mothers-to-be and decorating the nursery and interviewing nurses?

Well, Amy was Amy, and he liked her just the way she was. He grinned, thinking about the sweets and treats she'd been baking the last few weeks. If he had to choke down another one, he would need to see an apothecary to secure something stronger for his stomach than Cook had been providing him.

Sometime later, right about the time William was preparing to go up to their bedchamber to make sure Amy was ready for dinner, Filbert entered the library. "My Lord, you have a visitor."

"Not a visitor, just me." Michael's voice followed Filbert. "I'm here to drop off your kitten." He walked into the library, plopped the demon kitten onto William's lap and turned to leave.

William sneezed.

"Wait. This isn't our kitten."

Sneeze.

"Eloise said she and Amy were sharing the creature. I hate cats. I won't have it in my house."

Sneeze.

"I cannot abide cats either. I'm highly allergic to them."

Sneeze.

Michael placed his hands on his hips. "You have Persephone."

Sneeze. "She's a dog."

The man waved his hand around. "Same thing. Small, furry, annoying."

"Michael, what are you doing here?" Amy entered the library, a slight crease in her cheek announcing she'd just awoken from her nap.

"Returning your kitten."

"It's not my kitten, it's Eloise's kitten."

Sneeze. William held the creature out. "Amy, get rid of this thing."

She took the kitten out of William's hands and pushed it at Michael who raised his hands in the air and backed up.

Persephone came skittering through the door and began

barking at the kitten, who leaped from Amy's hands and raced around the room, wailing and screeching to wake the dead.

"Oh, don't let Persephone bite her," Eloise said as she waddled into the room, watching the two animals racing in circles.

Sneeze.

"Wife, I told you to stay in the carriage. I will handle this," Michael said.

William bent to scoop up Persephone, missed, tripped over the kitten, and landed on his knees.

Sneeze.

"Amy!" He barely got out before he sneezed again.

Michael finally grabbed Persephone, holding her up by her collar, the poor animal dangling in the air.

"Michael, let her go. You're strangling her," Amy yelled.

He shifted the dog around, so she was tucked into his arm, but still barking.

Eloise collapsed onto the settee and laughed while Michael glared at her, cupping Persephone's jaw together. "I want to know right now. Who owns that kitten?"

Sneeze.

Eloise and Amy pointed at each other. "She does."

Amy shuffled over to Eloise. "How can you say that? You know it's your kitten, and it's about time you told my brother about it."

Sneeze. "Amy, get rid of that cat!"

The animal had hidden itself behind the window drapes that hung to the floor. Amy eased herself down on her knees, admitting it was a foolish move because she would have a hard time getting back up again. "Come here, sweet kitten. No one will hurt you."

Sneeze.

She scooped it up, dragging it off its hold on the draperies, and left the room.

"Where is she going with my kitten?" Eloise said as she struggled to get up from the settee.

"Aha! So, it is your kitten," Michael said, pointing his finger at his wife.

She pushed at the back of the settee and finally made it to her feet. "Yes. It is my kitten, and I want to keep her." She burst into tears.

William leaned his forehead against the wall, a handkerchief pressed up against his nose. "Someone please remove that cat from my house." He looked over at Michael and Eloise who were in each other's arms, him patting her back and her sniffling in his shirt.

Amy returned with the kitten wrapped in a large cloth. "I got this from our housekeeper. You can take her home in this." She smiled at her brother and Eloise and turned to William. "I think she won this one."

Sneeze.

A half hour later, a sniffling Eloise, a grumbling Michael, and the wailing kitten were gone, Persephone had calmed herself and everything else had settled down. Amy had sent word to Cook that dinner should be pushed back a half hour so they could gather their wits about them.

Amy placed her empty sherry glass on the table in front of her chair. "I am quite hungry. Now that everything is peaceful again, I say let us proceed to the dining room."

"I agree." William finished the last of his brandy and reached his hand out to Amy, pulling her up. Hand in hand they walked down the corridor and took their places at the dining room table.

William had taken one bite of salmon when a female voice drifting from the entrance hall caught his attention. He wiped his mouth with his napkin and placed it alongside his plate. "Now what?"

"Mother!" He stood and walked over to her as she passed

through the doorway. She had been crying and looked quite distraught. Amy stood and joined them. "What is wrong, Lady Lily?"

She waved them off as if they asked her a strange question. "I need a cup of tea."

William pulled out a chair for her. "You came all the way across town for tea?"

She withdrew a lace-edged handkerchief from the sleeve of her dress and wiped her eyes "No. I just know tea will ease me."

William and Amy looked at each other and shrugged. "Please bring a pot of tea for my mother-in-law," Amy said as she took her seat.

"Are you ill?" William asked.

His mother shook her head and patted her eyes. She took several deep, dramatic breaths, then looked up at the footman who placed a teapot, cup, and saucer in front of her. "Thank you. You are very kind."

Since his mother didn't look physically bruised, William picked up his fork and continued eating, knowing she would have her say in due time. He couldn't help wondering where Mr. Colbert was. The man never let her out of his sight.

Finally, after a few sips of tea, Mother took a deep breath and said, "I am moving in with you. I want nothing more to do with that horrid man."

Just then a knock sounded at the door.

"That will be my luggage." His mother stood and left the dining room. Her voice carried from the entrance hall. "Just bring everything upstairs to the blue bedchamber on the right-hand side. I will be up to unpack shortly. My maid, Susan, should arrive in another half hour with the rest of my things."

Amy looked over at William. "Your mother is moving in?"

William closed his eyes and shook his head. "As soon as this child is born, we are moving to my country estate." He pointed to her plate. "Eat your dinner. Heaven only knows what will happen next and you need your strength."

14

"*L*ady Lily has moved in with us." Amy dropped that bit of news onto Aunt Margaret as she settled herself in her aunt's sitting room the following Wednesday.

Her hostess's brows rose as she poured tea for Amy. "Indeed? Did Mr. Colbert lose his home?"

Amy shook her head and took a sip of the tea fixed exactly as she liked it. "No. Just my mother-in-law moved in. Apparently, she had some sort of a tiff with Mr. Colbert and left him."

"Left him as in she doesn't plan to go back?"

Amy sighed and picked a small cucumber sandwich. "If the numerous pieces of luggage mean anything, I think she'll be with us until my baby is a grandparent."

Aunt Margaret folded her delicate hands in her lap. "Of course, I don't know them as well as you do, but from what I've seen myself and heard from you and William, I thought their marriage was one of the rare love matches."

"It is—or was. She won't tell us what happened, but she cries a lot. Also, Mr. Colbert has visited at least once, and in some cases twice a day since she arrived. Lady Lily refuses to see him."

"Where is the poor Lady Lily now?"

Amy shrugged. "Most likely in her bedchamber. She spends a great deal of time there. From what I've seen when I visit her, she is penning a great deal of letters. Or she's attempting to write a book."

"What does William have to say about this?"

Amy sighed and chewed on the sandwich. "Poor William is a tad overwrought lately."

"I didn't know men became overwrought."

"I didn't either, but several things have happened recently that has him claiming to move us all to the country once the baby is born."

"Do tell." Her aunt poured herself more tea and dropped in a cube of sugar and a drop of milk.

"Remember the other night when you were all at my house for dinner before Lord Exeter and William left for London?"

"Yes."

"And remember Papa arrived at the end of the dinner and requested to speak with William?"

"Yes. I forgot about that. We left shortly after Franklin appeared. What did he want with your husband?"

"It seems his investments aren't going well, and he wanted William's advice. He wasn't happy when William told him he should get back together with Michael since he is doing well. He left in a bit of a storm. We haven't heard from him since."

Aunt Margaret nodded. "That sounds like Franklin."

"Then Eloise and Michael showed up at our house with that kitten she's been hiding. There was a bit of a row with them—poor William sneezing the entire time—until Eloise became so distraught that Michael gave in, and they took the kitten with them."

"My goodness. I can see why William is threatening to move."

Amy smiled. "There's more."

"Oh, dear. Perhaps I should send for more tea." She stood and rang for the footman to bring more tea. She turned to Amy. "Perhaps I should make it sherry?"

"No. I find of late any sort of spirit beverage disagrees with my stomach."

"That is what you get for attempting to increase the world population." She took her seat and waved at Amy. "Continue."

"The police detectives came again."

Aunt Margaret's eyes narrowed. "I thought they had already arrested someone. I assume they came to discuss the case?"

"Yes. And to warn us off again." She leaned back and shifted in the settee. "These things are very uncomfortable. You need better seating here."

"There is nothing wrong with my seating, dear niece. It is your increased size." She stood and rang for a maid, and requested she bring a pillow for Amy's back.

Amy smiled and continued. "It seems they've released Mrs. Garfield. They didn't say why, but I assume their case wasn't strong enough." Amy leaned forward. "I think they have their eye on a Mrs. Devon."

"Who is she? Do you know her? Is that why they were asking questions again?"

"Wellll." She dragged the word out. "I might have met her when I attended St. Michael's Church Sunday last."

"St. Michael's?"

Amy felt uncomfortable, realizing if she acknowledged what she had done, fingers crossed or not, she would be admitting that she was, indeed, pursuing the murder of her midwife. "Lady Forester from my book club mentioned that Mrs. Devon and Mrs. Fleming had been battling in court over a piece of heirloom jewelry. I'm assuming the police are now looking at her as the murderer."

Aunt Margaret shook her head. "My dear, I believe your husband is right in this matter. I don't believe you should be involving yourself in this." She eyed her middle. "When is the child expected to make itself known?"

"In a tad more than two months. But from what I hear, the first child is generally late."

Her aunt grinned. "Depending on the morality of the bride and groom there are many 'first offspring' who arrive early."

That was true. Not so much now as in the previous generation—before the influence of Queen Victoria—many couples had 'anticipated their vows'. Since she and William were married months before she realized she was enceinte, they had no worries.

Amy cleared her throat, not sure now if her aunt would answer her question, but she had to try. "Aside from that—and I promise I will not get myself into trouble—"

A chuckle came from her aunt.

"—I spoke with Lord Exeter at our dinner party, and he told me he was not surprised Mr. Fleming was set to remarry shortly after his wife's death. In fact, probably any day now."

Aunt Margaret placed her teacup down. "He did tell me once that he knew Mr. Fleming from his school days, but he never mentioned anything else about him." She eyed Amy. "Although, I would have no reason to ask anything more about the man."

"I find it telling that Exeter would not be surprised by Mr. Fleming's remarriage so soon. It makes me wonder if he knows that Mr. Fleming was seeing someone while still married to his wife."

When Aunt Margaret did not offer any insight into her observation, Amy said. "I don't suppose—"

"No."

"I just wondered—"

"No."

Amy let out a huge sigh. "Honestly, Aunt, I only want to

know because I might want to use some of this information in a forthcoming book."

"Amy. Remember I practically raised you. I know precisely why you are interested in Mr. Fleming. I won't ask Exeter about him, but I will let you know that we will be at the Assembly this Saturday."

"That is quite helpful. Thank you very much." Amy broke into a huge smile.

She pointed a finger at Amy. "Do. Not. Tell. William I passed this information along to you. The only reason I did is because I'm afraid of what you will do if you decide to gather this information on your own."

Amy finished the rest of her tea and stood. "Well, I must be on my way. I have a new recipe I am trying for tonight's dinner that I think William will be quite fond of."

"I thought you said you haven't been able to bake recently because your cook always seemed to be out of ingredients you need."

She pulled on her gloves and picked up her reticule. "That is true, but I have a list of what I need," she patted her reticule, "and will stop at the market on my way home and buy them."

* * *

"Mother, it's time this nonsense ended. Your husband has been here every day since you arrived, yet you refuse to see him. You hide in your bedchamber, doing God knows what. You cry all the time and won't tell us what is wrong. Is it necessary for me to visit with him and tell him to name his second?" William addressed his mother as the three of them sat down for dinner.

His mother flipped her napkin and placed it on her lap. "Is it troublesome for me to stay here, William? Is my upkeep costing you too much? I can take up some duties to alleviate any problems. I believe I can cook or dust the drawing room."

William dropped his head into his hands. Although he had been considering moving his wife and child to the country after the baby was born, at present, America or perhaps Australia seemed like better choices.

"No, Mother. You are not a burden. I don't need you to clean the fireplaces or change the linens, either. I have sufficient staff to do all those things." He placed his hand over hers. "I just don't like seeing you so unhappy."

She sniffed and he prayed she was not about to cry again. "I am not unhappy. I have adjusted well to my new life." She fumbled with her silverware and took deep breaths.

Yes, she was about to cry.

Pulling herself together, she looked over at him while the footmen began serving dinner. "I assume you and dear Amy are attending the book club meeting this evening?"

William glanced at Amy who nodded. "Yes. Will you join us?"

"I believe I will." She sniffed and raised her chin. "That man will not keep me from doing the things I enjoy."

That was interesting since his mother only joined the book club initially out of curiosity and he was fairly certain she continued to attend because her husband was there.

The carriage ride to Atkinson & Tucker Bookstore was quiet. It was obvious his mother was nervous about coming face to face with Mr. Colbert. What confused William was why she chose to confront him in public after turning him away day after day when she could have spoken to him in private.

He was still puzzled by his mother's issues. Poor Mr. Colbert had looked like hell each time he arrived at William's front door. He felt awful having to turn the man away and hoped that this meeting tonight would resolve everything.

As they entered the room, the first person William saw was

Mr. Colbert. The joy on the man's face when he spotted his wife was almost heartbreaking. He hurried over to them, his eyes never leaving her. William took Amy's elbow and moved her away from the couple.

Smartly, his stepfather took hold of his wife's elbow as well and moved her out of the meeting room and into the bookstore.

"Do you think your mother came tonight to see her husband?" Amy asked as she and William moved to a small group of members.

"Yes. I can't think of any other reason she would come. I'm hoping she is ready to resolve whatever their issue was. I would certainly like to get back to just the two of us in the house. Not that she is any trouble, but the drama and constant tears are worrying on the nerves."

"Good evening, my lord, my lady," Lady Forester said as they joined their circle. "How are you feeling, Lady Amy? You are looking good."

Amy laughed. "Since I saw you only a few days ago at church, I'm happy to know you are pleased with my appearance."

Miss Gertrude O'Neill looked at Amy. "Have you abandoned us at St. Swithin's then, my lady?"

"Not at all," Lady Forester said. "Because his lordship was out of town this past weekend, I invited Lady Amy to our church—St. Michael's—for the service and a potluck luncheon following."

"I understand my wife met an old schoolmate while at your church," William said.

"Yes. It was truly amazing." She turned to Amy. "It is always nice to meet old friends."

Amy uttered a slight agreement and immediately changed the subject. William looked at the door to the bookstore to see his mother and stepfather returning to the meeting room.

Their hands were clasped together, and she was smiling for the first time in days.

He breathed a sigh of relief and nudged Amy, gesturing with his head in their direction. She looked over at them and smiled, mouthing "Thank goodness."

The meeting went swiftly with his mother once again sitting up at the front of the room with Colbert staring at her the entire time.

"I assume all is well, Mother?" William asked as she joined them once Colbert had called the meeting to an end.

"Yes, dear, it was all a misunderstanding."

Colbert walked up to them and shook William's hand and hugged Amy. "I will be over tomorrow morning to pick up my wife's things." He looked at her, and she looked back with the gooey eye of youthful love. "But tonight, she will return to our home with me."

"Do you wish to stop at our house first to pick up some things to sleep in?" Amy asked.

Colbert hugged Mother close. "She won't need anything to sleep in."

William coughed and cleared his throat. "Sir, please. This is my mother."

Colbert winked. "But my wife."

* * *

THE NEXT MORNING Lady Lily spent the time directing her maid to pack her things and prepare to have them sent back to her home. Amy was glad to see the couple had settled whatever issue it had been that caused the split to begin with.

Since her mother-in-law had only returned to Wethington House a short while ago, and went directly upstairs, Amy and William still had no idea what the issue had been. They ate their breakfast in peace and quiet.

Which, of course, did not last long.

Filbert entered the dining room. "My lord, the detectives you are so fond of are in the drawing room."

Amy's eyes flew open. Why in heaven's name were they here again? She'd done nothing since the visit at the church to arouse their concern and interest.

William gritted his teeth. "Tell the men this is not a convenient time. If they insist upon speaking with us, they will need to wait until we are finished with our meal."

Filbert gave a short bow and left the room.

Just then Lady Lily entered the room. "I think I am all packed. Susan is finishing up, and if you will allow her the use of your carriage, she will be ready in about fifteen minutes to return my things to my home."

"Are you leaving now? Or would you care for some breakfast?"

Her mother-in-law sat and gestured to the footman to bring her tea. "I have time for a cup. My dear Edward will be returning momentarily to fetch me." She blushed. "He has taken the day off from his work to spend the time with me."

"Mother, I probably will be sorry I asked this, but what was the issue that had you fleeing your home in such a state?"

She took a sip of her tea. "I had read in a woman's periodical that many men were beginning to wear wedding rings. So, thinking Edward would like one, I purchased him a ring, but he didn't want to wear it."

"I don't know that I would care to wear one, either," William said. "Do you care, Amy?"

She shook her head.

"Well, I soon found out that since dear Edward had never heard about the practice before, he merely refused, and when I pushed, he laughed at me, said he was not a woman!"

Just then Mr. Colbert entered the dining room. "Are you ready, my dear? I have a wonderful day planned for us."

Lady Lily actually blushed and stood to take his hand, which, Amy noticed, sported a gold band.

They left together and William let out a sigh of relief. "All is well that ends well, as Shakespeare said."

William threw down his napkin and stood. "We might as well see what the detectives want now." He glared at her. "You haven't done something I would need to know about before this meeting, have you?"

"No." She glared back at him and raised her chin. "And I resent the question."

His mere response had been raised eyebrows. They left the breakfast room together to find the detectives comfortably settled in their drawing room. She was amazed when they both stood as they entered.

Once they were all settled, Carson said. "Lady Amy, I've said this before. You are not a safe person to be around."

Amy and William looked at each other, confused. They turned back to the detective. "What does that mean?" William asked.

Carson looked directly at Amy. "Your recently rediscovered schoolmate, Mrs. Devon, was found dead in her bedchamber this morning."

15

*A*my merely stared at the two men, her heart pounding. Mrs. Devon was dead? It seemed unbelievable. Her reaction to this latest development almost made her decide to stay out of this, and any further, investigations.

"My dear, you look quite unsettled. I believe you should put your head down." William put his hand on the back of her neck and lowered her head to what was left of her lap.

Unsettled? In all the investigations they'd done before, never had she been so very rattled. Mrs. Fleming had visited with her and Eloise and the very next day she was dead. Amy met Mrs. Devon at church and within days she was dead. She was almost afraid to leave the house, lest she put someone's life in danger.

William.

Maybe she should move to the country by herself and save those she loved from a sudden death. She took a deep breath and calmed herself as William continued to rub her back. The detectives were speaking, but a buzzing in her ears kept her from hearing what they said.

William leaned down to speak in her ear. "I have no

problem escorting these men out of the house. I do not like the way you look. I think you need a tisane and a short rest."

She wanted nothing more than a way to escape what she'd just heard, but somewhere deep inside, she did not want to appear weak. She shook her head and sat up. She gripped William's hand as a wave of dizziness came over her, but she fought it and swallowed. "I apologize, detectives. I'm afraid that news took me by surprise."

"Detectives, it's obvious my wife is distraught. I know you have an investigation to conduct, but I ask you wait until another time to question us."

"I'm afraid I cannot comply with that request, my lord," Carson said. "Perhaps you can have someone bring her ladyship a glass of water."

Amy shook her head. "No. I am fine. Let's just get this over with. How did Mrs. Devon die?"

"A pair of scissors to her neck. Sliced the carotid artery, according to the coroner, and she bled to death."

Amy winced at that vision. "That is horrible. Was there a scuffle? Or perhaps a robbery?"

"We had her daily maid go over her things. It appears there was a recently acquired necklace returned from the courts that Mrs. Devon and the deceased Mrs. Fleming were fighting over. That was not to be found, but the maid was not sure that Mrs. Devon kept the piece in her room. She had no safe in the house, so it appears likely it was in her bedchamber, but that hasn't been confirmed."

"Aside from throwing my wife into grief and shock, is there another purpose for your visit?" William said as he frowned and continued to watch Amy.

Detective Carson stood and Detective Marsh held his pencil at the ready. "Lady Wethington, you stated at our last visit that you attended church at St. Michael's because a friend of yours —not Mrs. Devon—invited you. Putting aside my suspicions that you knew you would meet Mrs. Devon, was there anything the woman said to you that might help us?"

With all the encounters they'd had with the detectives, Amy never remembered them coming right out and asking for their help.

William looked over at her. "If you know anything, tell the detectives." He leaned in close to her ear. "If you help them, they might come up with the right person and we can put this aside since we have other matters that concern us right now."

Amy hated to agree with William, and she really did want to continue the investigation, but she had to admit she was quite rattled by this new murder. Of course, once the detectives were on their way, and Amy had time to calm herself and think about this, she would most likely come up with her own list.

"There really wasn't anything else. She told me she didn't get along with Mrs. Fleming, although they were apparently close at one time. I know there was a lawsuit between the two, Mrs. Devon claiming that Mrs. Fleming had stolen the necklace intended for her by tricking Mrs. Devon's mother, Mrs. Stoker into thinking Mrs. Fleming was her daughter. Apparently, near the end of her life, Mrs. Stoker was suffering from old age muddle-headedness."

Amy wanted to ask them about Mr. Fleming, who she thought should be at the top of the list since he planned to marry not long after his wife died and might have felt that the necklace that Mrs. Devon received from the court should be returned to him as Mrs. Fleming's husband. Although, truth be known, he really wasn't her husband anymore.

She began to feel befuddled. She cleared her throat. "I am sorry, detectives, but I know nothing more than you do."

"Then we are finished," William said.

He walked toward the door. "Filbert!"

The butler appeared in an instant which told Amy he was

listening at the door, although his expression never showed anything different. "Yes, my lord."

"Show the detectives out." He returned to where Amy sat and reached his hand out. "My dear?"

She took his hand, and they left the room, never looking back. William led them both up the stairs to their bedchamber. He closed the door, turned to her, and said, "I am suggesting a short rest. You have had a shock and your color has still not returned to normal."

"I am fine."

"No. You are not. If you don't take a short rest, I will find it necessary to visit with Dr. Stevens."

Not having the energy to argue, she merely nodded and crawled into bed and closed her eyes.

* * *

WILLIAM SAT at his desk in the library, gazing out the window, trying to convince himself that attempting to keep Amy from involving herself in this newest murder was futile. As much as he hated the idea, the only thing to be done was for him to join her.

They'd been a very good team in prior murders. Plus, it would be a way for him to protect her from any danger and make sure she didn't overtax herself.

As he sat there, he decided to put off his scheduled tour of a new factory in Bristol that he was considering investing money into and instead, spend the time with Amy going over all the information she had gathered—and of course had refused to admit to him before now—to see if they could come up with a solution to the two murders.

Amy arrived at the library looking much better than when he left her earlier. "I see the short rest has restored you."

"Yes. I do feel a lot better." She looked at the desk where he had a piece of paper with writing on it. "What are you doing?"

"I have decided to help you figure out these murders so you can concentrate on the baby."

She offered him a bright smile. "Indeed."

"Yes. As we learned before, two heads are better than one. The main problem I see is we need connections to people known to both Mrs. Fleming and Mrs. Devon."

Amy moved to stand behind him, staring at the paper. "What is this?"

"My list of suspects."

"There is only one name on there."

He huffed. "I'm just getting started." He motioned to the chair in front of the desk. "Why don't you take a seat, and we'll make a list."

Amy tapped her lips with her index finger. "First, of course, Mr. Fleming."

"For the first murder or the second?"

"If Mrs. Devon was his wife's cousin, then surely he knew her. Also, he was probably aware of the lawsuit regarding the necklace. I'm thinking he should go on both lists."

"Who do you have for the first murder?" William asked.

"Mr. Fleming and Mrs. Devon—who is now dead. I also added Mrs. Garfield only because she did find the body and the inept detectives seemed to think she was guilty at one time. To my way of thinking, it was merely one of those being in the wrong place at the wrong time."

William had been writing while Amy spoke. "As for Mrs. Devon, do we want to keep her on the list for the first murder?"

"Yes. Until we have reason to take her off, it is quite possible she killed Mrs. Fleming for the necklace and then someone killed her for the necklace."

"Mr. Fleming?"

"Possibly. Or someone who we haven't discovered yet. Husband, you are making me feel a tad foolish. These are things I should already have decided. I would never have let these things become so convoluted were I writing this as a book." She shook her head. "That is why I put my book aside. My mother-to-be brain is not functioning properly."

"I don't wish to insult you, but I do see a lack of your normal investigative skills."

Amy winced. "Then it is a very good thing that you offered to help."

"My thoughts are moving toward gathering more information on Mr. Fleming, also. I shall make a visit to my club while you take a rest."

"I just woke up from a rest! But I will need some time, however, to make the dessert for tonight."

William's stomach rebelled thinking of what his lovely wife would come up with tonight to torture him. "I think you should put your baking aside for now, Amy. Staying rested and working on this matter will take up all your time."

"No. I certainly feel well enough to bake something. I'll go through Cook's recipes and see what I haven't tried yet."

Once she was settled, flipping through Cook's notes, he strode to the mews and had the groom tack Major for the trip to his club. Since they'd passed on luncheon, he would have a meal there and visit with the members, seeing what information he could pull from them.

As he rode through the streets, he acknowledged that he should have reprimanded Amy for continuing with the investigation after he had forbidden her to do so. Of course, since Amy had never been a biddable wife, he had no reason to believe she would have done it this time, except he'd hoped impending motherhood might sway her.

Apparently not.

The club was typical for a Friday afternoon. Those who

engaged in business of any sort were there for a fast meal before returning to their work. Men like William whose work consisted of managing their money and meeting with investors, solicitors, and men of business, or dealing with Parliamentary matters when in session, were there for a more leisurely luncheon, being able to arrange their schedules as they see fit. And those few who still lived the life of a gentleman, spending their time in pursuit of pleasure, gaming, horse trading, garden parties, and such, spent a good portion of their day at their clubs, socializing and attempting to outdrink each other.

Since the large estates were no longer as profitable as they'd been a generation ago, many of the present crop of gentlemen had maintained their status quo by marrying wealthy American heiresses whose family sought a title for their daughters in exchange for a princely sum.

The rise of factories had changed the livelihoods of many estate owners with tenants abandoning farms that had been worked by their families for generations for better paying jobs in the cities.

William searched the room, looking for companionship as well as someone who might have information for him. It was growing close to the time luncheon would be served, but he had a bit of time.

He took a seat near two other members he knew from his Eton years who were living a good life. Because of their lifestyle, they could very well have gossip to share.

"Good day, Wethington. I haven't seen you here at this time for a while." Lord Pemberton nodded in his direction.

"Yes, normally I don't manage to visit here until later in the afternoon, but it being Friday, I decided to change things up a bit." He nodded to Lord Crawford, who sat alongside Pemberton. Both men had married rich wives, and both men were sipping on brandy. A bottle of the best the house had to offer sat on the table in between their glasses.

"Care for a drop before luncheon?" Pemberton asked as he filled his glass.

"Thank you, but no." William turned to signal a footman to bring him coffee. Not that he never imbibed before the sun went down, but this was a tad early for him. Plus, he wanted to remain sharp to gather information, not provide it.

He figured he might as well jump in. "Either of you seen Ronald Fleming lately?"

If they were surprised at his question, they didn't show it. "No. He disappeared shortly after his wife's death," Crawford said. "Talk was he planned on remarrying. Not waiting for the usual one year, it seems."

"That seems odd," William said as he nodded his thanks to the footman for the coffee he placed in front of him. He was not overly familiar with Fleming. He remembered meeting him over a card table once or twice but was never able to have a lengthy conversation with the man.

Pemberton shrugged. "I'm certainly not supporting what he's doing, rules of society and all that, but from what I've witnessed, he and his late wife were practically enemies."

"Indeed?"

"She was a nasty sort. He would come to the club on occasion after one of their bouts, bruises showing."

So far Amy hadn't uncovered anything good about Mrs. Fleming, and it appears there was a lot more. "I must say I'm surprised she has such a reputation because she was my wife's midwife. I would think a woman who is in a caring for others occupation would not be the type to succumb to fisticuffs."

Crawford shrugged and said, "From what I know, he had been nagging her for a divorce."

"A divorce! That's not easy to come by."

Crawford took a sip of brandy and shook his head. "No.

Word has it that she agreed but only if she could charge him with adultery."

William let out a low whistle. "That is about the only grounds I know for divorce. He must have been desperate."

"He wouldn't allow that. He's apparently a big man in his company and couldn't afford the scandal that would cause."

"I imagine remarrying so soon after his wife's death would be a bit of a scandal as well," William said, laying his cup down on the table in front of him.

"Any way you look at it, he was an unhappy man," Pemberton added.

What bothered William the most was he had approved using Mrs. Fleming to deliver his child. Why hadn't that information been presented by those who recommended her? Everyone he'd spoken to, including Dr. Dudley, were more impressed with her certification.

He hated sounding like a gossipmonger, but the sooner they could get this matter settled and handed off to the police, the quicker Amy would relax into her role as a mother. "I would assume if he were marrying quickly and asking for a divorce, there had to have been a woman in the picture while he was still married to Mrs. Fleming."

Crawford poured more brandy into his glass, not at all concerned about the questions William was asking. Given their way of life, gossip and scandal was very familiar to them. Something the *Beau Monde* thrived on.

He took a sip and said, "A chit in Bristol, I understand."

That explained why the banns were announced in the *Bristol Mercury*. Although, as far as he knew, banns were to be announced in both bride's and groom's church.

Just then one of the footmen approached their group, announcing luncheon was now being served. All three men rose and made their way out of the general area to the dining room. William would have preferred to partake with other members, hoping to get more or perhaps different information from them. He glanced around the room, but the only man he immediately recognized was Michael.

Not wishing to continue the conversation about Fleming with Crawford and Pemberton lest they begin to look at him in a peculiar way, William rested his hand on Crawford's shoulder as they arrived at a table. "I see my brother-in-law across the room. If you will excuse me, I need to speak with him about something. It was good seeing you both again, and I wish you a pleasant day." They waved him off, and he bowed slightly, heading toward Michael's table.

* * *

AMY LOOKED up and smiled as William entered the drawing room. "I thought I wouldn't see you until dinnertime. Did your visit to the club yield any information?" She laid a ribbon on the page of the book she was reading to hold her place and put the tome on the table in front of her.

"Indeed, it did," he said as he sat alongside her on the settee. "From what I learned, it seemed the Fleming marriage was a bit of a battleground."

Amy's brows rose. "Physical fighting?"

"Yes. Enough that Mr. Fleming arrived at the club sporting bruises. And he had also asked for a divorce."

"Oh, my. Isn't that almost impossible to gain?"

"Yes. Mrs. Fleming told Mr. Fleming she would petition the courts for a divorce but would charge him with adultery."

Amy shook her head. "My goodness, the more I hear about Mrs. Fleming, the less I doubt she pushed someone far enough that they did away with her."

They sat in silence for a moment, both considering what they'd learned. William shifted toward her. "Since I have the rest of the afternoon free, why don't we make a visit to Dr.

Stevens? Although Dr. Dudley and you both heaped praise upon her, I would like to meet her myself."

Amy stood and shook out her skirts. "That's a wonderful idea! Just give me a moment to freshen up and we can be off." She turned as she reached the door. "I just know you will love her."

"If you like her, dear, I am certain I will as well. While you are readying yourself, I will have the carriage brought around."

She hurried up the stairs, feeling better than she had in a while. She hadn't realized how much she missed having William as part of her investigation until he agreed to help.

Also, she was anxious for him to meet Dr. Stevens. With him home early and them making a visit to the doctor, it had turned out to be a very pleasant afternoon. After doing the best she could with her hair and finding two shoes that at least looked alike, she made her way downstairs where William awaited her.

He shifted her cape and rebuttoned the garment while she sighed like a recalcitrant child. It was rather embarrassing that she could not clothe herself. She would definitely see about hiring a lady's maid so she did not have to suffer these indignities.

Lord Sterling greeted them as they awaited Dr. Stevens in her waiting room. "Wethington, it's good to see you." He moved forward with a quick stride and extended his hand. He nodded in Amy's direction. "Lady Wethington, it is always a pleasure."

"My wife told me you had married Dr. Stevens and are now assisting her. I am quite impressed, Sterling," William said with a smile.

"Yes. Things change." He sat in the chair across from them and leaned forward, resting his elbows on his thighs. "My wife is finishing up with a patient, but she has time to visit with you once she's done. I wish to speak to you before you see her." He stopped for a minute, as if arranging his thoughts. Finally, he said, "I'm afraid she is not having a good day today, so she might seem a bit off."

"Is something wrong?" Amy asked. The man looked a bit off himself.

"I am sure if you don't know, you will soon find out about the death of Mrs. Petrina Devon?"

Amy and William both said at the same time, "Yes. We were aware."

Sterling ran his fingers through his hair and lowered his voice. "Mrs. Devon was one of my wife's patients." He stopped for a minute and took a deep breath. "It is always hard to lose a patient, but when it involves murder…"

16

*A*my's hand flew to her mouth. "Oh dear, I can see how that would be most disturbing."

Lord Sterling nodded. "Yes. Poor Rayne—excuse me, Dr. Stevens—is of course very upset. I've spent time since this morning trying to calm her down."

"Was she close to the woman? I mean, aside from Mrs. Devon being her patient?" William asked.

Sterling shook his head. "No. But she saw Mrs. Devon on a regular basis. I can't divulge why, but her death and the manner of it has hit my wife hard."

Wondering if Sterling and Dr. Stevens had spoken with the police, she asked, "I assume the police visited here this morning?"

"Yes. They wanted to see Mrs. Devon's medical records, but my wife will not release them unless she is ordered by the court."

William leaned forward, resting his forearms on his thighs. "What we heard was Mrs. Devon was stabbed. Whatever could that have to do with her medical records?"

Lord Sterling stood and began to pace. "That is precisely my wife's position. Medical records are private and unless there is cause for the police being concerned with why Mrs. Devon was under treatment, there is no reason for Dr. Stevens to release them."

Just as Amy was about to ask another question, Dr. Stevens came into the room. Both men stood, but Amy remained where she was. It was too hard to get up and down.

"Good afternoon, Lord Wethington, Lady Wethington." She glanced in Amy's direction. "It is so nice to see you." She walked up to William and put out her hand. "I am Dr. Rayne Stevens."

"My pleasure," William said.

If Dr. Stevens was 'off' it wasn't too easy to see. Amy did note the doctor seemed tense, and there were frown lines on her forehead she hadn't noticed the last time they'd met.

They all sat, and William said, "I must say, Doctor, that both Dr. Dudley and my wife are both very impressed with you."

Obviously used to praise, she gave a slight nod. "I am pleased to hear that. It is not easy being a female doctor in a man's world."

Sterling moved to sit next to her and linked her fingers with his. "But you have proved them all wrong, my dear. You are not only the best female doctor, but one of the best doctors."

Dr. Stevens laughed. "So says my husband. If I can't have him for support and praise, it would be a sad thing." She turned to Sterling. "Have you ordered tea?"

"Yes. Once John told me Lord and Lady Wethington were here, I asked him to have Cook put together a tea tray."

"Thank you. I can always count on you." She straightened in her chair and looked directly at William. "I assume you wish to interview me since your wife secured my services as her midwife." She paused for a moment. "I must ask you first if you have any objection to Lady Wethington being under the care of a female doctor?"

William grinned and took Amy's hand. "Since her former midwife was a woman, it would be quite foolish of me to object to a female doctor who is much more qualified and trained than a midwife."

"Thank you. I will tell you my mother and baby survival rates are excellent. I adhere to Dr. Joseph Lister's teachings on cleanliness. In my research and historical studies, I've learned that most cases of childbed fever come from dirty hands and implements, as incredible as that seems."

The man who had greeted them at the door entered the room, pushing a tea tray. He placed it alongside Dr. Stevens who began to pour for them.

"I see you are expecting a child yourself, Dr. Stevens," William said as he took the cup and saucer from her hand.

"Yes." Her face lit up with joy. "Lord Sterling and I already have a lovely daughter, Lady Madeline. We are hoping this one is a boy, but as long as the child is healthy, that's all that matters." She looked toward her husband who nodded his agreement.

Amy tried to think of a way to bring up Mrs. Devon, but since Lord Sterling already warned them that the doctor was upset about the death of her patient it seemed unkind to mention it. But she hated to pass up the opportunity to ask questions.

They chatted for about fifteen minutes, Dr. Stevens sharing stories meant to put William at ease about Amy's delivery as they drank the tea and ate the small sandwiches and ginger biscuits. She really should try to make them sometime. It was apparent William was quite fond of them since he was on his third one.

Dr. Stevens brushed crumbs off her lap and stood. "While I am enjoying this visit very much and am so happy to have met you, Lord Wethington, I do have to finish up some notes before my next patient arrives."

The rest of them stood. William took Amy by her elbow. "I certainly understand, Doctor, and I appreciate the time you've taken to speak with us."

The doctor looked at Amy's middle. "You are looking quite well, my lady. Perhaps you and your sister-in-law can drop by one day next week for a chat about how you are both getting on? Or I can meet you and Lady Davenport at one of your homes."

"Lady Davenport and I would be happy to come by. It is good for us to get out of the house. Do you have a particular day in mind?"

"Excuse me while I get my appointment book," she said.

"Your wife looks quite well," Amy said. "She seems to be holding up under the stress of her patient's death."

"Yes. She is a professional and a remarkable woman. But I can see the tension in her."

Deciding that continuing the conversation with Dr. Stevens about to rejoin them was not a good idea, Amy merely nodded.

"Here we are. It looks like Tuesday of next week in the early afternoon will work well. I can allot time to see the both of you then."

"I will make a note of it and inform Lady Davenport." Just as they reached the door, Amy turned back to Dr. Stevens and Lord Sterling. "Do you ever attend the Assembly on Saturday evenings? Lord Wethington and I often do, and we have friends who generally join us. You might find it entertaining."

They looked at each other and shook their heads. "To be honest, I am so tied up with my work that I never thought of that."

Lord Sterling took Dr. Stevens' hand in his. "It might be a nice idea to do some socializing." He turned back to Amy. "We will certainly consider it. We have friends, also, who go to the Assembly on occasion, perhaps we will meet them there, as well."

***

Relaxing after dinner in the library, William took a sip of his port and looked over at Amy who was reading a book that she hadn't turned the pages on in over fifteen minutes. "What is your opinion on these two murders? Have you come up with any theories?"

It was apparent with how quickly she answered that her thoughts had not been on the book, but on the murders. "I think the most pressing question is, are these murders connected? Mrs. Fleming and Mrs. Devon were fighting in court over a piece of jewelry they both claimed belonged to them. At one time I had Mrs. Devon on my suspect list, but now that she is dead, I don't know where to place her besides victim."

William frowned and looked out the window at the moonlit night for a few moments. "I find I must agree with you."

Amy pushed herself up off the settee and walked to the large wooden desk across the room that took up a good part of the library. She settled into the comfortable leather chair behind the desk and opened a drawer, taking out the list they had already begun.

"We have to continue with our lists," she said, reaching for the pen sitting on the pen rest.

If William truly wanted to help her solve these suspicious deaths, this was his opportunity to contribute. To her delight, he said, "If I remember correctly, we already have Mr. Fleming, Mrs. Devon, and Mrs. Garfield on the list. Perhaps we might add reasons?"

"Yes." Amy tapped her lips with the end of the pen. "Mr. Fleming first."

William stood and walked to the desk, resting his hip on the edge. "He wanted a divorce that Mrs. Fleming would not give him. He quickly arranged to remarry while Mrs. Fleming was barely in her grave."

"Agreed." She looked up. "What about his wife-to-be?"

William shrugged. "Until we learn more about her, I don't think we can add her. I don't know if it is worth our time to pursue Mrs. Devon."

"Why not? Even though she's dead, there is the possibility that she killed Mrs. Fleming and then she was killed."

"Mr. Fleming again?"

Amy studied him for a moment. "Yes. I shall add his name to the list of suspects for Mrs. Devon's murder, also."

William turned, looking directly at Amy. "Mrs. Garfield?"

"That one has me stumped. I know nothing about her, so if she is to remain on our list, I will have to do some research into her. Right now, all I know is she found Mrs. Fleming's body."

William crossed his arms over his chest and smiled. "Are we going with the theory, then, that the murders are connected, oh great mystery writer?"

She blew out a breath and sat back. "I don't know. I don't believe in coincidences, so what are the odds of two women, who are known to each other, who were in fact, related to each other, and fighting in court, both being killed within weeks?"

"For two different reasons?" William added.

"Or the same reason." Amy picked up the pen and continued to write. She sighed and studied the paper, then glanced up at William. "You know, Mrs. Fleming was truly not a very nice person."

William slid off the edge of the desk and began to pace. "You know who needs further scrutiny?" He stopped and looked at Amy. "The woman who wanted to take over the midwife duties for you and Eloise who'd been maligned by Mrs. Fleming."

"Yes. That is a good point. Plus, Eloise and I have heard that she was known to have a bit of a temper."

He gestured toward the paper. "How many is that?"

Amy glanced over the list. "Three. If we include Mrs. Devon for the first murder, there are four. Mr. Fleming, Mrs. Garfield, Mrs. Penrose, and possibly Mrs. Devon."

William stretched and yawned. "I believe we should put this all aside for now. It has been a long day and you need your sleep. Tomorrow I must meet with your brother and father who wanted me to act as arbitrator in their business issues."

"Really?" She took William's outstretched hands and stood. Botheration, it was getting harder and harder to get up from a chair. "When did this all come about?"

"I saw Michael at my club earlier, and he asked if I would attend a meeting with him and your father tomorrow. It seems most meetings between them have turned into shouting matches and he thinks my calm presence might help."

She took his arm, and they made their way upstairs to their bedchamber. "My father has always been a tad difficult to deal with. But he does have a good heart and only wants what's best for his family."

William opened the door to their room. "You mean by forcing you to write under a fictitious name, years browbeating Lady Margaret to marry, attempting to keep Michael from marrying Eloise, even though it was obvious their hearts were engaged?" He grinned as he removed his ascot. "Yes, he does want what's best. What *he* deems is best."

Amy walked up to him and tapped him on his chest. "He never had anything bad to say about our relationship. He didn't object to you, as I recall."

William removed his collar and grinned. "I never said Lord Winchester wasn't a smart man."

* * *

AMY TOOK careful note of how she was dressed before she went downstairs to join William for their trip to the Assembly. Her hat was straight, for once her shoes matched, her hair was at least tidy, and her cape was buttoned correctly. Satisfied there was nothing for him to adjust or fix, she left their bedchamber.

She hadn't seen William all day. He had the meeting with her father and brother and decided to have a tray sent to the library since he arrived home after she had already had dinner. She was in her bath at the time he arrived, so this was their first opportunity to speak all day.

Reaching the bottom of the stairs, she looked up at him. "How did the meeting go with my father and brother?"

William rubbed his eyes with his thumb and index finger. "I prefer to forget it for now and enjoy the evening. I will tell you all about it tomorrow."

He put his hand on her lower back to direct her out the door and stopped. "Where is your reticule?"

She stopped and closed her eyes. For goodness sake, whatever was the matter with her? Here she thought this time she had it altogether. She slumped. "I left it upstairs."

He grinned and said, "Wait here, I'll get it for you."

LADY FORESTER HURRIED up to Amy as she and William entered the Assembly room. She linked her arm with Amy's as they strolled along. "Did you hear about poor Mrs. Devon?"

"Yes, I did. It was such a surprise. We saw her only last Sunday at your church. Do you have any news about her death?" Amy figured feigning ignorance might work to gain information from a woman who seemed to be friends with Mrs. Devon, or at least knew her for some time.

They continued their walk while William joined the group of Aunt Margaret, Lord Exeter, Eloise, and Michael. She looked around but didn't see Dr. Stevens or Lord Sterling. She hoped they would come so she could speak with the doctor about Mrs. Devon. Hopefully by now she would be less troubled by the woman's death.

Lady Forester leaned in close and lowered her voice. "The information I got was Mrs. Devon was found stabbed in her throat." Lady Forester shuddered. "How horrible."

"Indeed. You knew Mrs. Devon; are you aware of anyone who might kill her?"

She bit her lip and shook her head. "No. She was a somewhat pleasant woman and made it to church most Sundays. Aside from her dispute with her cousin over the diamond necklace, I am not aware of any other discords. Although, I do admit she was a private person, so who knows what she might have been hiding."

Well, it appeared the information Lady Forester possessed about the recent victim was not extensive.

She thought back to Mrs. Fleming's funeral and tried her best to recall all the mourners present and didn't remember seeing Mrs. Devon. Although they were disputing, she was still a cousin.

Lady Forester waved at a friend and turned to Amy. "I must speak with Lady Newport, if you will excuse me."

"Certainly," Amy said. She then made her way to the small group of friends and family. She edged her way into the circle, next to William. He took her hand and linked their fingers.

Eloise moved to her side and leaned close to her ear. "Do you see anything different about Lady Margaret?"

Amy looked over at her aunt who was chatting away, Lord Exeter at her side. "No."

Eloise sighed. "Look at her hands."

Just then the light from one of the chandeliers caught a very nice diamond ring on Aunt Margaret's finger. On her left hand. She looked at Eloise. "They are engaged?"

17

Amy left Eloise's side and circled the group until she was squeezed next to her aunt. "Aunt Margaret," she said softly since someone was speaking.

She turned to her. "Amy, how lovely to see you, dear. You are looking well."

Amy huffed. "Is there something you want to tell me?"

Her aunt didn't offer more than a slight smile, but her eyes were full of mirth. "I don't know. Is there something in particular you are interested in?"

"Goodness, aunt, did you and Lord Exeter become betrothed?" There was no point in playing around. Now that she was closer, she could see the ring quite clearly. A lovely ring that fit perfectly on her aunt's graceful finger.

Her aunt lifted her left hand and gazed at the ring. "Yes, I believe so." At the look on Amy's face, she burst into laughter. "I'm sorry to tease you, Amy, but I couldn't pass up the opportunity to do so."

"I knew you and Exeter were friendly, but I had no idea…"

"When the right man comes along, it doesn't take much time." Realizing they were interrupting Michael who was telling some sort of story, Aunt Margaret took Amy's hand and drew her away from the group. "I think we are disturbing the others."

They linked arms and began to stroll. "You are always so very closed-mouthed about things, I'm not terribly surprised your feelings for each other are so strong." Amy reached for her aunt's hand and took a better look at the ring. "It's a lovely ring."

"Thank you. Exeter insisted I help pick it out." She held her arm out and admired the diamond. "I think it fits me well."

"Yes. But I can't imagine any piece of jewelry not fitting you well."

Aunt Margaret cupped her chin in her hand. "Thank you, my dear. You have always been a very sweet young lady."

"Hmm. Not so young anymore, and if you ask William, I am not so sure he would agree about the sweetness. Sometimes this extra weight I am carrying makes me a bit grumpy."

"It doesn't matter, you are still sweet, and William adores you." They veered off to the edge of the ballroom to continue their visit. "I sense more questions."

"Ah, yes. You do know me well, always full of questions." They ended up near the refreshment table where they each took a glass of lemonade. "Are there wedding plans yet?"

Aunt Margaret shook her head. "It is too early. Besides I want you for my attendant, and we must wait until after the baby is born."

Amy felt her face flush and tears begin to gather in her eyes. "I am honored."

They hugged, both wiping their eyes. "My dears, is everything well?" Lady Forester joined them, concern on her face.

"Just fine," Amy said. "Allow me to introduce my aunt, Lady Margaret Lovell. Aunt, this is Lady Forester from my book club."

Her aunt smiled warmly at the woman. "Yes, I believe we

met before when Lady Wethington invited me to one of your meetings."

Amy had to think back, then remembered she had asked her aunt to draw a sketch of a club member who they were considering as a suspect in one of the murders she and William had found themselves involved in.

Lady Forester studied her for a moment. "Yes, now that you mention it, Lady Margaret, I do recall meeting you. Your memory is better than mine, it seems."

"Are you ready for a dance, my dear?" William had arrived at the refreshment table along with Lord Exeter. Amy considered the man for a minute, now that he was no longer just a friend of Aunt Margaret's but soon to be part of her family. He was a nice-looking gentleman, well-dressed, mannerly, and seemed to be quite taken with Aunt Margaret. She decided she approved.

She took William's hand, and he led her to the dance floor just as Dr. Stevens, Lord Sterling, and another couple entered the Assembly rooms. She recognized Mr. Nick Smith as someone she had seen before at the Assembly, but not very often. He had owned a very fashionable and successful gaming club, but news about town was that a couple of years ago, he sold it and was now the owner of a hotel and a few restaurants. She assumed the pretty blonde woman was his wife.

"I'm glad you waited for a waltz to ask me to dance," Amy said as she tried her best to follow William with her center of gravity missing these days.

"Ah, I can assure you it was planned. I'm thinking the slower dances are better for you now."

"Dr. Stevens and Lord Sterling just arrived. I'm glad they decided to come. I hope by now she's over her distress with Mrs. Devon's death."

Amy hung onto William's shoulder as he swung her around.

"Husband, be careful with these fancy steps. My center of gravity is a tad off these days."

He grinned. "I've got hold of you." He studied her carefully. "I would never let you fall."

That brought a wave of warmth to her middle. William could be very sweet, but if she told him he was sweet he would probably leave her in the middle of the dance floor and return home. Men did not like to be thought of as 'sweet'.

"To change the subject, did you know that Lady Margaret and Lord Exeter are betrothed?"

"Yes, I just found out tonight. I assume you were unaware of it before now?"

"Indeed." She shook her head as William tightened his hold and moved them into another dip and sway. "I guess I just never expected Aunt Margaret to marry. She never seemed interested in nuptials."

"When you meet the right person, it becomes more acceptable." He pulled her close to avoid another couple. "I think we are a fine example of that."

"Hmm. Except we knew each other for more than a year through the book club."

His eyes twinkled. "Ah, but I had my eye on you for a while."

Amy felt herself flush—again. "Is that true?"

"If you remember, you were engaged to another man for part of that time." He smiled and gave her a hug as the music ended. "How about another lemonade?"

The musicians took a break, so the refreshment area was busy, and it took William some time to get them drinks. As she sipped her drink, Dr. Stevens and Lord Sterling walked up to them. "Good evening, my lord, my lady," Dr. Stevens said.

"The same to you as well. I'm glad you decided to treat yourselves to an evening out," Amy said, glad the couple approached them instead of her having to figure out how to hunt the good doctor down.

Lord Sterling carried a plate with two biscuits and a small sandwich on it. "Why don't we take seats over there." He waved in the direction of the grouping of tables near the refreshment table.

The four moved to one of the tables and settled in. "I see Mr. Smith and his wife joined you tonight," Amy said, eyeing the plate Dr. Stevens had in front of her.

Most likely noticing her look, William stood. "Allow me to fill a plate for you, Amy."

He was so considerate. When he wasn't ordering her about.

Dr. Stevens patted her mouth and swallowed before speaking. "Since we are here, this saves me from sending a note around. I would find it most helpful if you can somehow obtain Mrs. Fleming's records of your and your sister-in-law's pregnancy since she had been seeing you, I assume from the beginning."

"Yes, that is true." She tapped her chin. "I have her direction, so it would be no problem to request the records."

She was excited by the doctor's request for their records. It would give her the perfect excuse to visit Mrs. Fleming's home and speak with any staff. Or with any real luck, perhaps Mr. Fleming would be at home.

William rejoined them, setting a small plate of tiny sandwiches and a sweet in front of her.

"Something I learned recently that I was unaware of, Lady Wethington. You are an author. Have you had any of your work published?" Lord Sterling asked.

Since her mouth was full, William answered for her. "Yes, indeed. My wife has several murder mysteries available for sale. She writes under the pseudonym of E. D. Burton."

"That is very interesting," Lord Sterling said. "I have never met an author in person. But then, I'm embarrassed to say I do not read a great deal of fiction. Reading all the reports from my land steward and trying to make sense out of my wife's ledgers is enough for my poor eyes."

Dr. Stevens poked her husband in the side. He just laughed.

Amy cleared her throat. "I believe it would be most helpful if you wrote a short note for me to present to Mrs. Fleming's staff."

"From the little I know of her, I believe there is a husband, and I assume he still resides there?"

That was something Amy hoped would be the case. Of course, the home he and his wife had lived in would belong to him, and most likely he brought his new wife there. This made the trip to secure the medical records even more interesting.

"I would think so. Then perhaps you should pen your note to him."

"I will do that. You can expect to receive the note requesting the records tomorrow or Monday."

Lord Sterling watched his wife carefully and turned to Amy. "I'm sure Dr. Stevens will be happy to receive those records, but it was my intention to take her away from medicine for the evening." He stood and reached out for the doctor's hand. "Now that the music has started up again, I'm sure you would like another dance, my dear?"

The dismissal was polite, but obvious. Amy did feel a bit uncomfortable if her questions had brought the woman's work back to her when she was here for a chance to relax and not think of medicine. "He is very protective of his wife."

William leaned back on his chair legs and studied the couple as they entered the dance area. "As all good men are."

Within minutes Lady Forester joined them at their table. "I wanted to tell you, Lady Wethington, that Mrs. Devon's funeral is Monday. I know you didn't spend much time with her, but since she is an old schoolmate of yours, I thought if you were not busy you might want to attend."

Since most funerals ended with some sort of a meal for the

attendees, it would give Amy the opportunity to speak with people who knew Mrs. Devon. "Yes, I would like to do that. What time is the service?"

"Ten o'clock. I can send my carriage for you."

William jumped in. "That won't be necessary, my lady. Our carriage is available for her use. But thank you for the offer."

Well, then. The men at the Assembly tonight seem to be protective of their women.

Lady Forester patted Amy's hand. "Then I will see you Monday morning."

She wandered off to join a group of book club members. Amy rubbed her stomach, more out of habit than anything else.

"Is all well, Amy?" William asked.

"Yes." She shifted in her seat to face him. The chair was not the most comfortable, but she didn't want to worry her husband. She'd noticed he watched her more carefully the last couple of weeks.

After a few minutes of silence while Amy drank the last of her lemonade, William said, "I see Lord Exeter and Lady Margaret are making it an early night." He gestured with his chin toward the door.

Amy looked at the exit. Lord Exeter was helping Aunt Margaret with her cape and solicitously assisting her down the stairs to the door. Amy turned to William and smiled. "Another protective man."

They had one more dance, and then Amy decided she was growing weary. William walked her to the door and left her there while he saw about having their carriage brought around.

She was ready for her soft, comfortable dressing gown and a nice cup of tea in the library with the book she'd been trying to finish. Socializing was very nice and she certainly enjoyed it, but she found as she grew larger and bulkier that resting at home was more appealing.

She waved to Lord Sterling, Dr. Stevens, and their friends

as they left. It was growing crowded in the entrance area, so she stepped outside to wait for her carriage. It took only a few minutes before William bounded up the steps to help her down. A couple walked alongside them, and she glanced over.

The man looked very familiar. She continued to study him, poking her tired brain for where she saw him before. He turned to the woman with him to help her into a carriage, and Amy got a good look at his face.

William helped her into their carriage, and she twisted and turned trying to see the couple.

"What is it, Amy? Is something wrong?"

"I don't know. Or rather I'm not sure." She pointed out the window as their carriage began to move. "Do you see that carriage going the other way?"

"Yes. Why?"

Amy turned back. "I am almost certain the man in the carriage is Mr. Fleming. I only saw him briefly at his wife's funeral. At least I think it was his wife's funeral."

"My dear, you're not making sense."

"What I mean is, I never learned if that man was Mrs. Fleming's husband or not, but he played a dominant role at the funeral. He sat in the front of the church, slumping over, and stood the same way at the graveside. Then he was the one who announced the attendees were invited to a meal in the church Fellowship Hall."

"If that is him, then he is here in Bath now, so it appears you might get to speak with him when you fetch the records for Dr. Stevens."

Amy leaned back on the comfortable cushion. "Yes. I assume that woman with him was his new wife."

"Unless he is already cheating on the new wife, I assume that is her," he said with a smile, then rested his elbow on the armrest and stared out the window as they made their way through Bath, the stores all dark and empty, giving the area a ghoulish feeling.

She rested against the comfortable seat and with a stream of thoughts running through her mind, she felt as though they were making some progress on their investigation.

After Filbert opened the front door, he said, "My lord, your favorite detectives called this evening while you were out."

"Saturday evening? If I didn't think they were incompetent, I would praise them for their dedication to their job."

"They said they would return."

William shook his head and linked his fingers with Amy's. "Of course, they did." With a sigh, they climbed the stairs.

18

Amy always found comfort in the Sunday Services at St. Swithin's Church. Her visit to St. Michael's the week before had been pleasant, the music lovely, and the pastor's sermon inspiring but St. Swithin's was her church home.

It was a very old church in the Walcot area of Bath. Amy and her family had been members for years. It was where her parents had been married, and where she'd been baptized and married.

The sunlight shimmering through the colored glass, the wooden pews, shiny from all the bodies that sat there over the years, and the smell of the building itself were all soothing and uplifting.

She and William shifted over as Aunt Margaret and Lord Exeter entered their family pew. They were soon joined by Eloise and Michael, right before the service began. As usual Mrs. Edith Newton, a very sweet woman who had played the church organ for years—off key—began the first hymn as the congregation rose.

The pastor's sermon was heartening as always. She glanced down the row to see Aunt Margaret and Lord Exeter holding hands. She shook her head in wonder. It would be a while before she became accustomed to the idea of Lady Margaret as a married woman.

She remembered hearing the story of how her aunt was desperately in love with an ill-suited man as a young girl, but her brother, Franklin—Amy's father—broke the couple up and Aunt Margaret swore she would never marry. Perhaps being older now, she realized by sticking to that vow she was only depriving herself of happiness.

Thinking of her papa, Amy wondered how he was faring. He and Michael had split their businesses, and she and William never had a chance to talk about the meeting they held where they wanted him to act as arbitrator. She must remember to ask him about that.

Her papa could be a difficult man. He and her mother had lived in separate places while Amy was growing up; Amy and Lady Winchester in Bath, with Aunt Margaret, who later took over raising her when Mama died, and Michael and her papa in London. When her parents were together, they were cordial, but she never saw the type of touching and comforting looks she and William and Eloise and Michael engaged in.

Poor Papa was on the outside now with no family support it seemed. She made a vow then that she would invite Papa for dinner. A family dinner to celebrate Aunt Margaret and Lord Exeter's betrothal would be nice. She perked up at the idea of finding the recipe for some elaborate dessert for the dinner party. She had neglected her baking while she and William had gotten more involved in the investigation.

Once the service ended, with Amy feeling happy and uplifted, they made their way outside to greet the Pastor and do a bit of socializing with the rest of the congregation.

Somehow word of Aunt Margaret's betrothal had spread, and well-wishers kept joining their little circle to congratulate

Lord Exeter and wish Aunt Margaret well. It was a social *faux pas* to congratulate the bride-to-be.

"I hope you will all join us for luncheon," Amy said to her family members who were looking like they were ready to head for their carriages. I believe Cook is making a fine fish stew."

Michael, who was always hungry, and Eloise who was the same way lately both agreed immediately. Lord Exeter and Aunt Margaret declined, saying they had planned to meet another couple for luncheon.

They parted ways and Amy and William settled into their carriage. "I just now realized your mother and Mr. Colbert weren't in church this morning." She paused and grinned. "Perhaps they are still enjoying their second honeymoon."

William raised his hand. "Amy, please. That is my mother. I don't like to think of her having a honeymoon." He shivered. "Some things are better left not imagined."

Poor William did have a time accepting his mother being pursued by a man. Perhaps she would feel the same way if Papa found another wife. Not likely. Both that he would find another wife or that it would trouble her.

"I forgot to ask you about the meeting with my father and brother. You were not anxious to speak of it when you returned yesterday. Was it truly that bad?"

"Not as dreadful as it could have been, but your father is a stubborn man. He refuses to consider any way except his own."

She felt bad that her husband had to come between the two men. She was sure it wasn't a pleasant place to be. "Michael can be a tad stubborn himself."

"Yes. But while he was willing to make some concessions, your father held firm. It made me wonder why he even agreed to the meeting."

"Perhaps he thought you would take his side with everything he wanted and that would strong-arm my brother."

"If that is so, then he chose the wrong man to act as intermediary." He shook his head as the carriage came to a rolling stop in front of their townhouse. "The meeting ended with nothing really being accomplished. The one thing I got out of it, is that your brother and father are better off going their separate ways." He paused as the footman opened the door. "For both their sakes."

"That's unfortunate since they'd been in business together for years."

William shrugged. "Things change. Times change. Your father is not willing to look at those changes. He keeps fighting the inevitable."

They greeted Eloise and Michael as they all made their way up the steps and into the house. "Filbert, tell Cook to give us about fifteen minutes to relax before you serve luncheon." William placed his hand on Amy's lower back and they all made their way into the drawing room.

"Care for a sherry before luncheon?" William asked.

Amy and Eloise both declined, but William and Michael imbibed. By the time the men had finished their drinks, Filbert announced luncheon.

The fish stew, along with cheese, fruit and bread, warm from the oven, was delightful and from the lack of conversation during the meal, it appeared everyone agreed.

Amy had just taken her first sip of tea after the meal had ended, and the leavings taken away when Filbert arrived. "My lady, there is a visitor for you." He held out a card which Amy took from his hand.

Mrs. Priscilla Penrose, Midwife

"Oh dear," Amy said. She looked up at William. "It is that midwife who wanted to take over my and Eloise's care when Mrs. Fleming died. I never did give her an answer and I'm sure she's anxious to see if she has two new clients." Amy tapped the card against her lips. "Eloise, why don't you join me?"

William took the card from her hand and frowned. "Why don't you merely send a note to her that you are in the middle of luncheon and you have already secured services elsewhere?"

"No," Amy said, shaking her head. "That would be rude, or at least unkind." She stood and a footman pulled her chair back. She glanced at Eloise. "I think it's best if we speak with her. It won't take long."

"Do you want me to speak with her as well?" William made to stand, but Amy waved him off. "No, that's not necessary."

Eloise and Amy left the dining room and walked the short distance to the drawing room. Mrs. Penrose was looking around the space, smiling and touching a small China bowl filled with dried flower petals. She looked very impressed with the room and Amy imagined her adding numbers in her head on what she could charge them for her services.

"Good afternoon, Mrs. Penrose." Amy waved to one of the comfortable pink and green flowered chairs. "Please have a seat."

Eloise took the seat across from Mrs. Penrose on a settee, Amy joining her.

Before Amy got a chance to ask Mrs. Penrose why she was here, the woman jumped in, "I'm sorry to disturb you on a Sunday, my ladies, but I am still awaiting your decision on using my services. I am assuming that by this time you have had an opportunity to visit with some of the mothers on the list I gave you to discuss my skills and professionalism."

Amy always hated disappointing someone. It was not in her nature to say 'no', which, in many cases, had gotten her into trouble. "I apologize for not sending a note around before now, Mrs. Penrose, but I have been quite busy preparing for the baby." Blatant lie. "However, both Lady Davenport and I have secured the services of Dr. Rayne Stevens for our maternal care."

After a few moments of silence, with anger radiating off the woman, Mrs. Penrose jumped up. "Dr. Stevens! She just killed one of her patients."

Amy's jaw dropped at the outburst from the woman.

Drawing herself up, she said, "I beg to differ with you, Mrs. Penrose, but I believe you have incorrect information with regard to Dr. Stevens."

She leaned forward, in a most aggressive manner. "I do not have the wrong information, my lady. A woman died just a few days ago from a horrible wound. Word has it she was in Dr. Stevens' office when the doctor inadvertently stabbed her in the neck with her scissors. Right there in her office. She dropped dead at her feet."

Amy was completely shocked at the woman's words. It was truly amazing how stories were spread around and changed to suit whoever wanted things their way.

Attempting to remain calm, she said, "I must once again disagree with you. I happened to speak with Dr. Stevens just recently and her patient who died was found in her own bedchamber in her own home, with a pair of her scissors stuck in her neck." Amy drew herself up. "I do hope you will not go around spreading this lie about a very competent doctor."

Mrs. Penrose stabbed the air. "Ha! A female doctor. Of course she would make mistakes. Women are not meant to be doctors." She sat back down in her chair and smoothed out her skirts. "I would like to offer information to you that I hope will change your mind."

Tired of the conflict and anxious to get the woman out of her house, Amy said, "I'm sorry, Mrs. Penrose, but our decision has been made." She looked at Eloise who nodded.

Amy lumbered to her feet, and Mrs. Penrose stood. Thinking this was the end of it, Amy said, "Thank you for stopping by. I am sorry things did not turn out the way you had hoped they would."

Mrs. Penrose leaned forward and stuck her finger out. "You will be sorry you made this decision when you end up dead."

"Excuse me, madam, but did I just hear you threaten my wife?" William's outraged voice echoed through the room. He moved forward and put himself between Amy and Mrs. Penrose. "My wife *and I* have made our decision. You are now requested to leave my house and if you come anywhere near my wife, I will see that you are arrested and charged with making threats to a peer."

The woman was brave, to be sure. Or unbalanced, because she snarled at William and didn't immediately remove herself, but straightened her hat, smoothed her skirts, then, her chin thrust forward, marched out of the room.

"Filbert, see Mrs. Penrose out," William said as she passed through the doorway.

Amy looked down at her hands which were shaking. She hated confrontations and this one had been especially frightening. The woman looked almost deranged.

William wrapped his arm around her shoulders. "Come, my love, let's return to the dining room and have some hot tea sent in."

Michael was embracing Eloise in a similar manner, who seemed as upset as Amy.

Once they were all settled in the dining room, William said. "That is the woman from the Assembly who you mumbled something about not telling her we had secured other midwife services, is that correct?"

Amy ran her palms up and down her arms. "Yes. She was recommended to me by a Mrs. Oldbridge. I didn't know her, either, but she stopped me right after Mrs. Fleming's death. It was at the Assembly, and you were with me at the time. You gave her your card so she could pass it along to Mrs. Penrose to secure an appointment with Eloise and me."

"I vaguely remember that. You were weary and I was

anxious to get you home. But to return to this woman, I find her reaction to your refusal to use her services as threatening and worrisome."

Amy nodded. "I admit I found her outburst surprisingly hostile. She told Eloise and me that she had a sick daughter and apparently Mrs. Fleming had spread rumors about Mrs. Penrose's services which she claimed cost her clients."

"Yes, that I remember. We discussed how unprofessional it was for a woman to cast aspersions on another colleague."

Michael stood and reached for Eloise's hand. "I think it's time we left, my dear. You look as though you could use a lie-down."

Eloise wearily climbed to her feet. "Yes, I agree. I must admit Mrs. Penrose's outburst was rather disturbing and now I am feeling wrung out."

Once her brother and Eloise had left, Amy made herself another cup of tea with the hot water Filbert had brought in. William poured a glass of wine and studied her. "If I remember correctly, Mrs. Penrose was already on our list of suspects," William said.

"Yes. But I think I'll move her name to the top. Her visit this afternoon will now spur me to find out more information about her. I hate to make a judgment without knowing her very well, but she certainly seemed unbalanced to me. And there were those two drownings of her family members."

* * *

WILLIAM STUDIED Amy while she drank her tea. The poor woman looked tired and stressed. "Why don't you take a lie-down as well? I'll even rub your feet until you fall asleep."

Amy pushed back her chair, not waiting for him or the footman to pull it back. "You have said the magic words, my lord."

After slipping off her matched shoes—which she pointed out to him—Amy laid down, sinking into the soft bedding. He began to rub her feet which brought interesting sounds from his wife.

Once she was fast asleep, and lightly snoring, William stood and covered her with her favorite fuzzy blanket. He tiptoed out of the room and downstairs to the library. A quiet Sunday afternoon was just what he needed after the craziness of yesterday's meeting with his in-laws and then the unhinged woman who threatened Amy earlier.

He considered hiring someone to follow her to make sure her threat to Amy was merely referring to Dr. Stevens' patient dying, and not that she intended to harm Amy. His country estate was looking better and better every day. Even more reason to wish this confinement over.

He shook his head and searched the shelves for something to read—to take his mind off everything for a while. His brain could surely use a rest.

He'd barely read a few pages of a very thumbed-through copy of A Tale of Two Cities when Filbert entered the room. The man, who rarely showed any type of emotion on his face, looked resigned.

"I am so sorry to disturb you, my lord, but the detectives are here again."

19

"Let's look at our list of suspects again," William said.

Amy had arisen from her nap, thankfully after the detectives had left. Nothing had come of their visit. He was thoroughly perplexed as to why they kept coming to talk with them, always ending the visit with 'stay out of our investigation'. Yet based on their questions, it seemed to William that they were trying to get information from *him*.

Amy pulled the folded piece of paper from the middle drawer of the desk. "Here it is."

"Read it to me."

She smoothed the paper out on the desk. "Mr. Fleming, the new Mrs. Fleming," she looked up at him, "I added her after our last talk—Mrs. Penrose, Mrs. Garfield, and the late Mrs. Devon, although she can only be considered for the first murder."

William frowned. "All women, except for the husband. Perhaps he's the one we should look at first."

Amy glanced at him from the list. "Excuse me, husband, but if I recall correctly, we had female murderers before." She tapped the paper with her finger. "You need to visit your club as you said and see if anyone has seen Fleming. I'm not one hundred percent that was the man I saw at the Assembly last night. If he is back in Bath and most likely living with his new wife in their home, I'd like to know that before I go."

"I'm not sure I like the idea of you going to his house to ask for the medical records. It might be dangerous."

Amy shook her head. "Not likely. A pregnant woman asking for her medical records from her former midwife is not threatening at all."

William sighed, imagining his country estate where he would be far from murders, detectives, and in-laws who wanted him to take sides in business battles. "I'd like to get this over with, Amy. That is the only reason I offered to help. You don't need the stress of trying to find a murderer—"

"—or murderers."

He nodded. "That is true." Apparently, the only way to remove Amy from this matter was to find the killer, or killers, await the birth of the baby and then hustle his family out of Bath and off to his country estate. With resignation, he said, "I assume you are going to Mrs. Devon's funeral tomorrow?"

"Yes. I'm hoping members of her staff will be there. I know nothing about her except that she stole a story from me when we were in school together."

"Truly?"

"Yes. She took it off the desk in my assigned bedroom, when neither I nor my roommate were there. She recopied it in her own handwriting and turned it in. Then she won first prize."

William's brows rose. "And you didn't tell those in charge what she'd done?"

"Of course, but they didn't believe me. I may be a good author, but she is one fine actress." She made a face. "And her father was a huge donor to the school."

William shook his head and finished the last of his drink. "It seems everyone has a price."

"My lord, my lady, dinner is served." Filbert had entered so quietly William hadn't even heard him.

"Thank you."

They made their way to the dining room and settled into their seats. "It is nice to have a quiet evening at home," Amy said as she settled into her chair and placed her napkin on her lap. "Perhaps your idea of retiring to your country home once the baby is born is good one."

"*Our* country home," William said with a smile.

Amy reached for a pork chop and set it on her plate. "Since I've only been there a couple of times, I've yet to feel like it's ours. But I will take your word for it."

"I spent most of my childhood there. My father was a true country gentleman. He loved the smell of the air that he called sweet, although to my young nose it was a nasty smell of manure."

The memories that flashed through his mind were both welcoming and poignant at the same time. He had a happy childhood, him, and his sister. But when he was ten years he was sent off to school. Years later while he was at university his father died. He still missed him.

"As much as I love Bath, having lived here my entire life, I must admit I look forward to moving to the country. I think it's a much better place to raise a child."

Her remarks surprised him since he always felt it might be a tug of war to get Amy to move. Apparently not.

Once dinner ended, they retired to the sitting room next to their bedchamber and enjoyed tea and brandy and good books. A very pleasant way to end a stressful few days.

William pondered whether to tell Amy about the detectives' visit, but since nothing of importance was said, he decided to keep it to himself. One less thing for Amy to get annoyed at.

***

Amy settled in her carriage and stared out the window at the gloom of the day. She was on her way to Mrs. Devon's funeral. Even though the woman had pulled that dirty trick on her when they were schoolmates, Amy still felt a sense of sadness that Petrina had suffered an early and unexpected death. And in such a horrible way.

She couldn't help but believe whoever killed Mrs. Fleming also killed Mrs. Devon. Mayhap Mrs. Devon knew who killed Mrs. Fleming, and that person killed her to keep her quiet? But if Mrs. Devon did know the killer, why wouldn't she go to the police?

Also, if they were, in fact, connected crimes, the expensive piece of jewelry might be the reason for both crimes. To get this investigation moving, she had to find out more about the necklace.

Only ten minutes from her house and she already had worked herself into a nasty headache.

William had plans to work on his ledgers and send a report off to his land steward and then visit his club to learn if anyone had seen Fleming, who as far as they knew had not been seen around Bath since his wife's funeral. Unless it was him Amy had seen at the Assembly. Of course, since his home was in Bath, he would have to return there sometime. She just preferred to know before she went there to ask for the medical records.

She was well into her seventh month of pregnancy, and truth be told, she was beginning to feel a tad nervous about the ordeal. She wanted it to come soon so her body could go back to normal, but at the same time she wanted to put it off, trying not to think of the stories she'd heard and books she'd read where the idea of childbirth was painful and frightening. And in some cases, deadly.

At least she had the comfort of knowing Dr. Stevens would be in attendance.

All the energy she had felt the last couple of months had vanished and now she felt herself dragging out of bed and thinking about returning there almost all day. Dr. Stevens did mention that the first three months of confinement were generally filled with nausea and fatigue, the second three months with a great deal of energy and the last three months as the longest period of time on earth.

She sighed and looked out the window as the carriage rolled closer to St. Michael's church, rubbing her temples to ease the headache. Perhaps it was just the weather that had her feeling morose. Or the thought of another funeral. Two in a row. Both women. Both murdered.

Despite her interest in finding out who killed Mrs. Fleming as well as Mrs. Devon, she really needed to begin looking for a nurse for the baby and doing some interviews. Picking out furniture for the nursery would also pass the time. It didn't seem to make sense to redecorate the room since William planned to move them all to the country soon after the baby's birth. She went through excitement and nervousness about being a mother.

She was forever losing her shoes and forgetting things. What if she took the baby out in a pram for a stroll and forgot it? Or misplaced it? William might tease her and grin about her inattention, but she doubted he would think his child missing was humorous.

Aunt Margaret had done a wonderful job of raising her after Mama died, but Amy had already been ten years old. She never saw anyone change a nappy, or deal with a crying baby or a feverish one. And what if the baby was a boy and he climbed trees and did other things lads did and ended up with a broken arm?

Wiping the perspiration from her forehead, she realized she

was tying herself in knots with worry and 'what ifs'. Didn't all new mothers fret about these things? She needed to have a conversation with Eloise, although if the poor girl hadn't given these things much thought Amy might end up with both of them nervous ninnies.

While she'd been amusing herself with one fearful event after another, they had traversed the distance between Wethington House and St. Michael's church, but her headache had eased. Apparently thinking of new mother issues was not as stressful as trying to solve murders.

She climbed from the carriage with the help of the footman and made her way into the church. There were enough mourners, and since Amy didn't really know that much about Mrs. Devon since they parted as schoolmates, she had no way of knowing if the woman had a husband or children.

The front pews, which were traditionally reserved for family members held two elderly women and a woman around Amy's age. A few more people entered the church, but no others joined those in the front pew.

The Pastor entered the sanctuary in an appropriately somber mood and began the service. He gave the eulogy, and from his sermon, it was obvious Mrs. Devon had been a member of St. Michael's for some time.

He told a few stories about Mrs. Devon and Mr. Devon, who it seemed from his speech had passed onto his eternal reward a few years before. No children were mentioned. There was no muffled crying, or other speakers to extend the service. It was a short liturgy and the mourners all found themselves standing next to the gaping hole in the ground in less than an hour.

After a blessing, and few more comments, the graveside service was over, and the crowd moved to the Fellowship Hall at the behest of one of the elderly women who had been in the front pew.

Lady Forester walked up to Amy and linked their arms. "It's nice to see you again, Lady Wethington, even though this is a somber event."

Amy nodded and they moved along, following the clusters of mourners going to the church hall. "As you know I haven't been in touch with Mrs. Devon for years. Did she have family? I assume the three women in the front pew were all she had?"

"You assume correctly. The two older ladies are her aunts. Both her mother's sisters. A third sister, Mrs. Devon's mother, passed away over a year ago, as did the fourth sister, Mrs. Fleming's mother. From what I knew the two remaining sisters never married. The other younger woman is a companion, I believe to the two aunts."

"Then, it would seem that it was at her mother's death that Mrs. Devon learned the jewelry she'd been promised from her mother had been taken by Mrs. Fleming?"

"Yes. It was very sad to see cousins unable to settle their differences without turning to the courts."

Amy nodded her agreement. "No children for Mrs. Devon?"

Lady Forester shook her head. "No. She told me one time she had miscarried a child but had never conceived again. In fact, if memory serves, her cousin was her midwife at the time."

Amy absently rubbed her stomach, wishing she could get away from the subject of childbirth. But it was interesting that the cousins had another connection beside the necklace. Mayhap that was another point of contention between them.

Lady Forester patted her hand, guessing her thoughts. "Do not fret, my lady. You are looking remarkably healthy, and I'm sure all will be well with your child."

The room was slowly filling up. They found two chairs several tables from the door. Lady Forester leaned back in her chair and fiddled with the end of the tablecloth. "Mrs. Devon was still young enough to have a child, and if her betrothal to Mr. Long hadn't ended, she might very well have."

"She was engaged to be married?"

"Yes. The wedding was set and then we heard the engagement had ended. She never spoke of it to anyone, as far as I know, but rumor has it that he was quite angry, and told someone she refused to return the very expensive ring he'd given her."

Another interesting piece of information. "Mr. Long you say?"

"Yes. Mr. Jeffrey Long. A nice fellow. I met him a couple of times when he escorted her to church."

They reached the Fellowship Hall as Amy tucked away that bit of information, and possibly someone to add to their suspect list. Wanted his ring back and didn't get it. The rule generally was the ring was returned if the betrothal ended. Very angry. Yes, his name would be added.

It annoyed her to see Detectives Carson and Marsh at the funeral, and then they followed the group to the church hall, as well. Carson had cast a glance in her direction once or twice, but she ignored them.

Most likely because their superiors were pushing them for results. Since they had released Mrs. Garfield, there had been no new arrest. Not that she knew of, at least. And now they had another murder to solve.

She and Lady Forester found seats together, and soon they were joined by two other ladies. Lady Forester made the introductions.

"Lady Wethington, may I introduce two other church members, Miss Adeline Smith and Mrs. Rosemary Garfield."

Amy smiled and began to greet them as she always did, when she realized what Lady Forester had said. Sitting across from them was Mrs. Garfield, one of the people on her and William's suspect list, and the one who had been arrested for Mrs. Fleming's murder, then later released. Of course, it was possible that there was more than one Mrs. Garfield in Bath. It was not such an unusual name.

The notion passed through her mind that the last funeral she attended, right here at St. Michael's, was when she met Mrs. Devon. Then Mrs. Devon was murdered. Would Mrs. Garfield turn up dead in a few days, then? She shuddered at the thought.

And it was quite interesting that Lady Forester, the deceased Mrs. Fleming, Mrs. Devon, and Mrs. Garfield all belonged to the same church.

If she was, indeed, the Mrs. Garfield who found Mrs. Flemings, body, this was turning into a very nice opportunity. She hadn't known the woman at all, so she could have passed her by on the streets, or in stores many times and not known. While Mrs. Garfield spoke with the woman next to her, Amy took time to study her features. Since Amy had been to the Baths many times, she had to admit this woman did look a bit familiar. Or it could be her hope that she was the right woman.

To continue, first she had to establish this woman was the right Mrs. Garfield. However, it would be ill-mannered of her to ask if she had been charged with murder. That would be considered bad manners. It would be better to ask her one of those 'tell me about yourself' questions, hoping she would mention she worked at the Roman Baths.

If the conversation went well, she might ask to set a date to meet for tea, also. Women were generally chatterers and loved to talk about themselves. If Mrs. Garfield was one of them, it might be easy to strike up a pseudo-friendship.

Yes, things were looking up. Now she just had to relegate all the fear mongering she'd subjected herself to about motherhood to the back of her mind. She was much happier concentrating on murder.

Admittedly, that did give her pause.

Both ladies returned polite acknowledgement of the introductions Lady Forester had made. While Amy ruminated on the murders again, the ladies spoke of typical British subjects, the weather, the traffic, and the Queen. No one seemed to want to discuss the deceased, or her manner of death.

After about ten minutes, the announcement was made that the food was ready. Occupants of each table moved in turn to the lengthy tables against the wall holding all the scrumptious offerings made by the ladies of the church.

She filled her plate, realizing she was, in fact, quite hungry. About three steps from her chair a voice behind her said, "We would like to speak with you, Lady Wethington."

She turned and groaned, wanting to dump the contents of her plate on Detective Carson's head.

20

William groaned as Michael waved at him as he entered his club. It was not his intention to get into another hassle with the man about his father, but it was impossible to pretend he hadn't seen him.

"It's rather on the early side to see you here, Davenport," William said as he settled in the chair across from him.

"I'm meeting Mr. Dobish about an investment he is involved in. It sounded interesting, and I thought I would get more information. He's supposed to be bringing documentation on a diamond mine in South Africa."

Bells went off in William's head. There was no reason for him to believe Dobish was attempting to swindle Michael, but William had heard many stories of men investing in 'diamond mines' in South Africa that turned out to be worthless.

He thanked the footman who delivered the coffee and a light repast of cheese, fruit, and bread he'd requested when he first entered the club. He had passed on breakfast since Amy had already left for the funeral and he was anxious to have some interviews and get this entire mess behind him.

"Has Dobish been involved in this for a while?" William asked as he placed a piece of cheese on a thick slice of bread.

"He said he was involved, didn't mention for how long. Would you be interested?"

The last thing William would do is invest in something with as sketchy a history as diamond mines, and never would he consider one without consulting his man of business first, but because Michael was Amy's brother, he decided to stick around and listen to Dobish.

"I would be interested in hearing what the man has to say and what his documentation looks like." He took a sip of coffee. "When is he expected?"

"Any minute now," Michael said, checking his timepiece.

William nodded and took a quick glance around the room. It was still early, and there weren't a lot of members present. As usual, mostly older gentlemen who spent a good part of their day at the club, discussing politics, horses, gaming wins and losses, and how useless the next generation was. Of course, the current generation had been saying that about the next generation since the beginning of time.

He remembered a quote from his philosophy class at university from Horace, uttered around 20 B.C. *"Our sires' age was worse than our grandsires'. We, their sons, are more worthless than they; so in our turn we shall give the world a progeny yet more corrupt."*

Michael stood and waved. "Here he is now."

It barely took a minute for a man about a decade or so older than William and Michael to arrive. William didn't recognize him, but he looked like a pleasant sort. Of medium height, he was well-dressed, his light brown hair already showing wisps of gray. He had a hard-to-read face.

It was always difficult to discern who was dishonest, or being swindled themselves, but William had decided to give the man a chance to produce his information.

He stood and extended his hand as Michael made the introductions. Once Dobish was settled in a third chair, with a small table in front of them, he pulled out a portfolio and began removing papers.

"Wethington might be interested in your venture, Dobish. He just happened to wander in here today."

The man's eyes lit up, which gave William pause. Dobish might merely be an enthusiastic investor, or he was glad to have another victim to hoodwink.

The man rubbed his hands together and spread out the papers on the table. He began his presentation which went on for a good fifteen minutes, waving papers in their faces, stabbing various documents with his index finger and trying his best to sell them on the project.

To say William was skeptical was an understatement. He'd negotiated many contracts and investments over the years and this one left him wondering why anyone would be interested in this. He'd produced nothing of substantial worth and relied heavily on what he claimed others said about investing in South African mines.

Dobish shuffled his papers and stacked them, grinning as he leaned back in his chair. "So how much can I depend on from the two of you to invest?"

"I never make a decision immediately," William said. "If you can send around copies of the documents that indicate the money invested so far, the men also involved in the project, and the expected outcome, I will have time to study it and consult with my man of business."

Dobish's bright smile dissolved and he frowned. "I don't think I can do that, Wethington. The list of investors is growing every day and I am quite certain there won't be room for more than a few more men before we close it out."

"I'm in, Dobish," Michael said. He turned to William. "You might be missing out here, this looks good."

Another negotiation tactic William had used was to never show enthusiasm for the presentation. Even if he had every intent of entering this 'investment' he would not let Dobish know until he had time to think about it, and maybe do some research on his own.

William shrugged. "Unfortunately, a good deal of my capital is tied up at present, so even if I wished to be included, right now is not a good time for me."

Unfortunately, Michael, who didn't understand the finesse needed during negotiations, said, "I can advance you your part of the investment, Wethington."

Bloody hell. Is this what Lord Winchester had dealt with when he and Michael were partners? As much as he felt that Amy's father was overbearing and arrogant about things being done his way, Michael didn't seem to show the restraint needed to guard his money.

After speaking with Winchester alone, and then the two of them together, and now this, William believed the two men were better off working together. Michael appeared to be ready to rush into something that could become a disaster while his father was stuck in the mud. They did seem to balance each other out.

Apparently aware that William was not to be pushed since he didn't respond to Michael's offer, Dobish turned his attention back to Michael. "How soon can you get your funds to me? The other investors want to wrap this up. As soon as we can get the blunt to the current owners, the sooner we can start making money."

"Unfortunately, my previous partner and I are going our separate ways, so money is tied up right now. I can probably get it to you by the end of next week."

Dobish frowned. "Hmm. I can wait until then as long as I have your word that you are definitely committed. In fact, I am planning a meeting of all the investors tomorrow afternoon at my home. Say around two o'clock. I'd like you to join us." After a slight hesitation, he added, "You as well, Wethington. You might learn something there that will change your mind."

William merely dipped his head, making no promise.

Michael stood and held out his hand. "I definitely want to do that. Just leave your direction with the footman at the door and I'll get it when I leave. I am happy to join the group."

Dobish nodded and strode from the room, his portfolio tucked securely under his arm.

"You might be sorry you didn't get into this, Wethington."

William took a deep breath, wanting to have his say, but reluctant to alienate his brother-in-law. "I have reason to believe that some of these South African diamond mines don't produce what is promised."

Michael shrugged. "I know there is always a bit of a gamble, but I liked what Dobish said, and his numbers looked good."

"They were projections. And one wonders if this mine is so successful, why are the owners selling it?"

His brother-in-law shrugged and waved at the footman for a whisky. "Care for one, Wethington?"

William shook his head. "A tad early for me. I'll stick with coffee."

"I'm to my office when I finish this," Michael said. "If I'm going to have the funds to invest in Dobish's diamond mine, I need to visit with my father and insist we resolve this business matter post haste."

They spoke business for the next twenty minutes or so, then Michael downed the last of his whisky and stood. "It was nice talking to you Wethington. I still think you're making a mistake with Dobish's plan."

Michael snapped his fingers. "By the way, Eloise mentioned you and my sister are again trying to outmaneuver the police on this murder business."

William grinned. "You might put it that way. I don't think

Amy is going to let go of this until she has her answers. I need her to focus on the upcoming birth of our child. I agreed to help her to speed things up."

"What I wanted to tell you is I heard Fleming is back in Bath. He made an appearance at a few places, with his new wife." Michael shook his head. "Rather poorly done to marry so soon after his wife died. However, what I wanted to tell you is I heard from someone, who heard from someone else—you know how these things go—that he returned to Bath because he was about to inherit some sort of jewelry that he already had a buyer for and needed the funds for an investment he was anxious to join."

William's brows rose. "Perhaps it is Dobish's South African mine?"

Michael checked his timepiece once again. "The timing seems right."

William thought for a moment, then said, "I believe I will join you at Dobish's meeting tomorrow."

"Good. I'm glad you decided to go. Eloise told me she and Amy have a doctor's appointment tomorrow afternoon. I'll bring Eloise to your house, and you can ride in my carriage to Dobish's house."

William nodded and watched Michael leave the club.

The piece of jewelry had to be the one both Mrs. Devon and Mrs. Fleming had been fighting over. It was an interesting fact that according to Amy, Mrs. Devon got the piece after Mrs. Fleming died, and now that she is dead, Fleming was apparently making claim to it. Tricky business, that. It would be interesting to know whatever became of the heirloom once Mrs. Devon died. Unless he took the jewelry from Mrs. Devon's home once she was dead. Or before she was dead.

Another point to ponder.

* * *

"WE ARE AT A FUNERAL, DETECTIVE," Amy said to the annoying Carson. "If you wish to speak with me, please make arrangements with my husband to visit at our home." Amy set her plate on the table and turned to them. "I do not understand why you continue to harass my husband and me. We have nothing to do with these cases you are working on. Neither one of us found the bodies. My only connection to Mrs. Fleming was regarding her midwifery skills. I know nothing about her life. The same with Mrs. Devon. I hadn't seen her since school, which I can assure you was many years ago."

Detective Carson smirked. "Yet, here you are at her funeral."

Well, that certainly took the wind out of her sails. Before she could think of a comeback, Carson gave a short bow. "I suggest you eat your meal, Lady Wethington before it grows cold."

With those words he turned on his heel and left her glowering at him.

Lady Forester deposited her full plate on the table, scooted her chair in and looked over at Amy. "Who was that man? He certainly didn't look pleasant."

She didn't want to shock the poor woman by telling her the truth. "He is an associate of my husband's."

"Why is he troubling you? Especially at a funeral." She tsked and picked up her fork. "I don't like the way things are these days. People seem to have no sense of manners or decorum."

Soon Mrs. Garfield and the other woman who was with her, who's name Amy could not recall settled in their seats across from them.

After everyone remarked on how all the food looked delicious, Amy absently asked, "Mrs. Garfield you look vaguely familiar to me, even though we haven't formally met."

At first she seemed to stiffen up, which almost convinced her she was *that* Mrs. Garfield. Then she relaxed and said, "If you visit the Roman Baths, you may have seen me there."

"Do you visit that often?" It was best to play dumb.

"No. I mean, well I do, but I work there."

Amy hoped she looked as surprised as Mrs. Garfield most likely wanted her to look. "Yes. That must be where I've seen you. I visit regularly since I do partake of the water even though it tastes vile."

Mrs. Garfield nodded. "Yes, I've heard those complaints before."

"What is your position at the Baths?" Lady Forester asked.

Thank heavens for that. With Lady Forester also asking questions, it didn't look like Amy was interrogating the woman.

"I work as what they call a Tourist Guide. I greet the visitors and direct them to where they can get the most out of their visit."

"That is very interesting," Amy said. "I think they would mostly have men working as guides."

"But they do. I am one of only two women who work at the Baths. I was fortunate to get the job because my father was a guide and when he passed away, I received his position. And that was only because the curator was quite fond of my father."

"I thought your family was in the clergy?" Lady Forester asked.

"You are thinking of my grandfather. He is an Anglican Bishop." Mrs. Garfield took the last bite of her food and pushed her plate away.

"That is most interesting." Amy moved the leftover food on her plate around with her fork. "Mayhap the next time I visit the Baths, we will see each other."

Mrs. Garfield nodded. "Most likely."

"I have a better idea. I planned my trip to the Baths for Tuesday next. If you find the time, perhaps we can have tea."

The woman shook her head. "I don't think so, my lady. I am not allowed to leave my shift while I'm working."

"I see."

She was trying to figure out another way to possibly meet up with the woman when Detectives Carson and Marsh arrived at their table. "Lady Wethington, we would like some of your time Wednesday. In the afternoon. Is that notice enough?"

She turned to give them a scathing retort when her attention was drawn back to Mrs. Garfield who hopped up from her seat and with a strangled sound, turned and left the table.

The woman hurried across the floor, dodging other attendees, almost knocking over a large plant at the end of one of the tables. She arrived at the door of the Fellowship Hall and barreled through it.

"I wonder what that was all about?" Lady Forester said.

Amy huffed. "It's apparent the presence of this man has frightened her," she said as she glared at the detective. "I will not speak with you now, and that is the end of it."

Lady Forester had also turned to glare at the man. "If you have business with Lord Wethington, I assume you can make arrangements to speak with him." She turned her back and engaged Amy in a conversation about the weather. After a few moments, Carson turned on his heel and left.

"A very obnoxious man, Lady Wethington. You must speak to his lordship about him. If he is a business associate of your husband, he needs to be put in his place."

21

When Amy arrived home from Mrs. Devon's funeral, all she could think about was a nice, warm, comfortable nap. But it seemed that was not to be had.

"Lady Wethington, this note arrived for you this morning." Filbert held out a folded paper with the Sterling seal on the back.

"Thank you." She strolled up to her bedchamber, breaking the seal on the note as she climbed the stairs. It was as expected, a note from Dr. Stevens asking for medical records for Lady Wethington and Lady Davenport who were now her patients.

They had an appointment the next afternoon with Dr. Stevens, so it was in her best interests to visit with the Fleming household now. Hopefully, if Mr. Fleming was not at home, whoever oversaw the household—most likely a housekeeper—would feel comfortable turning over the records to her.

It might be a good opportunity to speak with staff members to get more information on Mr. Fleming and his new wife.

She walked the length of the corridor to the washroom where she refreshed herself, fixed her hair and returned back downstairs. "I am sorry, Filbert, but can you have the carriage brought around again?"

"Of course, my lady. If you care to wait in the drawing room, I will fetch you when it's ready."

"Actually, I will be in the library." She entered the room and headed for the large desk. She pulled out the piece of paper with the names of their suspects so far and added Mr. Jeffrey Long to the bottom of the list. Men usually did not like being tossed over and then refused return of the ring.

She studied the list and no one, so far, stood out. Every person had a reason to kill either Mrs. Fleming or Mrs. Devon or both. She sighed, replaced the paper, and stood.

"The carriage is ready, my lady. Randolph had not released the horses yet."

"Thank you, Filbert." She picked up the note from Dr. Stevens, tucked it into her reticule and walked to the door.

"Your bonnet, my lady," Filbert said.

Drat. She remembered taking it off when she fixed her hair. "I will be right back." She trudged up the stairs and retrieved it from the washroom and returned to the front door.

She nodded at Filbert, who was busy hiding a smile and once again made her way back to the carriage. Even though Mrs. Fleming always examined her and Eloise at their homes, Amy still had her direction from a card she'd given them when they first hired her.

The house was in a nice middle-class neighborhood, where most people worked hard for a living, but were able to afford at least one servant. Thrift and responsibility were the traits that had pulled some of them out of the lower class. Others came from middle class beginnings, had a decent education, and worked at respectable jobs.

Had she time after Dr. Stevens' note had arrived, she would have sent around a note herself, but since her appointment with Dr. Stevens was tomorrow and anxious to get the matter settled, she hoped she wasn't turned away.

At the rate she and William were going, she might be traipsing around Bath, babe in arms, as she tried to find the murderers. Wouldn't William love that!

She climbed the steps and dropped the knocker. It took a few minutes, and she was about to knock again, when the door finally opened. "Yes, miss, how can I help you."

The woman was stout, wearing an apron over her dark wool dress that identified her as the cook. She didn't seem happy that she'd been forced to open the front door. Was she their only employee?

"Good afternoon, I am Lady Amy Wethington."

The woman immediately changed her demeanor and did a slight dip. "Yes, my lady."

Amy pulled the note from her reticule. "I am here on behalf of Dr. Rayne Stevens."

When the woman just stared at her, Amy said, "May I please come in?"

Now flustered, the woman stepped back and allowed her to enter. "Of course. I am so sorry, my lady."

"As I said I have a note here from Dr. Stevens requesting the late Mrs. Fleming's medical records for myself and Lady Davenport. Is Mr. Fleming at home?"

"Yes, my lady. Let me see if he is accepting visitors." She waved to a small room next to the entrance hall. "If you wait there, I will check for you."

Before Amy could ask her any more questions, she hurried away. It would be interesting to see if Mr. Fleming was indeed, the man she'd seen leaving the Assembly.

Amy wandered the room, assuming the former Mrs. Fleming was the one who had done most of the decorations. The wedding should have taken place by now, so she assumed the new Mrs. Fleming was in residence.

After about five minutes, a tall man, nice looking, with a slight smile on his face entered the room. He was the man she'd seen leaving the Assembly.

"Lady Wethington?"

"Yes, I assume you are Mr. Fleming?"

"That is correct. My housekeeper, Mrs. O'Reilly, said you were requesting medical records?"

Apparently, Mrs. O'Reilly did double duty as Cook and Housekeeper. "Yes, I assume she gave you the note I brought from Dr. Stevens?"

He whipped the note out of his trousers' pocket. "This one?"

"Yes."

He waved to the grouping of comfortable looking chairs. "Won't you please have a seat, my lady?"

Amy settled in one of the seats and Mr. Fleming took the chair across from her. He cleared his throat. "I have not had the opportunity to go through my late wife's medical papers. It's been a difficult time."

She would have had more sympathy for the man if he hadn't run off and remarried so quickly. But then, from what she knew about Mrs. Fleming, and the stories she's heard since then, she probably did not fulfill her marital role very well.

"You might have heard that I have already remarried."

Well, then. That was a surprise. Although, it was also a smart thing to say since most likely everyone in Mrs. Fleming's circle had already heard about his new wife.

"Yes." She was left in the awkward position of trying to decide if she should offer her condolences on the death of his wife, or congratulations on his marriage. A difficult situation to be sure. She elected to say nothing.

"Darling, Mrs. O'Reilly said we have a guest." A woman no more than five or six years older than Amy entered the room. Mr. Fleming stood and smiled at her. It appeared she was a much better match than his previous one.

This new Mrs. Fleming was tall, with bright red hair and a scattering of freckles across her nose. She spoke with a distinct Scottish accent.

"Yes, my dear. This is Lady Wethington. She is here to collect Jane's medical records for herself and," he glanced at the paper in his hand and said, "Lady Davenport. They were Jane's clients." He turned to Amy. "This is my wife, Mrs. Darlene Fleming."

The woman gave a slight curtsey. "It is a pleasure to meet you, my lady."

"And you as well, Mrs. Fleming."

"If you will wait here, I will be happy to get you the records you are looking for. I was just starting to organize all the papers that were left behind." Mrs. Fleming turned and left the room.

Mr. Fleming stood. "I will assist you, my dear."

Amy sat back in the chair and considered the new Mrs. Fleming. She was soft-spoken, pretty and gracious.

And slightly pregnant.

* * *

"And then she jumped up and ran for the door like the devil was at her heels," Amy said.

It was Tuesday afternoon. Amy and Eloise were on their way to their visit with Dr. Stevens. William and Michael had some sort of business meeting, so they had both gone in the Davenport carriage and she and Eloise were using her and William's vehicle.

Amy had seen little of William yesterday, since he had an emergency to deal with presented by his land steward that had tied him up all afternoon.

After having secured the medical records, Amy stashed them away. She attempted to read a page or two, but it was medical terms she was not familiar with, so she shoved the page back into the box Mrs. Fleming had given her.

William had gone out that evening to meet friends for dinner and cards at the club. Amy had fallen asleep before she could tell him about the funeral, meeting the new Mrs. Fleming, and securing the records for Dr. Stevens. He was up and gone when she came down for breakfast, then he rushed in again right before Michael and Eloise had arrived.

Amy had just related the story to her sister-in-law about Mrs. Garfield's odd reaction when Detective Carson had walked up to her at Mrs. Devon's funeral the day before.

"Well, since the poor woman had been wrongly arrested for Mrs. Fleming's murder before the detectives released her, I can see why she might be a bit unnerved at seeing the men at the funeral. Especially as he approached you, who, as you said, were sitting right across from Mrs. Garfield."

"Yes, I guess that is true."

Eloise grabbed onto the strap alongside her to hold on as the carriage hit a rather nasty gouge in the road. "Not that I consider it a social event, but how was Mrs. Devon's funeral? A lot of weeping and gnashing of teeth since her death was unexpected?"

Amy held onto her own strap as the rocking in the carriage continued. "Actually, no. It was a very calm and sedate affair. There were only two family members there, Mrs. Devon's two aunts and their companion."

Eloise stared out the window and spoke softly. "Do you worry sometimes that there won't be a sufficient number of mourners at your funeral?"

Amy gasped. "Eloise, for heaven's sake! No. I never think of such things. I am sure the good Lord is not ready to remove me from William's side anytime soon. He needs my presence to keep him amused."

Eloise seemed to think seriously for a moment. "What about childbirth?"

Here it comes. Amy closed her eyes, her stomach clenching. Just what she had been troubling herself about recently. "I will admit I am a tad concerned. But I don't believe the percentage of women dying in childbirth is very high. Especially those—like us—who use qualified midwives and doctors."

"You don't sound very sure. Are you attempting to convince yourself?"

Amy shrugged. "Probably." Before they could dwell any further on the subject, the carriage came to a halt and the door opened. Randolph reached in and took her hand and helped her out, and then did the same with Eloise.

"Will you be so kind as to carry that box up to the door?" Amy pointed to the box on the floor between the two seats that one of her footmen had carried down earlier.

"Of course, my lady." He lifted it to his shoulder and climbed the steps right behind them.

The man who had met them at the door the last time they visited escorted them to the drawing room. "My ladies, Dr. Stevens has sent for tea for you to enjoy. She sends her apologies because it might be about another fifteen minutes before she has finished with her current patient."

"That is no problem, and thank you very much," Amy said. "What was your name again?"

He gave a slight bow. "John, my lady." He glanced at her driver. "Is that something for Dr. Stevens?"

Amy answered. "Yes. They are medical records. Where should he put them?"

"If you follow me, I will show you to Dr. Stevens' office. I'm sure that is where she would prefer to have them."

John turned and led Randolph from the room.

"I could use some tea," Eloise said. "I hope her cook sends in some small sandwiches as well."

Amy eyed her best friend and sister-in-law. "You know I would never criticize, and I don't mean this as such, but you are growing quite large."

"I know." She sighed. "I have merely reconciled myself to the fact that my child will enter the world demanding steak dinners."

Tea arrived and they chatted for a while. Amy managed to steer clear of conversations about childbirth and the risks thereof.

"Here you both are." Dr. Stevens entered the room looking quite chipper. Amy had a feeling she was just that sort of person. Because she had a few inches on Amy, she also looked much more graceful with her pregnant self. It had always been Amy's regret that she stopped growing around thirteen years.

"I apologize for keeping you waiting." Dr. Stevens took a seat across from the settee where Amy and Eloise sat. She touched the tea pot with her fingers and said, "I will be right back. I need a cup of tea, and the water is cold."

Just then Lord Sterling entered the room. "I will get the hot water, my dear. You have kept these lovely ladies waiting long enough." He kissed the doctor on her head and left the room.

"It was no trouble, I assure you, Dr. Stevens," Amy said again. "Eloise and I had a lovely chat while we waited. And the cream biscuits your Cook sent in were delightful."

Dr. Stevens patted her bulge. "I know. I must force myself to not eat more than one. I should just probably ask her not to make them so often, but Sterling loves his sweets."

As if her words conjured up the man, he returned, carrying a teapot of hot water and placed it in front of his wife. "I am off to my meeting with Lord Danvers. We are getting close to agreeing on the wording for the bill we want to present at Parliament's next session."

Dr. Stevens smiled and waved him off as she poured herself

a cup of tea. "I am so delighted that Cook keeps water on the stove all day." She grinned at them. "I enjoy my tea."

After a deep sigh as she took a sip of the liquid, she said, "Now ladies, we can discuss any concerns you have. Then I will want to weigh you and check you over."

Eloise glanced at Amy. "One thing Lady Wethington and I were discussing was childbirth."

The doctor took another sip of her tea. "Yes, and are there concerns I can address for you?"

"Will we die?" Eloise blurted out.

Poor Dr. Stevens almost spit out her tea. After swallowing and wiping her mouth with a napkin, she said, "Whatever made you think about that?"

Eloise looked over at Amy for support.

Clearing her throat, Amy said, "I think we only worry about what all women in our condition do. Will we survive the birth? Will our baby be healthy? Will the baby even survive? How common is childbirth fever?"

Dr. Stevens nodded and smiled softly at them. "Yes, my ladies. They are truly questions that all expectant mothers worry over. However, I can assure you that you both are in good health. You seem to get enough nourishment. Your babies are growing at a respectable rate, and you both told me your babies are very active."

She picked up a small sandwich and said, "As far as childbirth fever, once it became known that keeping things clean was very important, the rate of the sickness dropped considerably. As I mentioned before, I follow Dr. Joseph Lister's teaching on keeping all surfaces and instruments scrupulously clean."

Amy and Eloise nodded as she spoke. Amy did feel a tad better, then glanced over at Eloise who was smiling brightly at the doctor. Most likely whatever concerns she had were mollified by the doctor's words.

Brushing off her hands, then her skirt, Dr. Stevens said, "Let's go into my examining room and I'll assess both your conditions."

After thoroughly examining Amy and then Eloise, the doctor declared them and their babies healthy and congratulated them on how well they were taking care of themselves. "Nothing stressful, ladies. You are more fortunate than some of my mothers in that you have no other children to care for and have household help. Please take advantage of your station and use the services of your servants as much as possible."

She packed away the instruments she'd used as Amy and Eloise fumbled to right their clothes.

"Do you have any idea when my baby will be born?" Eloise asked the doctor. "I feel so cumbersome and swollen. You must notice that I am larger than Lady Wethington, yet she is due before me."

Dr. Stevens tapped her chin. "Some women put on more weight than others. Also, it is possible your baby is bigger than hers. Or perhaps you've miscalculated your last courses and you are farther along than you believe."

"Before I forget, I secured the medical records you requested from Mr. Fleming. I believe my driver put them in your office at John's request."

"Thank you very much. I will set aside time to go over them."

She smiled as she walked them to the door. "One thing I can recommend is a daily walk in the fresh air. Exercise is good for you and the baby." She nodded at John who opened the door. "I will expect you in another two weeks unless anything happens that you feel should be brought to my attention."

They thanked the doctor and headed to their carriage. She did feel somewhat pacified after discussing childbirth with Dr. Stevens.

22

William waved his wife off to her doctor appointment and climbed into Davenport's vehicle. His first inclination had been to talk Michael out of attending Dobish's meeting. He had no confidence that his brother-in-law would not get himself into trouble. Which was another reason it was good for William to attend.

The primary reason, of course, had been to seek out Mr. Fleming. He really didn't expect to gain much information from the man since it was a business meeting, but once committed to going, he felt he could at least hear what Dobish had to say and get a look at the other men who were involved.

Once they both settled in, William said, "Did you have a chance to speak with your father? You mentioned you had hoped to finish up the partnership break-up so you would free up some funds for this venture."

Michael scowled. "Very briefly. Once I mentioned South African diamond mines he exploded. The man really does need to calm down. He will collapse one day with the way his temper flares like that."

"He must have been hard to be in business with."

Michael shook his head. "Actually, no. It's only since we moved to Bath and brought all our businesses with us that he's been acting so peculiar. He doesn't seem to trust my judgment. I agree, up until the move I did go along with most of his suggestions. After all, he'd been successful for years."

"What changed?"

"I want to be my own man, not go along with everything he suggests."

"Does he not listen to you?"

Michael leaned his elbow on the carriage seat armrest and rested his chin in his hand. "He does. But he always seems to have a better way to do things." He looked over at William and shrugged. "Most times he's right."

After about twenty minutes of weaving in and out of traffic, they finally arrived at the direction Dobish had left with the club footman that Michael had given to his driver.

"It looks like we've arrived," Michael said. He opened the door and jumped out, William following him.

Once they entered the home, they were directed to a large drawing room, filled with about twenty other men standing around, some smoking and most of them sipping on whisky.

"Help yourselves to a drink while we wait for everyone to arrive." Mr. Dobish stood at the front of the room, looking quite satisfied.

William and Michael made their way to the table where several bottles of various kinds of spirits were laid out. They each poured a drink and began to wander the room.

William found quite a few of his cohorts at the meeting. No one he felt comfortable enough with to say he believed this was not a genuine investment. The only one he felt he needed to convince was Michael, but from what he'd said about the meeting with his father, it sounded as though he might not be able to come up with the money anyway. Perhaps another time that Winchester was right.

Although he hadn't had a great deal of time to study this investment, he did speak briefly with his solicitor, Alfred Lawrence the night before at the card games. Lawrence said he didn't know very much about this particular venture, but he did know of two others originating in London that had fallen through, leaving some irate investors. He said the information he had was that most of the South African mines have been worked to death and he doubted if there was one as active and well-paying as Dobish claimed.

William greeted several of the men, taking note of all the wealthy men Dobish had assembled. It was quite an impressive bunch, which amazed him. One would think anyone who had money to invest in a diamond mine would have consulted with their people first.

After stopping at two groups and moving on to the third he was thrilled when Mr. Johnson, an old school mate, introduced him to the man next to him as Mr. Ronald Fleming.

The man looked ordinary. But then does a murderer look like one? Not from what he and Amy had found out so far, but an uncooperative wife could push a man to do things he might never consider.

"I believe we have a connection, Fleming," William said, studying the man.

Fleming took a sip of his drink. "Indeed? And what is that?"

"Mrs. Fleming was midwife to Lady Wethington. My wife."

If Fleming was surprised, he didn't show it. He merely dipped his head in acknowledgement.

"I am sorry for your loss, Fleming," William said.

Fleming shrugged. "I doubt anyone believes I was too broken up. I met your wife yesterday. Charming woman, a former patient of my late wife."

"Yes, from what I believe Dr. Stevens—your late wife's

replacement, had asked my wife to obtain the medical records regarding her and my sister-in-law, Lady Davenport."

"Did she tell you my new wife is expecting a child?"

"No." Since he and Amy hadn't had the opportunity to speak since she visited with Fleming, he was surprised to hear this.

He ran his fingers through his hair. "I know it doesn't look good." He waited a minute, studying his empty glass. Saying no more, he just wandered away, apparently heading toward the table with the spirits set out.

The meeting was a repetition of the presentation Dobish had given them in the club the day before. In some ways it reminded him of the fire and brimstone sermons some preachers were wont to do to get people all whipped into a frenzy.

Nothing Dobish had said changed William's mind, and thankfully, on the ride home, Michael seemed less enthusiastic about it. When questioned, he said, "The last thing I want to do is make a major mistake and give my father fodder for his already sketchy opinion of my business decisions."

* * *

"I HAVE DECIDED to take the day off," William said as he and Amy lay in bed the next morning, the pale sun shining through the open window. "The last two days were quite hectic and I feel the need to relax and assess all that's happened recently."

Amy rolled to her side to face him and placed her cheek on her folded hands. "I am happy to hear that. I have several things to tell you—"

"—About the investigation?"

"Yes." She sat up. "Would you like me to ring for breakfast to be sent up here?"

William threw the covers off and stood. "No. I don't believe

I want to be that much of a sloth. I suggest we dress and go down for breakfast. Then we can take a stroll in the garden to discuss the past two days."

"You are correct. Dr. Stevens mentioned that Eloise and I needed to take a daily walk." Amy sat up and stretched. "She said it is good for the baby. And me."

They took their turns in the washroom, dressed, and headed downstairs. "Amy, I think it is time to retire that frock until after the baby comes. You can barely close the buttons."

She looked down at the haphazard way her dress hung. "That's because I misbuttoned it. Although this, along with a few others, really need to be set aside. "I should visit my dressmaker and have a few garments made for the next couple of months."

Hand-in-hand they entered the dining room where breakfast had already been laid out. After selecting sausages, eggs, tomatoes and beans, Amy took her seat with William following.

"I suggest for digestive purposes we enjoy our meal and then discuss matters when we take our walk."

"Very good idea, husband."

THE SUN SHONE brightly as they stepped out the back door of the house. "I find the heat this summer is bothering me more than other years, yet it is truly not that warm. I remember much worse summers. I believe it might have to do with the extra burden I'm carrying," Amy said as she tied the ribbons of her bonnet under her chin.

He took her arm and they began their stroll. "First, I'd like to tell you about Mrs. Devon's funeral."

He nodded and she continued, "To my surprise, Mrs. Garfield was there."

"Indeed?"

"Yes. She is also a church member of St. Michael's. She did look vaguely familiar to me, but since I visit the baths often, that was no surprise. Also, our friends Detectives Carson and Marsh were there."

"Don't they always go to the funerals of victims?"

"Indeed they do, and I'm sure they haven't moved along on either murder or they would be here questioning us again."

William turned them in another direction. "Actually, they were here Sunday afternoon when you were taking your nap."

She drew back, her eyes wide. "And you didn't tell me?"

"My dear, there hasn't been much time for anything, which is precisely why I've taken the day off."

"What did they want?"

"What they always want. To ask questions and then leave with the very tedious reminder to stay out of the investigation. One would think if they wanted us to truly stay out of the investigation, they would stop involving us."

She shook her head and kicked a pebble that had wandered from the grouping of colorful stones around the water fountain.

William moved them slightly to keep her from tripping over a loose branch. "Did meeting her gain anything for you?"

"A bit. I found out she's still working at the baths. It seems she inherited the job when her father passed, since he'd worked there for ages. But a very odd situation occurred when Detective Carson came up to me at the table where we were seated. Mrs. Garfield was right across from me. When he stepped up and spoke to me, Mrs. Garfield jumped up and raced—literally raced—from the room."

She winced and said, "May we sit for a minute? I believe I have a small pebble in my shoe."

"Of course, my dear." He led her over to one of the stone

benches that were scattered all around the garden. Amy attempted to reach her shoe but sitting down it was near impossible. She looked at William with imploring eyes. He picked up her shoe, loosened the fasteners and shook it out. A small stone fell to the ground. "I can't imagine how this got in there, but it's out now."

"Speaking of Mrs. Garfield racing from the room, I also learned that her grandfather is an Anglican Bishop."

"How interesting," William said as he refastened her shoe "I met Mr. Fleming yesterday."

"You spoke with him?" Amy asked.

He nodded. "I attended an investors' meeting with your brother yesterday afternoon while you and Eloise were seeing Dr. Stevens. Mr. Fleming was there. I found him to be quite pleasant."

"Not the murderer type?"

"I think we've learned, my love that there is no 'murderer type'. I was introduced to him, and he told me you had visited with him and his wife to pick up the medical records Dr. Stevens had requested."

"Did he say anything else?"

"He did mention that his new wife was pregnant and wanted to know if you had told me."

Amy nodded. "She seemed like a lovely person. Tall for a woman, with bright red hair and freckles. I would say no more than a few years older than me."

William stood and reached out his hand. "Come, let us walk some more. You said it was good for the baby."

Once they were on a new path through the beautiful flowers their gardener had taken great care with, Amy said, "As you know, Eloise and I had an appointment with Dr. Stevens yesterday."

He covered her hand on his arm with his and linked their

fingers. "And what does the good doctor say about your condition and the baby?"

"She believes we are doing well. The little one is growing and so am I," she laughed as she rubbed her belly.

"That is very good news." He turned to her and stopped their progress. "We really must get this matter resolved. I don't mind telling you I am quite concerned for the stress this entire thing is having on you and the baby. I was so happy when you decided to put your book off until later, but it seems what we are involved in right now is even worse."

They moved from one path to another one that connected and took them past the rose garden, her favorite place. She sniffed deeply. "Oh, I do love the smell of roses." She continued, "I understand, truly I do." She sighed. "We just have to work harder." She snapped her fingers. "Do you happen to know a Jeffrey Long?"

William stared at her. "I do. He rents space with my solicitor. He is a barrister, and they share some work. Why?"

"It seems that Mr. Jeffrey Long was engaged to Mrs. Devon. She broke off the engagement and refused to return the engagement ring."

William huffed. "Jewelry again."

He glanced around the garden, as they continued to walk, enjoying the sight and smells. With summer coming to an end in another month or so, this would all dry up until next spring.

"I imagine a man would be quite angry to be thrown over and then refused the return of an expensive ring."

"Are you suggesting we put Mr. Long on our suspect list?"

She grinned. "I already have."

William turned them to head back to the house. "I can make a visit to my solicitor. I have something I need to discuss with him anyway. It will give me the opportunity to ask him about Jeffrey Long. His temper, how upset he was at the break-up, that sort of thing."

They ended up at the back door of the house and William opened it and ushered her through.

"That stroll was refreshing." Amy untied her bonnet and handed it to Filbert. "Now that you have the day off, what do you want to spend your time doing?"

"Come, I have a suggestion."

They entered the drawing room and after brushing Persephone off William's favorite chair, which Amy knew the animal did on purpose, they settled in. "What is your suggestion?"

"There are several nice restaurants in the Roman Baths area. I propose we spend time visiting the shops, especially the bookstore. I am quite fond of Atkinson and Tucker, as you know, but it's always nice to peruse a new bookstore."

"I agree."

"Then, we can stop at the Roman Baths for luncheon and possibly have the opportunity to get more information on Mrs. Garfield since she obviously was rehired once she was released from jail."

"Brilliant, husband. Especially the part about visiting the shops. I do have to begin to purchase some tiny items of clothing for the baby. Plus, it is a good opportunity to visit my dressmaker and commission a few dresses for the rest of my pregnancy."

William held his hand up. "But I don't want to spend all our time shopping." He ran his finger alongside his ascot as if it had just shrunk.

Amy laughed. "No. I know how much men despise walking along going from shop to shop, balancing armfuls of packages and boxes, and you are no different. However, if memory serves there is a nice furniture maker in the same area. Perhaps we can find something appropriate to commission for the nursery."

He grinned. "I think it's about time you concentrated on the arrival of our child which is not too far off. We should also discuss wallpaper and carpeting for the nursery. And hiring a nurse."

Amy waved him off. "I don't think it's wise to spend money on wallpaper and carpets if we are moving to the country."

"My dear, we can afford it, and we won't be trekking off to our estate the minute the little one arrives. And of course we will be visiting Bath from time to time."

Amy nodded. "I know there is a lot to be done, but until these murders are solved, I'm afraid my mind can't think of other things. It is almost as if I'm writing one of my books and planning the murders and who committed them. I promise once this is all put to rest, I will concentrate on nothing but motherhood."

"My lord, a missive has arrived for you." Filbert handed William a small cream-colored envelope.

"Since we know the detectives never announce themselves beforehand, I'm sure it's not from them," William said.

Amy studied it. "It looks like my father's crest on the back there."

William turned it over and broke the seal. "We shall find out." His eyes skimmed over the paper and looked up at Amy. "It appears your father is hosting an impromptu dinner party Sunday and would like us to attend."

"How very odd. I'm assuming as it says a dinner 'party' that others will be attending." She took the paper from his hand and studied it. "Father rarely hosts dinner parties, and to do one expecting whoever he's invited to this 'dinner party' to be able to attend with such short notice is suspicious." She tapped the vellum against her lips.

"Just so." He retrieved the paper from her and said, "If we are to spend time shopping—" he grimaced, "we should be on our way."

Amy tried to stand but ended up looking like an upside-down turtle. Finally, in desperation, she reached her hand out and asked a grinning William to please help her up.

"It will take me only a few minutes to freshen up." She walked off, trying her best, he was sure, not to waddle very much.

23

*A*my yawned as she entered the dining room. "You are looking quite cheerful this morning," she said to William who was already eating his breakfast.

She took a seat, and the footman placed a teapot of hot water in front of her. She nodded her thanks and fixed her tea, fighting more yawns.

"Why don't you return to bed, my love. You look as though you can hardly keep your eyes open."

Amy shook her head. "No. This is the final months of my pregnancy. Only about another six or seven weeks to go. I'm supposed to be tired."

She looked over the tempting dishes and chose to have her tea first. "I have decided to bake something special for Papa's dinner party."

William stared at her, his coffee cup halfway to his lips. "Dessert?"

"Yes." She yawned again. "I saw a recipe in Cook's notes that looks very impressive and tempting."

"Indeed." He paused for a moment. "Perhaps taking on a brand-new recipe might be too much for a dinner party."

She shook her head. "No. Remember the two pies I made for our dinner party that had been accidentally destroyed? I was so pleased with how they turned out, and really wanted everyone to try them. I was very disappointed at the accident. So, this time I will be sure the pudding is set in a safe place." She sighed and took a sip of tea.

William patted her hand. "You go right ahead and make dessert if you want to." He looked at her with a slight grin. "I shall eat two helpings."

"Thank you, husband." Noticing he was fully dressed, she said, "Are you off somewhere?"

He wiped his mouth and set the napkin down. "Yes, I have a question for my solicitor, but I decided instead of sending around a note I would visit him in his office. I intend to get some information on Jeffrey Long while I'm there."

"Very good. I feel as though there is something I should be doing." She rubbed her tummy. "Or maybe I will take your advice and return to bed after breakfast."

"That is a very good idea." He stood and leaned down to kiss her on the head. "I will see you later today."

She nodded just as Filbert entered the room. "My lord, the detectives are back again."

William looked over at Amy. "Perhaps we should fix up one of the extra bedchambers for them. It will make it much easier for them to tell us to stay out of their business."

"I believe we considered that when we were in the middle of Cousin Alice's murder investigation."

William smirked. "Had I known that solving murders was going to become our life's work, I would have done it."

"Please, William." She shuddered. "No more. The only murders I want to solve from now on are the ones I write about."

William looked up at Filbert. "Are they in the drawing room?"

The butler nodded.

"Tell them we will join them momentarily. My wife hasn't even had her breakfast yet."

Amy made to stand, and William helped her up. "I would rather get this over with. If I can have my tea, I can wait for breakfast."

William nodded at the footman. "Please bring your lady's tea into the drawing room."

The man quickly picked up the teapot, the small cream pitcher, sugar and her cup and saucer and placed the articles on a tray. He led the way to the drawing room, William and Amy following.

The detectives were standing when they entered. Amy settled herself in her favorite chair and William took the one alongside her. The detectives sat and Marsh took out his notebook.

Deciding it wasn't worth it to chastise the men for coming since that didn't seem to have any effect on where or when they chose to visit, she took a sip of tea and waited for Detective Carson to start.

"Lady Wethington. We have reason to believe you are in possession of information that should have been turned over to the police."

Indeed.

Truly puzzled this time, she said, "I have no idea what you are referring to, detective."

Marsh scribbled and Carson stood, his hands behind his back. "It has come to our attention that you obtained written information from Mr. Fleming."

Things became clearer. Apparently, the lame detectives had finally gone to Mr. Fleming's house and found out she'd taken the medical records.

But that didn't mean she had to surrender so fast. "Can you

be a bit more specific? A note? An invitation? A recipe for a new cake for me to try?"

Carson growled and moved toward her. William stood, blocking the man from her. "I suggest you take a seat, detective. I don't like the attitude you are taking with my wife."

Carson fiddled with his ascot and sat. William didn't return to his seat, but sat on the armrest of Amy's chair, his arm relaxing on the back of the seat. A very protective move.

"I am referring to notes that belonged to Mrs. Fleming, which should have been turned over to the police."

"Then why hadn't you retrieved them before now?" William asked.

Ignoring William's question, Carson turned to her. "Lady Wethington, I am trying to make this easy for you. I can escort you down to the police station for questioning if I so choose."

William stood. "You will take my wife nowhere. If you attempt to, I will have my butler physically remove you and I will immediately visit with my barrister."

Apparently listening close enough, Filbert slipped into the room, standing near the doorway, his arms crossed.

Marsh spoke up, one of the few times Amy ever heard his voice. "Why don't we all calm down?" He directed his attention to her. "Lady Wethington, what were the papers you received from Mr. Fleming?"

At last, a clear question. "Medical records."

"Why?"

"Because my present doctor, Dr. Rayne Stevens requested them since Mrs. Fleming was my midwife before her."

Marsh nodded and returned to scribbling in his notepad.

Carson returned to his seat. "What do you know about a diamond necklace that both Mrs. Devon and Mrs. Fleming were in a court battle over?"

Amy shrugged. It appeared the men were finally doing their job. "Not much. Just as you said, they were in a court battle and when Mrs. Fleming died, Mrs. Devon went to the courts and had the necklace returned to her."

"It's missing."

William and Amy both said, "What?"

"The necklace. It's missing. As well as a very expensive diamond ring. It was apparently an engagement ring. We had our men search Mrs. Devon's entire house." Carson leaned forward and looked at Amy. "What do you know about that?"

She licked her lips. "Nothing."

Carson sat back and studied her. "For your sake, Lady Wethington, I hope you are telling the truth."

William narrowed his eyes at the detective. "I assume you are not suggesting my wife stole a necklace and a ring, things I could easily purchase for her."

"No," Carson said quickly, taking a quick glance at Filbert, apparently not wishing to be physically removed from the house. "We just want to see what Lady Wethington knows about the missing jewelry."

"I know nothing except that Mrs. Devon possessed both."

Marsh snapped his notepad closed and stood. "We are finished here."

Carson frowned but rose from his seat. "We intend to retrieve the medical records from Dr. Stevens that should not have been removed from the house. If you would be so kind as to give us her direction, it would be appreciated."

Amy nodded and made to stand, but William placed his hand on her shoulder. "Stay there, I will get it from the library."

The two detectives and Amy remained silent in the short time William was gone. "Here you are Carson." He held out a small piece of paper.

"One thing, detective," Amy said, "I suggest if you intend to take the records from Dr. Stevens, you might secure a court order first."

They left the room and Amy let out a huge sigh of relief.

William remained standing, studying the door they just left. "Do you realize what information they just gave us?"

"The necklace and the ring?"

"Yes. It can be assumed whoever killed Mrs. Devon stole the necklace and ring."

"Hmm. I think it's important if you speak with Mr. Long today. Perhaps he stole the ring back since she had refused to give it to him."

"And the necklace?"

Amy shrugged and leaned on the chair's armrest, struggling to rise, shaking her skirts out. "I don't know. Right now, I need some food and will probably take a short nap."

"My dear, you are truly pregnantly—is that a word?—muddle-headed. It now gives us motives for Mr. Fleming for both murders: his pregnant new wife and the money gained by selling the jewelry to finance his investment in the South African diamond mine deal."

Amy blinked a few times at his words. "Thank goodness I am not writing my book. My publisher would most likely send it back to me with a terse note to rewrite." She yawned and waved at him. "I must eat now. If I am asleep when you return, please wake me."

William crossed the room and gave her a kiss. She grinned and said, "You were quite the protective husband with Detective Carson."

He placed his hands on her shoulders. "Always."

* * *

Mr. Alfred Lawrence had been William's solicitor for years. He mostly worked with William's man of business to handle his contracts, leases, and investments.

They met occasionally at their club, but aside from that they had no social interaction, but William relied heavily on the man's honesty and integrity after having been swindled by his former man of business, Mr. Harding.

Lawrence's office was in a three-story building in the heart of Bath. There were various types of businesses housed there. William rode his horse to the meeting since it was a pleasant day, and he was able to maneuver the traffic better than if he'd been riding in his carriage.

He left his horse at the mews and climbed the two sets of stairs to reach Lawrence's office.

The man at the desk, Mr. Timothy Clark, who had been Lawrence's secretary for years, greeted him.

William smiled back at the man. "Is Mr. Lawrence available? I don't have an appointment, but if he has a few minutes, I'd like to speak with him."

Clark stood and waved to a chair against the wall. "If you will have a seat, my lord, I will check with him. He doesn't have a client now, but I believe he was working on some files."

"Thank you."

He could hear the voices behind the closed door, and within minutes, the young man returned. "You may go in, my lord."

"William, didn't I just see you a few days ago?" Lawrence stood and reached out to shake his hand. Despite the differences in their stations, they'd always had a less-than-formal arrangement.

William took the seat in front of Lawrence's large desk. "Yes, you did. I was questioning you about that diamond mine deal."

"Ah, yes. How did that all work out?"

"I didn't invest in it, and I'm trying to talk my brother-in-law from doing so, but that is not why I came today."

Lawrence leaned his arms on his desk. "How can I help you?"

"How well do you know Mr. Long?"

"My Mr. Long?"

"Yes."

"Well, I wouldn't say we're the best of friends, but we work well together when we must, I respect him, and I believe he feels the same about me. Is there a reason for this question?"

William certainly didn't want to cast aspersions on the man, but perhaps if he could speak with Long, under the pretense of needing legal advice, that might work. "Do you think it possible that I may speak with him now? Is he in the office?"

"No. He's been out of town for two weeks working on a matter that involved the two of us."

If that was correct and accurate, then Long wasn't even in Bath when Mrs. Devon was killed. Which means he also didn't attend her funeral. But then, if she broke her engagement to him, why would he?

"And you are certain he's been out of town all this time?"

Lawrence looked at him strangely. "Yes. He sends me telegrams every day with updates on his progress." He sat back and studied William. "I assume there is a reason for these questions, Wethington?"

"Yes. There was a reason but with Mr. Long out of town, it no longer applies."

"And that is all you are going to say on the matter?"

William sighed, sorry to have involved his solicitor. "Yes. I am afraid so."

They briefly discussed the question William needed to have cleared up about one of his leases, and then he stood as did Lawrence.

Lawrence walked him to the door, and grinned. "I have a feeling you and your charming wife are trying to solve a crime again."

Feeling both embarrassed and annoyed at the man's humor, William nodded. "Just so."

With a chortle, Lawrence opened the outer door. "Tell Lady Wethington I send my regards."

William nodded and left the office. He retrieved Major and rode home, thinking about his conversation with Lawrence.

Amy was indeed still enjoying her nap when he returned. He tried to keep from waking her, but she rolled over just as he was about to leave their bedchamber. "How did the meeting with Mr. Lawrence go?"

He returned to the bed and sat alongside her. "We can cross off Mr. Long."

She shifted, raising herself up on her elbows. "Why?"

"He's been out of town for two weeks, sending updates via telegrams to Mr. Lawrence the entire time. Unless he snuck back to kill Mrs. Devon and went right back to where he's been staying, I doubt if we should keep him on our list."

Amy swung her legs over the side of the bed and stood. She stumbled slightly and William had to grab her arm to keep her from falling. "Are you well, Amy?"

"Yes. Just a bit off balance these days."

They left the bedchamber and holding tightly to his wife's arm, they made their way downstairs. They moved to the drawing room and settled into two chairs.

"I guess we're down to fewer suspects now," Amy said.

He nodded. "Yes. If I remember correctly, it's Mr. Fleming, Mrs. Penrose and Mrs. Garfield."

"Right now, I'm leaning toward Mr. Fleming. As you pointed out earlier, he had a strong reason for both murders."

"Yes, but Mrs. Penrose is a bit on the peculiar side, and she has two family members who drowned."

"But why would she kill Mrs. Devon? Mrs. Fleming I can see."

"The woman was always short of money for her daughter's medical bills. It's possible she knew about the necklace and decided to steal it from her bedchamber, Mrs. Devon surprised her, and Mrs. Penrose killed her."

William studied the pattern on the rug under his feet and thought for a minute. "And Mrs. Garfield?"

"She found the body, by herself, and she raced off at Mrs. Devon's funeral when she spotted the detectives."

William laughed, then stood and called for tea to be sent in. "I wish I could run off when I spot the detectives, but they're always in my house."

24

*A*my proudly carried her Sussex Puddle Pudding into the Winchester townhouse for her Papa's dinner party. "I think this one turned out very well," she said to William as he dropped the knocker on the front door.

"I'm sure it's wonderful, my dear."

The door opened and Charles, Winchester butler for years, following Papa when he moved from London to Bath, greeted them. "Good evening, Lord Wethington, Lady Wethington." He smiled brightly.

They offered their greeting in return and removed their outer garments to hand them off.

"Is this the dessert you have brought for the party, Lady Wethington?"

She held it out and Charles took it. "Yes, it is. I made it myself." She glowed with pride.

He took the dish from her and said, "The others are in the drawing room. I don't think you will have a problem finding it. I will be off to bring this to the kitchen."

Papa, Michael, Eloise, Aunt Margaret, and Lord Exeter were all in the room, sipping on before dinner drinks. Papa looked quite lively and enthusiastic. Something she hadn't seen in a while.

"Daughter, I am so glad you have arrived." Papa walked across the room and gave her a hug.

"Thank you, Papa, I'm so happy to be here." She leaned in close. "I brought the dessert for tonight that I made myself."

"Indeed?" He tried hard to hide a smirk, but she was sure that was because he doubted her ability. Well, he was in for a surprise.

"What are you drinking?" Michael asked from where he stood near the sidebar.

William asked for a sherry, Amy passed since spirits were still not sitting well with her tummy these days. She wandered over to where Eloise and Aunt Margaret were in the midst of a conversation.

"You are looking fine, Amy," Aunt Margaret said as she kissed her on the cheek. "Are you feeling well?"

"Yes. But mostly I'm feeling ready to give birth."

"Me, too," Eloise said. "I feel like I was born pregnant."

They chatted about a few mundane things while Lord Exeter, Papa, Michael and William discussed, from what Amy could assess, politics. At least they weren't yelling at each other.

"My lord, dinner is ready," Charles said as he stood at the drawing room doorway.

"Thank you, Charles." Papa waved his hand in the direction of the doorway, and they all moved that way.

Amy was pleased to see her assigned seat was between Michael and Lord Exeter. Not that she intended to question him tonight. She would enjoy the rare dinner party Papa arranged and forget all about murders. But it would be nice to learn more about the man that had snagged Aunt Margaret. Michael, of course, she saw all the time.

The footmen immediately began to pour what Amy thought

was wine when she noticed it was champagne. What was Papa about?

Once the drinks were poured and the footman out of the way Papa stood and picked up his glass. "I arranged this dinner party to announce and honor a couple of happy events in my family."

They all picked up their glasses and studied Papa.

He cleared his throat. "Of course, the first thing I wish to honor is the upcoming birth of my grandchildren. He looked at Amy and Eloise with a warm smile. Amy was glad to see his smile encompassed Eloise as well as her.

Papa continued. "Next I have the great privilege of welcoming Lord Exeter into our family." He looked down at Margaret. "I am so happy you have finally done what I've been trying to get you to do for years."

Lord Exeter coughed to try to cover his slight grin. Aunt Margaret glared at Papa.

"And finally, it is with great pleasure that I announce that my son, Michael, Lord Davenport, and I have found a middle ground and we are joining together in a new business that encompasses some of the old, and some of the new."

All eyes swung to Michael who smiled brightly and raised his glass. "Here is to success."

Papa raised his glass higher and since apparently all his announcements were ended, took a large gulp of his champagne.

Congratulations came from all dinner guests before they drank their own champagne.

Amy turned to Michael once they returned their glasses to the table and the footmen began to serve dinner. Amy passed on the raw oysters since they brought an unwelcomed twinge to her belly but was happy to eat the bowl of clear broth. "I am pleased that you and Papa have mended your rift."

Michael nodded. "We both made concessions, but I feel we

can work out any little matters that come up. Father is willing to listen to some of my ideas that I think will improve our financial security."

"William mentioned that you were interested in a South African diamond mine. Are you still planning on doing that?"

Michael wiped his mouth with his napkin and shook his head. "No. It was me being stubborn when Father was trying to talk me out of it, but I did some investigation on my own when William decided against it and I don't believe it's a solid investment."

"I'm glad. I know William didn't see the value in it at all."

"Others pulled out, also. Melrose, Sanders, Wolcroft, Fleming, Waterford."

"Mr. Fleming pulled out?"

Michael nodded and took a sip of wine. "Yes, I believe his reason was that now that he'd gotten his inheritance, he intended to use the money to move to Scotland."

That gave Amy pause. Was the inheritance the necklace? If it was, and included both the necklace and the ring, it pointed to him as the murderer. A move to Scotland was not unbelievable since his wife was obviously Scottish.

She thought on that all through dinner, wondering if William would agree with her, and if she had come to the right conclusion, what should they do about it.

Once the meal was finished and the leavings cleared away, Charles entered the dining room. "Shall we serve dessert here, or shall you all retire to the drawing room?" He looked directly at Aunt Margaret, which was proper since she was the oldest female in the room, and the host's sister.

"I believe we can enjoy our tea and dessert in the drawing room."

After about ten minutes, they all trooped out of the dining room into the drawing room where Charles had already set up a tea cart with pieces of her pudding on dishes.

Amy was excited for everyone to taste her creation.

William gave her a warm smile as Charles carried a tray with the puddings on it, offering it to each guest.

Tea was fixed and they all began enjoying her treat. She took one bite and closed her eyes and relished the pudding. It had turned out delicious. She looked at William whose eyes were wide as he swallowed and quickly took another bite.

Aunt Margaret licked her lips. "This is quite good, Amy. You certainly have some baking skills."

Everyone else complimented her and she scraped the dish, wishing her piece had been larger.

After about another hour of visiting, she felt weary and looked across the room at William who was again in a circle with Exeter, Michael, and Papa discussing politics. Trying to catch William's eye, she waved a bit, and he glanced over. She gestured to the doorway.

He nodded and said something to the men and walked over to where she was. "Are you ready to go home, my love?"

"Yes. I am feeling fatigued."

William helped her up and they walked to the circle of men. "We will be on our way, Winchester. Thank you for a wonderful dinner."

Papa nodded and looked at Amy. "Thank you, Daughter, for the lovely dessert." He reached over and kissed her on the cheek.

She was almost falling asleep on her feet when they arrived home, but the information she received from Michael had to be shared.

"William, I believe we've come closer to solving the two murders."

He smiled at her weary face. "Why don't we put that off until tomorrow? You need to find your bed."

What he said was true. Nothing would change between this

night and tomorrow when she would be refreshed and able to hold an intelligent conversation.

She nodded and he walked her to the bedroom, helped her to undress and tucked her into bed. "Good night, sweetheart."

He went back downstairs to enjoy another brandy before bed. He was settled with a book and a brandy and feeling quite at peace when Cook came into the room.

He laid the book in his lap. "What are you doing up so late, Mrs. Tomlinson?"

She stood twisting her hands. "I have a confession to make, my lord, and I cannot sleep until I do."

The poor woman looked like she feared for her position. "What is it?"

She took a deep breath. "Her ladyship's dessert."

He frowned and leaned forward. "What of it?"

"I know how much she loves making those desserts. And I know she was quite proud of bringing it to her Papa's dinner tonight."

William had an idea where this was going, but held back, letting the woman make her confession. "Yes, go on Mrs. Tomlinson."

She continued to wring her hands. "You know how much we all love Lady Wethington. We were never happier when you married her, and we found her to be so very pleasant. So many households are turned upside down when a new mistress arrives."

"Yes. I agree my wife is quite easy to get along with."

After a pause, she took in a deep breath, and with rushed words, said, "I made a pudding and had Filbert bring it to Lord Winchester's house and asked his cook to switch the puddings, explaining that Lady Wethington had brought the wrong one."

William ran his hand down his face, trying very hard to hide his smile. "Mrs. Tomlinson, since I love Lady Wethington, too, I can only thank you for what you did. It would break my heart to see everyone trying their best to eat the pudding when we both know it would have been hard to swallow."

Mrs. Tomlinson let out a huge breath. "Then you won't dismiss me?"

"Of course not. You are the best cook in all of England."

She dipped, relief on her face. "Thank you so much, my lord."

"Don't concern yourself. Enjoy the rest of your evening."

* * *

"And everyone absolutely loved my pudding! I was surprised myself, truth be known, that it turned out so well." Amy had stopped in the kitchen the morning after the dinner to tell Cook how thrilled she was with the results of her pudding.

Cook smiled brightly as did the others in the kitchen. "I am so happy for you, my lady."

Amy tapped her lips. "I think perhaps I should spend more time baking, maybe even open a bakery."

"No!" The resounding response came from Cook as well as the others in the kitchen.

She must have looked quite startled because Cook said. "My lady, soon you will be a mother. Having raised a few children myself, I know how time consuming it is. Plus, with you being such a famous author, you will be busy between caring for your little one and writing your books."

Amy nodded. "I believe you are right. As much as I feel my baking skills could be put to good use, it is now better to turn to other things."

She glanced around when she heard what could only be called someone letting out a deep breath. They all just stood and smiled at her.

"Well, then. I shall be off to enjoy my breakfast."

William was already seated, a full plate in front of him. She sat next to him and shook out her napkin. "What are your plans for today?"

He swallowed a sip of coffee. "I believe it might help if I tried to track down the necklace. I'm quite sure at this point whoever took it sold it. Hopefully they didn't go all the way to Bristol or London to sell it, but since time seems to be of the essence for Fleming, I'm thinking he sold it in Bath."

"That is a very good point, husband, I think—"

"Excuse me, my lady but this package just arrived for you." Filbert held out a small, book size item wrapped in paper and tied with string.

"Thank you," she said, taking the object from his hand. She looked briefly at the card attached to it. "It is from Dr. Stevens. It must be a book on childbirth. Eloise and I both badgered her about what to expect the last time we were there." She looked up at Filbert, still standing there. "Can you please put it on the desk in the library?"

He bowed and took it and left.

"Are you concerned about the birth?" William asked. "You have the best doctor to attend you, and even though you've been quite tired of late, you still look healthy to me."

"And our child is forever swimming around, knocking me in the stomach," she laughed.

William reached over and covered her hand. "I will not allow anything to happen to you. In fact, while I am out and about, I will stop in to see Dr. Stevens to assure myself of your health and the baby's health, so I can reassure you."

Amy burst into tears. He handed her his handkerchief, picked her up and placed her bulky body on his lap, rubbing her back and speaking nonsense to get her to calm down. "What's wrong, sweetheart?"

She blew her nose and sighed. "You're so nice."

He grinned and placed his forehead against hers. "And you are so nice, too." He shifted to lift her off. "I suggest you go to the library and read that book Dr. Stevens sent you. I'm sure anything she provided to you would calm you down."

Amy looked at the now cold food on her place. "I'm not really hungry, so I think I'll have tea sent to the library while I read it."

"You go on ahead and get settled in a nice comfortable chair and I will ask Cook to send in tea and maybe some light food you might want to nibble on."

She wiped tears from her eyes again. "You are really so nice."

Apparently concerned that he was about to witness another outburst, William took her hand. "Come, I will get you settled."

INSTEAD OF READING THE BOOK, Amy had fallen asleep, annoyed at herself for wasting the morning away. After a light luncheon, she received a note from Eloise suggesting they take in the fresh air and maybe do some shopping for their babies. She mentioned that Amy had already scouted out the best shops when she and William had visited the week before.

Eloise had been anxious to begin purchasing clothes for her little one and Amy had agreed that when the time came, she would go with her.

As she consumed her meal, she spent time going over their notes. While they had agreed Mr. Fleming was their main suspect, all they had were coincidental facts. Certainly not enough to summon the detectives to lay out their case so they could put it all behind them and plan for their baby. And, truthfully, Amy didn't trust them with their information anyway.

This time they took Eloise's carriage since William was out with theirs, the weather having been rainy when he'd left earlier. The sun had broken through the clouds now, and the warmer air made for a pleasant stroll while they took in the stores.

After an hour of giggling and sighing over little pieces of clothing and soft blankets, they decided it was time for refreshments. "Before we have our tea, I would like to stop over at the Roman Baths and see if Mrs. Garfield is working," Amy said as they handed off the last of their purchases to Randolph to load into the carriage.

Eloise frowned. "I truly wish you two would finish this up. I want to speak of our babies and plan for that, instead of always talking about murders." Eloise shuddered.

"We are close."

She huffed. "I've heard that before."

They strolled arm-in-arm to the Roman Baths area, noting the crowds continued to descend upon the famous area with it still summertime. "It will be so nice when we can enjoy our strolls here without so many people," Amy said as they barely dodged a young lad chasing after a ball. She huffed. She would never allow her offspring to race around public places like that.

They entered the Baths and began their promenade around the waters. They spotted several tourists guards but didn't see Mrs. Garfield. After about fifteen minutes of searching, with Eloise complaining loudly and frequently about her desire for tea, Amy stopped one of the guards. "Excuse me, I am a friend of Mrs. Garfield, and I was wondering if she was working today."

"Mrs. Rosemary Garfield?"

Amy nodded. "Yes."

"Oh, she no longer works here. It was odd because she'd been here for years and they even hired her back after she had some difficulties a couple of months ago, but she left quite suddenly merely saying she had decided to move from Bath." The guard shrugged and walked off.

25

William began his quest to find the seller of the necklace and ring. He tried several jewelry stores, but without a description of what the piece looked like, he was stymied.

He took a break after a few hours and rode his horse to his club. William caught Michael waving him over.

"Glad to see you, Wethington. I wanted to talk to you about a few things."

William continued to stand next to Michael's chair. "I stopped in for luncheon, did you want to join me?"

Michael downed the rest of his drink and stood. "Excellent idea. I just met with a man who proposed a new venture to me. I'd like to discuss it with you."

"Why aren't you discussing it with Winchester? I thought the two of you were back together again."

Michael nodded as they arrived at a small table in the dining area. White tablecloths adorned all the tables, with china and crystal set at each place. A footman bowed to them and pulled out William's chair. "Welcome to the dining area, my lord."

"Thank you, Martin."

"Would you care for a drink before luncheon?"

William looked over at Michael who shook his head, which made up William's mind. "I would like tea."

Michael added, "Me as well."

His brother-in-law explained how it had been decided between both him and Winchester that he would investigate this particular project and give a report to his father. He continued to outline the business deal during their meal of turtle soup, grilled salmon with a pepper sauce, small potatoes and glazed carrots.

When they were finished, Michael sat back and said, "I am quite impressed with my sister's efforts at baking. That pudding we had at Father's house was quite tasty."

"Yes," William said as he stirred his tea. "It was, wasn't it?" He grinned as he took a sip.

* * *

AMY RETURNED from her shopping with several boxes of items for the baby and very sore feet. It was far enough off from dinner to allow her time to relax before William returned home. She decided changing into comfortable clothing and her house slippers was a good idea. Since she was dressed so informally, having dinner trays for her and William, if he returned soon, sent to the library would be appropriate.

After changing, and feeling much more comfortable, she retired to the library. The first thing that caught her eye was the book from Dr. Stevens sitting on the library table. With not much else to do, she picked it up, undid the string and unwrapped the book. She was taken aback when the book was not, indeed a book on childbirth, but what appeared to be a journal.

She settled into her favorite blue-flowered chair and opened a note from Dr. Stevens and read it.

Lady Wethington, while going through the box of medical records you so kindly dropped off, I found this book which appears to be Mrs. Fleming's journal. I thought I would send it to you so you can see that Mr. Fleming receives it.

Mrs. Fleming's journal? How very interesting. Settling down for a long perusal of the journal, she made sure the oil lamp next to her was lit and began to read.

She skipped the beginning part since that seemed to be notes on various mothers, but after about three-quarters of the way through, the author began to write personal items. After about ten pages, it was obvious this woman was evil. She was even blackmailing people.

One of those people was Mrs. Garfield, who now moved to the top of the suspect list. She had a very good reason to murder Mrs. Fleming, and she had quit her job of many years and moved. She leaned back and thought about that. Was this enough evidence to hand to the police?

Her heart thumped as she skimmed the pages, looking for more information on Mrs. Garfield. After a while she got tired of reading all the hate and angst in the book and flipped to the end.

Her eyes grew wide and she dropped the book as her hands flew up to cover her mouth.

She had a burst of energy, feeling the need to jump up and do something. She walked in circles, her heart thumping.

"My lady, you have visitors." Filbert looked at her. "Are you well, my lady? Is there something wrong?"

Amy pulled herself together and offered a slight smile. "No. Everything is fine. Who are my callers?"

"Mr. and Mrs. Ronald Fleming."

Maybe everything wasn't fine. "They are in the drawing room?"

"Yes, my lady. Shall I send for tea?"

She shook her head furiously. "No. That won't be necessary. But I will ask you to join me in the drawing room."

His brows almost reached his hairline. "My lady?"

"It is hard to explain, but I would feel better if you were with me."

Bowing slightly, he extended his arm. "Then we shall both greet your visitors."

Ronald and Darlene Fleming had remained standing as they waited for her. Amy and Filbert entered the library. "Won't you please have a seat?"

Mr. Fleming glanced at Filbert. "There is no need for sitting and socializing, my lady. We have learned that a journal belonging to my deceased wife was inadvertently sent to Dr. Stevens with the medical records. We have just returned from her office, and she said she sent it to you."

There didn't seem to be any reason to dispute that, so she nodded. "Yes."

Mr. Fleming cleared his throat. "I would like to retrieve it."

It was important for her to act blasé, as if she had not read the book. "Of course, Mr. Fleming. I believe my butler put it in the library." She turned to Filbert. "Isn't that where you said you left it?"

Without a flicker of an eye, he said, "Yes, my lady."

Amy smiled at her visitors. She had to fetch it herself since it was out of the wrapping the doctor had put it in. "I will be just a moment."

Her heart in her throat, she made a graceful exit from the room, then ran to the library. She grabbed the book, placed it back into the wrapping paper and quickly tied the string. Taking a deep breath, she returned to the drawing room.

She held the book out. "Here you are."

Mr. Fleming took the book and studied it for a moment.

Then he looked at her. "Thank you, Lady Wethington. We will be on our way now."

"Filbert will see you out."

The butler ushered them both out and closed the door. He returned to the drawing room where Amy sat on the settee since her legs no longer held her up. "Filbert, you must send a note to the Bath Police Department."

"Yes, my lady. Anyone in particular?"

"Detectives Carson and Marsh. I will write a quick note for you to send. Have one of the kitchen helpers deliver it."

On shaky legs, she made her way to the library, fumbled through the desk drawer for a piece of paper. Her fingers trembled as she scrawled the note asking the detectives to come immediately.

* * *

WILLIAM ENTERED yet another jewelry store beginning to believe his efforts were useless. The necklace could have been sold out of town, or even to a private buyer.

An older man, glasses perched on the end of his nose and gray hair leading into a scanty beard walked over to him. "Good afternoon, my lord. How can I be of assistance today?"

"I am looking for a particular necklace that might have been sold to you, along with a ring, although I'm not sure of that. Can you tell me if you've purchased such items recently?"

"Ah, young man. Despite my age, I have an excellent memory." He waved at William as he hobbled toward the end of the counter. "Come with me. I keep such items in the back room so I can study them further, think about potential buyers and such."

The two of them entered a small room at the back of the store, closed off from the rest of the store by a flowered curtain. The storekeeper lit two oil lamps which gave the space a cozy feel.

He waved him over. "Is this what you are looking for, my lord?"

Since William had never seen the necklace, he couldn't say for sure this was it, but since there was a diamond ring sitting alongside it, chances were he'd found the missing jewelry. "Can you tell me how long you've had these items?"

If they had been here for months, it would not be what he was looking for.

"Recently, my lord. The seller was quite anxious to get rid of them quickly. In fact, the price I paid for them was below market, but when one is in a hurry to change jewelry into money, they don't often make the best trade."

"Since you pride yourself on your memory, can you describe the person who sold these to you?"

The old man cackled. "I certainly can."

As he went on to describe the seller, William's lips tightened in recognition. Once he was finished, William said, "Thank you very much. That is quite helpful. To thank you for your assistance, I will be purchasing jewelry for my wife. She is about to give birth to our first child, and I think a nice bracelet or ring would be an appropriate gift."

The man nodded. "I look forward to serving you, my lord."

With his heart in his throat, hoping Amy hadn't gotten herself into trouble, he headed home.

* * *

AMY PACED IN THE LIBRARY, anxious—probably for the first time in her life—for the detectives to arrive. A knock on the door drew her attention.

Filbert stepped into the library and closed the door. "Mrs. Fleming has returned, my lady."

"Alone?"

"Yes."

"Do not allow her in. Tell her I am asleep, or in the bath, or anything you can think of and escort her out."

Where were the detectives? Or William? No, that wasn't a good thought. If things got dangerous, she didn't want him here.

She left the library and waddled down the corridor to the closet where William had stored his gun. He thought she had no idea where he put it, but she'd known for some time since she found it when she was rummaging around in there one day looking for something.

Careful to carry it correctly, she returned to the library. She'd barely entered the room when Filbert arrived, his face flushed. "My lady, Mrs. Fleming is no longer here."

Amy breathed out a sigh of relief. "That is good."

He shook his head, his eyes wide. "No, it is not good. Her carriage is still out front."

Panic hit her like a sledgehammer. "She's somewhere in the house?"

"So it seems. What do you want me to do?"

A million thoughts raced through her mind. After a minute, she said, "Have my carriage brought around. I will go to Lady Davenport's house until the detectives arrive. When they do, send them to me there."

Filbert nodded and hurried away. Amy walked to the library door and locked it.

"Thank you for locking us in, Lady Wethington."

Amy spun around, almost losing her balance. Mrs. Fleming stood across the room from her. Her brain, already muddled, was now almost dead. She kept telling herself to think, to do what she needed to do until the detectives arrived.

She raised the gun with trembling hands.

Mrs. Fleming laughed and raised her own gun. "It seems we both had the same idea." She scowled. "Put yours down."

Amy shook her head. "Not unless you put yours down."

She waved her gun around. "You looked in the journal. I could see it in your eyes when you handed it to Ronald."

"I don't know what you're talking about." Bloody hell, she hated how her voice shook. But then again, most people would have shaky voices if a gun was pointed directly at them.

"Yes. You do. You read that I arranged to meet Jane Fleming at the Roman Baths." She waved the gun at the chair near Amy. "Sit down. You look like you're going to give birth any minute."

Amy sat, continuing to hold her gun, but the weight of it had her entire arm shaking. "Why the Baths?"

Darlene smiled. A truly frightening one. "I worked there years ago, and never turned in my key. It was easy to invite her inside and then knock her on the head and push her into the water." She shrugged. "Then I held her under until I was sure she was dead."

When Darlene laughed softly, Amy shuddered.

Her eyes snapped. "Don't look at me that way. She was an evil woman and deserved to die."

Her hand was growing slippery from sweating, and she was afraid the gun would slide right out of her hand. "Even if she was, that wasn't your decision."

When Darlene didn't respond, Amy said, "What do you want from me?"

"Silence. Now and forever. Ronald and I are leaving Bath. We're going to Scotland where I have family. But your nosy self is causing problems."

Amy opened her mouth to speak, but Darlene cut her off. "Don't try again to tell me you didn't read that blasted journal. Since you did, you know she was an awful person. Ronald hated her and loved me. But she wouldn't give him a divorce. I was pregnant, I needed a husband."

"And Mrs. Devon?"

"We required money to move to Scotland. Mrs. Devon wasn't to have that necklace. It rightly belonged to Rita. The Devon woman stole it from her, so I stole it back. If she hadn't returned early from her visiting, she would be alive today. She grinned. "But poor."

There was no point in attempting to convince this woman that what she had done was wrong, and she should turn herself in. All she needed now was to get herself out of this situation before she was killed.

"So I guess the plan now is to kill me so I can't turn you in?"

Darlene didn't answer but continued to stare at her.

"When will it end? Will you continue to kill anyone who stands in the way of what you want—what you need? Does Mr. Fleming know about this?"

"Yes. After I presented him with the money I received from the necklace and ring, he said we had to move to Scotland right away. He's a very protective man, you know."

All Amy could think was he was a very foolish man. This woman could very well turn on him one day and decide to resort to murder again to get him out of the way.

Darlene cocked the hammer back on the gun. "But now I have to deal with you."

* * *

WILLIAM JUMPED FROM HIS HORSE, noting the two carriages in front of his house. One was his, but he didn't recognize the other one. He raced up the steps and almost took the door off its hinges when he opened it.

Filbert stood in the entrance hall looking as if he would faint any minute. "What's wrong? Where is Lady Wethington?"

"My lord, Lady Wethington is in the library, but the door is locked. Mrs. Fleming is in there with her."

"Bloody hell." He thought for a minute. "Do you know if the police have been notified?" Not that he thought they were going to be much help, but every little bit counted.

"Yes, my lord. We sent around a note some time ago."

He could not leave the two women locked in the room, but he had to get an idea of what was going on. He left the house, climbed through the beautiful garden—which his gardener would have a lot to say about—and ended up on the small terrace outside the glass doors of the library.

The drapes were only partially open, but by maneuvering around he was able to get a limited view of the room. What he saw stopped his heart. Mrs. Fleming had a gun pointed at Amy. More frightening was Amy had a gun pointed at her. Damnation, were they planning on having a shoot-out?

He jumped when he heard someone behind him. "We got a note from your wife to come to your house," Carson whispered as he edged closer to him. Detective Marsh was right behind him. "But your butler told me to go around to the back of the house which is where you went."

"Yes. We have discovered who killed Mrs. Fleming and Mrs. Devon."

"Fleming." Carson said. "We already know. We're about to pick him up."

"No need," William said. "The one you should be picking up is Mrs. Fleming. She's the one who sold the jewelry and since she sits in my library, aiming a gun at my wife, I assume she's guilty of both murders."

While Carson digested this information, William said, "We must get my wife out of that room and away from that woman. We can discuss anything else you want to know later."

"Is this door locked?" Marsh asked, gesturing to the glass patio door.

"No. They are left open during the day and locked at night." He peeked into the room again. The two women were still talking but waving around guns. If it were two men one, or both, of them would be on the floor bleeding. Women just talked and brandished guns.

"Is the library locked?" Marsh asked.

"My butler told me yes."

"Do you have a key?"

"My housekeeper would have one." His heart in his throat, he couldn't think clearly, so it was good the detectives took over. All he could imagine was Amy getting shot, losing the baby, and maybe her life.

Marsh remained quiet for a minute, then said, "This is what we will do. My lord, go back into the house, get the key and unlock the door, as quietly has you can, but don't go in. I will give you five minutes. Then we will bang on this door which will startle Mrs. Fleming, and her immediate reaction will be to look behind her. You get inside and fetch your wife. Get you both out of the room, or if there isn't time, duck behind the settee by the door. We will go into the library through this door and arrest her."

"What about her gun?"

Marsh stared at him with disdain. "Grab you wife's gun before she shoots herself. As far as Mrs. Fleming, we are trained offices of the law, my lord. And it appears to me these two women are going to talk each other to death before any shooting starts."

William nodded and left. Going as fast as he could, trampling all the flowers, he rounded the corner, and almost hit Filbert with the door as he rushed in. "Where is Mrs. Adams? I need the key to the library."

"Right here, my lord." The woman walked up to him, and that was when he realized all the household staff were huddled together on the stairs.

William grabbed the keys. "Which one is the library?"

Mrs. Adams fumbled with the ring of keys and handed him

one. "This one."

He strode down the corridor, pushed the key into the lock, trying to be as quiet as possible. The lock turned. Waiting with his ear against the door, his heart pounding so loudly he was sure he'd never hear the detectives bang on the door, he waited. Filbert, Mrs. Adams, and the rest of the staff waited with him. The tension in the room was thunderous.

A loud bang had him rushing into the library. He grabbed Amy by the arm. "Drop the gun."

She did and it went off, the oil lamp next to the settee exploding. He could hear the scuffle with Mrs. Fleming and the detectives, but he was more concerned about the flames that had erupted from the lamp and now had the table underneath it on fire.

"Amy, get out of the room." He glanced over at the melee in the corner. It seemed Mrs. Fleming was not going to give up easily.

"What about the table?" she yelled.

"I don't care if the entire house burns down. Get out of the room."

Just then Filbert entered and handed William a bucket of water to douse the fire. He then took Amy by the arm and practically dragged her out. Another gunshot went off which told him the detectives had not gotten the weapon off her.

Once the fire was out, William left the room, looking for Amy. She was sitting on the bottom stair, pale as new snow. "I thought she was going to kill me."

William pulled her up and closed his eyes as he held her close. He thought she was going to be shot, too.

A lot of screaming went on, but eventually, Detectives Carson and Marsh walked out of the library with Mrs. Fleming between them, her hands behind her back in handcuffs.

"We shall return tomorrow to ask questions to get this all settled," Carson threw over his shoulder as the three of them continued to the door, down the steps and into a police carriage.

After smiles, hugs, and pats on the back, the staff returned to their duties.

William took in a deep breath. "I don't care what time it is, we are retiring to our bedchamber, getting into our nightclothes, having a nice bottle of wine, and asking for a dinner tray to be sent up. I want nothing more to do with Mrs. Fleming, murder, death, guns that go off and set fires in the library, missing necklaces, and floating bodies. In fact, I'm feeling that maybe reading the Bible to each other for a while is in order."

"Husband, I think you have a wonderful idea. I am a tad weary."

As they made their way up the stairs, he asked, "How did you find my gun?"

EPILOGUE

Two months later

"William."

Silence.

Amy nudged him. "William."

He grunted and rolled over, presenting his back to her.

She shook his shoulder. "William, you must wake up."

He pulled the pillow over his head. "It's too early. It's still dark outside."

"But I think the babe is on the way."

He hopped out of bed so fast he banged his head on the bedpost. "Why didn't you say so?"

"I just did."

"How do you know?" He grabbed a pair of trousers off the chair next to the wardrobe. "I mean are you sure?" He drew out a shirt and struggled into it. "Did something happen?"

Amy shifted in the bed, feeling the wetness under her. Goodness, it appeared in addition to her cramps, her water had broken. "I think you need to summon Dr. Stevens."

"And my mother. She knows what to do."

Amy gripped her stomach and groaned. "Whoever you get, please do it soon."

"I'm leaving right now." He opened the door and Amy called to him, "You forgot to put your shoes on."

He was back in a flash. "Right. Shoes would be good." He pointed at her. "Don't go anywhere."

Now where the blazes did he think she would go? For a stroll around the park? "Stop by Michael's house on your way to the doctor's office. Eloise can keep me company while I wait." She could also help her change the sodden sheets. She fell back against the pillows and prayed.

The sound of the front door slamming reminded her she was all alone. Why hadn't she arranged for the nurse to come? Probably because like most new mothers, she didn't know when the little one would decide to arrive. It would be silly to have the woman living in their home before she had any duties.

Another cramp started and she gritted her teeth. "Hurry up Dr. Stevens."

* * *

WILLIAM POUNDED on the Davenport townhouse front door. It immediately opened with Michael's butler staring at him wide-eyed. "I thought you were the doctor."

"The doctor? Is someone ill?"

"No, my lord. Her ladyship has begun her labour."

"What? No that can't be. It's not her turn yet." He rushed past the butler and shouted, "Michael!"

His brother-in-law came bounding down the stairs, his hair wild, his shirt unbuttoned. No shoes.

William grabbed Michael's arm. "Amy has gone into labour. She wants Eloise to sit with her."

Michael's eyes bulged. "She can't. She is doing that herself."

Forgetting what the butler just told him, he said, "Doing what?"

Just then they heard a bellow from the upper floor. "Michael! If that blasted doctor isn't here in ten minutes I want you to fetch her."

Michael looked at him. "She's in some pain."

"So it seems." William ran his fingers through his hair. "Did you send a missive to Dr. Stevens?"

"Yes. About twenty minutes ago."

William grabbed him by the collar. "Come, we're going to the doctor's office in my carriage." He looked down. "Go put shoes on."

After a race upstairs where William heard Michael speaking softly to a very loud Eloise, he practically tumbled down the stairs. "Let's go."

The race through the streets of Bath was perilous at best. The driver ignored the normal polite driving manners and barely missed running over a street vendor. Michael and William held onto the straps of the vehicle as if their lives were in danger. They might have been.

Just as they pulled up to Dr. Stevens' office, she was climbing into her own vehicle. "Whatever is the matter?"

"My wife is giving birth," Michael said.

"Yes, I know. I received your missive. I'm on my way." She turned to get back into the carriage.

"Mine, too."

Dr. Stevens reared back. "Oh, my goodness. Both?"

Becoming a bit frantic now that he'd been away from Amy for so long, he shouted. "Yes! You must come to my house."

"No," Michael leaned forward until William thought he would drag the poor doctor out of the carriage.

Dr. Stevens stepped out of the vehicle and held up her hand. "My lords, you must both calm down. Childbirth is a normal process. If the ladies had just begun their pains, they have plenty of time."

William glanced at Michael, then turned to the doctor, lowering his voice. "Dr. Stevens, it's not Lady Davenport's turn. Her expectant date is weeks away. I think you should come to my house first."

The doctor had the nerve to laugh. "My lord, please. There is no such thing as someone's 'turn' when it comes to birthing a child. But I will say this. Either you both begin to behave like grown men and be prepared to support your wives without this falling apart circus, or I will ban you from the house."

"I can do that," Michael said.

"Do what?" the doctor asked.

"Be banned from the house."

Dr. Stevens sighed. "No. You will both return to your own houses where you will comfort your respective wives. I will merely go back and forth because I know you live near each other." She climbed back into her carriage. "I have all of my necessary equipment ready to go." She waved her hand at them. "Return to your homes and I will see you there." With those words she slammed the door, tapped on the roof of the carriage and the driver rolled away.

William and Michael stared after the carriage. "I guess we should follow her," Michael said.

"Yes." They jumped into William's carriage and instructed the driver to return the two of them to their respective houses.

* * *

AMY WONDERED why so much time had passed and Eloise hadn't come. In between her pains she'd managed to strip the bed of the wet sheets but didn't have the energy to put new bed linens on. She had pulled off her soggy nightgown and found a clean one that she struggled into after drying herself off.

She climbed into the bed and breathed a sigh of relief when she heard the front door close and then footsteps after that. It didn't sound like William, though; they were too light. It was probably Eloise.

"Amy, dear. I'm here." Amy looked up from the stripped bed at her mother-in-law. Never was she so happy to see someone.

"Oh, thank goodness you're here. Where is William?"

"I'm not sure." She walked back out the door, continuing her conversation. "Does he know you're in labour?"

"Yes. I sent him for the doctor. I thought he would be back by now. I also asked him to stop by Michael's house and have Eloise come over to sit with me. How did you hear about this?"

"Filbert sent word with one of your grooms. I had left instructions with him weeks ago to fetch me the minute you began your labour." She returned to the room, holding linens over her arms. "We must get you set up for this, dear." She walked to her side and wiped her brow with her hand. "How are you doing?"

Amy wanted to be brave. She really did, but the fear that had been lingering in the back of her mind for weeks and then the soft brush of tenderness from Lady Lily's hand did her in. She burst into tears.

"Oh, sweetheart, don't worry, everything will turn out fine." She handed her a handkerchief she pulled from underneath her sleeve and patted her on the head as she cried into the cloth.

Just then the front door opened again and the pounding on the stairs told her William had returned.

"Where is the doctor?" Lady Lily said.

"She's on her way. Since we passed Michael's house first, she stopped there and said she would be here momentarily."

"Why did she stop at their house? I thought you were going to ask Eloise to come here to offer support." Amy wiped her nose, the tears coming to an end.

William ran his fingers through his hair again. "It seems Eloise is also giving birth right now."

"Truly?" Amy stopped and held her breath and placed her hands on her belly.

"Breathe, dear," Lady Lily said, rubbing her back. William looked as though he was ready to faint.

After about a minute, the pain subsided, and Amy took a deep breath. "That was painful."

"Here, let's get you up out of the bed. I found with my two children, walking in the beginning helped and it certainly didn't hurt."

Amy twisted around to look at William. "Why is Eloise giving birth now? She's three weeks after me."

"Apparently not. When I got to their house Michael was just racing around the place. He said he'd sent word to the doctor, but I decided to go to her office to make sure she got the message. Michael went with me."

Lady Lily studied her. "Amy, why don't you have a maid?"

"I do. I mean, we do have maids, but no, I don't have a lady's maid."

"She needs one," William added, attempting to put the linens on the bed.

"William, for heaven's sake, go find one of the other maids and have her fix the bed," Lady Lily said with a sigh.

After about an hour passed, with Amy now gripping the knotted end of the sheet Lady Lily had tied to the bedpost every time a pain hit, the sound of the front door opening, and quick footsteps drew their attention to the bedroom door.

Dr. Stevens hustled in. "I have Lady Davenport all settled with her lady's maid attending her."

Lady Lily and William both glared at Amy.

Dr. Stevens fussed with the bedding and then glanced up at William. "I will need to conduct an examination, and I think it best if your lordship waits outside." Looking at his tense posture and pale face, she added, "Maybe even retire to your drawing room or library. This will take a while and I don't think you need to be here."

"Yes. That is very good. I will do that." He left the room so quickly Amy thought he would tumble down the stairs.

"How is my sister-in-law doing?" Amy asked as the doctor placed her hands on Amy's belly just as a pain gripped her.

"Breathe, my lady."

Amy nodded, but closed her eyes, sweat breaking out on her forehead. It was amazing how the natural inclination was to hold her breath.

Once the pain passed, Dr. Stevens said, "Lady Davenport is doing well. I also chased her husband out of the room, and like yours, he was very happy to go. She has sent for the nurse she and his lordship hired."

Amy shifted in the bed, turning toward Lady Lily. "That is an excellent idea. Can you find William and have him send a note to our nurse?"

* * *

AFTER SEVERAL HOURS OF PACING, running his fingers through his hair and trying very hard to avoid the brandy bottle, William grabbed his topcoat and headed to the front door. He turned to Filbert. "I will be at Lord Davenport's home. If anything happens I should know about, please fetch me. As you know their home is a mere ten-minute walk."

The man nodded and opened the door. "I will send the fastest runner in the house if we need you, my lord."

The walk in the crisp early October air restored him and relieved some of the tension. He had learned in the past few hours that not being in the room was still taxing. Listening to Amy's howls had been too much and since there was nothing he could do to help her, it was time to leave the house. Perhaps

Eloise was in the same state, but her wails wouldn't disturb him as much as his own wife's.

Davenport's butler opened the door, looking as distraught as William felt. Men just didn't take these things well. "Where is his lordship?"

"In the library, my lord. I think he could use the company. How is Lady Wethington?"

"Noisy," he said as he walked past the butler and headed to the library.

Indeed, Eloise was quite noisy as well. He found Michael sitting in his leather chair, his elbows resting on the desk in front of him, his hands covering his ears. He looked up as William entered. "I refuse to have a drink, but I cannot remember needing one more."

William crossed the room and patted him on the back. "Good man. I heard enough stories of men showing up after the babe was born so soused, they collapsed before they learned if they had a son or daughter."

Michael stood. "I think a long walk is in order. I just heard from Dr. Stevens that everything is going well, but it will be another hour or so."

"Dr. Stevens was just pulling up to my house when I left. I agree, a walk in the cool air will help."

As they stepped out of the house, Michael said, "I have decided to no longer share a bedroom with Eloise." He tucked the collar of his coat around his neck as a quick breeze buffeted them. "I cannot go through this again."

William patted him on the back. "I thought the same thing, but we're not thinking clearly right now."

They walked for over an hour and feeling guilty at being away from Amy for so long, William parted ways with Michael and headed home. As he handed his outer garments to Filbert, the first thing he noticed was the lack of noise.

He immediately panicked. "Is something amiss?"

Filbert grinned and said, "No, my lord. Your mother just came downstairs not two minutes ago to find you. She said as soon as you return to send you up to the bedchamber."

Taking the stairs two at a time, William raced to the next floor, rounding the corner, and headed to their bedchamber. The door was closed, so he gently knocked.

"Is that you, William?" It was Amy's voice, sounding very, very tired.

"Yes, my love. May I come in."

The door opened, his mother smiling brightly. "You are a father, William."

He felt his knees buckle and hoped he would not embarrass himself in front of the doctor, his mother, the nurse, and his wife and fall to the floor in a faint.

Taking a deep breath, he moved to stand next to the bed where Amy sat, propped up, looking as tired as she sounded and holding a small bundle. She smiled at him and said, "Come and meet your son."

"I must be on my way," Dr. Stevens said. "Lady Davenport was getting closer when I left her." She patted Amy on the head. "All is well, my lady. Your mother-in-law and nurse will help you. I will stop by in a few days, but if you need anything, please send for me."

William blinked several times to clear the water from his eyes, most likely from the cold air outside and put out his hand. "Thank you, Dr. Stevens." Unable to say anything more he just nodded. She smiled back at him and turned to leave the room.

William and Amy spent a good half hour admiring their son as his mother left them alone to make herself tea. The nurse had finished straightening up things and left them as well. The room was very quiet.

They counted fingers and toes and marveled at the perfect nose and chin the child possessed. "He is beautiful," Amy said.

"Yes. But not beautiful, handsome."

The front door barged open, and footsteps sounded, then the door to their bedchamber flew open.

Michael stood there, a huge grin on his face. "We know now why Eloise was so blasted big!"

"Why?" William said, thinking that was a strange thing for his brother-in-law to say with all that had gone on this day.

"It's twins!" With those words, he collapsed into a heap on the floor.

William called for Filbert to assist the man, then he and Amy went back to admiring their son.

The End

Did you like this story? Please consider leaving a review on either Goodreads or the place where you bought it. Long or short, your review will help other readers discover new authors and make purchasing decisions!

I hope you had fun reading *Death and Deception*. If you are new to my Victorian Book Club Mystery series, start with *A Study in Murder*.

Bath, England, 1890. Mystery author Lady Amy Lovell receives an anonymous letter containing shocking news: her fiancé, Mr. Ronald St. Vincent, has been dabbling in something illegal, which causes her to promptly break their engagement.

Two evenings later, as Lady Amy awaits a visit from Lord William Wethington, fellow member of the Bath Mystery Book Club, her former fiancé makes an unexpected and most unwelcome appearance at her house. She promptly sends him to the library to cool his heels but later discovers the room seemingly empty--until she stumbles upon a dead Mr. St. Vincent with a knife in his chest.

Lord Wethington arrives to find Lady Amy screaming and sends for the police, but the Bobbies immediately assume that she is the killer. Desperate to clear her name, Lady Amy and Lord Wethington launch their own investigation--and stir up a hornet's nest of suspects, from the gardener who served time in prison for murder to a vengeful woman who was spurned by St. Vincent before he proposed to Lady Amy.

Can they close the book on the case before the real killer gets away with murder?

Want to read the rest of the story? Visit my website: https://calliehutton.com/book/a-study-in-murder/

You can find a list of all my books on my website: http://calliehutton.com/books/

ABOUT THE AUTHOR

Receive a free book and stay up to date with new releases and sales!
http://calliehutton.com/newsletter/

USA Today bestselling author, Callie Hutton, has penned more than 45 historical romance and cozy mystery books. She lives in Oklahoma with her very close and lively family, which includes her twin grandsons, affectionately known as "The Twinadoes."

Callie loves to hear from readers. Contact her directly at calliehutton11@gmail.com or find her online at www.calliehutton.com.

Connect with her on Facebook, Twitter, and Goodreads.

Follow her on BookBub to receive notice of new releases, preorders, and special promotions.

Praise for books by Callie Hutton

A Study in Murder

"This book is a delight!...*A Study in Murder* has clear echoes of Jane Austen, Agatha Christie, and of course, Sherlock Holmes. You will love this book." —William Bernhardt, author of *The Last Chance Lawyer*

"A one-of-a-kind new series that's packed with surprises." —Mary Ellen Hughes, National bestselling author of *A Curio Killing*.

"[A] lively and entertaining mystery...I predict a long run for this smart series." —Victoria Abbott, award-winning author of The Book Collector Mysteries

"With a breezy style and alluring, low-keyed humor, Hutton crafts a charming mystery with a delightful, irrepressible sleuth." —Madeline Hunter, *New York Times* bestselling author of *Never Deny a Duke*

The Elusive Wife

"I loved this book and you will too. Jason is a hottie & Oliva is the kind of woman we'd all want as a friend. Read it!" —Cocktails and Books

"In my experience I've had a few hits but more misses with historical romance so I was really pleasantly surprised to be hooked from the start by obviously good writing." —Book Chick City

"The historic elements and sensory details of each scene make the story come to life, and certainly helps immerse the reader in the world that Olivia and Jason share." —The Romance Reviews

"You will not want to miss *The Elusive Wife*." —My Book Addiction

"…it was a well written plot and the characters were likeable." —Night Owl Reviews

A Run for Love

"An exciting, heart-warming Western love story!" —*New York Times* bestselling author Georgina Gentry

"I loved this book!!! I read the BEST historical romance last night...It's called *A Run For Love*." —*New York Times* bestselling author Sharon Sala

"This is my first Callie Hutton story, but it certainly won't be my last." —The Romance Reviews

An Angel in the Mail

"…a warm fuzzy sensuous read. I didn't put it down until I was done." —Sizzling Hot Reviews

Visit www.calliehutton.com for more information.

Printed in Great Britain
by Amazon